Other books by PJC:

There's Always an Upside

I AM a Character

Sue, I'm glad you're in

the Winner's Circle

PJ Colando

Third novel in the "Faith, Family, Frenzy!" series:

Stashes

Hashes & Bashes

ACORN PUBLISHING

The Winner's Circle

First Edition

Acorn editor: Laura Taylor

Cover illustration by Damonza

Book interior formatted by Debra Cranfield Kennedy

www.acornpublishingllc.com

Paperback ISBN: 978-1-947392-35-9 / Hardcover ISBN: 978-1-947392-36-6

Dedicated to Ed and Narelle Cree who ignited the story

with me on the return trip from the Blue Mountains, AU

*and **Larry**, my adventure partner for life...*

"I love you all my heart!"

One | *Fran*

UNLIKE JACKIE, FRAN WAS irked by "Amazing Grace". Especially when Bonnie's ringtone interrupted steamy Tom Selleck dreams. She groped the nightstand for her cell, clicked it on, and croaked, "How—"

Fran swallowed to regain her voice and attempt cordial. She needed to reply, "How sweet the sound." It was the obligatory response among friends, but just now the ritual undermined behavior management principles. One shouldn't reinforce disruptions like nighttime phone calls. Though she was a late-in-life newlywed, who didn't require beauty sleep, she did need peace. How did Jackie Breeden sleep with grandfather clock chimes every quarter hour through the night?

Fran opened one eye to sneak a clock peek: 10:33 p.m. In the jostling, her phone dropped to the floor, but their carpet prevented clatter. She gratefully rolled over, mindful not to bump her snoring mate. His guzzle-snort camouflaged a phone call that would awaken him and ignite his potential to pray.

Joan Baez's famed anthem resumed. Fran suppressed a groan. Her clumsiness had disconnected the call of a persistent friend. Rolling to a crouch on the floor, she scooped up the phone and clicked on.

"The new sweet sound will be cha-ching," Bonnie said. "Write these numbers down!"

"Hold your horses if you want to remain friends. I didn't

hear *please.* Also, speak softly. Paul's asleep and I need to locate paper and pen, plus my bookmark. I'm reading the new Jan Karon book."

This was a half-truth, a misdirect to cover her irritation. *Somewhere Safe with Somebody Good* lay spread-eagled on the nightstand. A moment ago, it covered her phone.

"Trying to learn how to be a pastor's wife?" Bonnie joked.

"Bad move, Bonnie. Thank your stars you're long distance. Do you want me to write the number or not?"

Fran bustled into the robe draped across the foot of the bed. A double bed shared with a pastor, who performed un-puritanically beneath the sheets, then cozied her onto the mattress edge where she tried to read herself to sleep. Marriage was unexpectedly exciting. Apparently abstinence did make a body grow fonder. Fran was considering an additional wedding gift—purchase of a king size bed to ensure her own space.

She grabbed her phone and held it low, amidst the rustle and swish of the silken fabric, hoping the noise would infuse sense into Bonnie's head. Fran padded to her office down the hall and Brailled the desktop. A tablet and pen aligned in their always-place. The silver patina of her recent wedding photo's frame twinkled in the moon glow.

Fran startled. She'd never noticed Paul's tie skewed to spoon the folds of her wedding suit sleeves. Significant lust hidden in plain sight.

She smiled as she recalled squeezing her nosegay during the ceremony and the subsequent photo shoot. Moments later, she lofted the roses over her head backwards for a perfect landing into the hands of Bonnie, Paul's secretary. The same still unmarried woman who'd quit her job and left town a few days ago with Carl, Steve Breeden's half-brother. California bound, they said. What an upended apple cart to accept, to explain, and, eventually, to embrace.

Bonnie Voss. The same woman who'd lost her morals and her mind. The same woman who called her for a favor in the middle of the night. *Please.*

Fran's chair rewarded her careful sit with silence. Her knees complied, noiseless too. She poised the pen and drew her cell to her ear. "I'm ready. Shoot me the numbers." Fran cleared her throat to underscore her great effort.

"Please? 10. 11. 31. 41. 44. 14. 24."

"Okay. Let me repeat them to make sure I got them right." Fran adjusted her robe. "10. 11. 31. 41. 44. 14. 24." After Bonnie's confirming purr, she continued, "What are these? Sounds like high school locker combinations."

"Good guess, girl! It's Carl's combination from his junior and senior years of high school. He was excited to have a locker in the jock block twice."

"Is that the hell why he remembers the numbers?" Fran snapped so harshly she almost bit her tongue. She nursed a grudge about entitled high school athletes, a remnant of fending off Coach's over-protection when his star players missed grades. She smiled at a memory of hoisting her paddle in the general vicinity of his over-stuffed ass. Hell, she'd have whacked him if her office door had been closed.

Emboldened by the memory, she pressed on. "What the hell am I supposed to do with these numbers? Memorize them and then eat the note? Global nuclear war didn't start after the nightly news, did it? You giving me the combination to Carl's underground bomb shelter or his safe deposit box?"

"Watch the Boffo Lotto drawing tonight at 11:00. We can't, because we're deadheading to Rock Island, Illinois. I knew you stayed up late and would do a favor for a friend." Bonnie didn't pause to allow Fran to object. "I have a question for you, Fran. What the hell are you saying *hell* for? You're a pastor's wife now!"

"I'm off-duty." Fran slammed down the phone.

Fran stood, hoisted her robe so she wouldn't trip over its hem—and to shake off Bonnie's rebuke—and swished into the family room. She turned on the TV, already set on FOX, and heard the same news pronounced by another bauble head, part of the daily parade, all interchangeable, most often blondes with hair sprayed into helmets. Cement-smiled with chunky gold jewelry coiled at the crest of vibrant high-necked, sleeveless dresses. Clothing to frame the toothy truths spread by big mouths on pedestal necks. Lipstick like dual blood streaks cheek-to-cheek. Yip-yap-yip. It was exhilarating to watch.

Fran settled in. She'd never monitored the lottery picks before, never even bought a ticket, considering the act beneath her station in the small, close-knit community. Maybe she'd made a mistake. A buy was frivolous for certain, but watching the drawing promised the simplest high on the planet. Its pep counterbalanced the bite of the recycled news' spew.

The numbered ping-pong balls bubbled, perked, and popped into round channels, the Plexiglas contraption reminding her of the junior high science teacher's elaborate gerbil cage.

Glad to perch on her chintz-covered chair, swimming solo in a household of beige leather and brown corduroy, Fran felt secure. She'd moved into the parsonage under extreme protest, put her Craftsman cottage up for sale. Paul didn't know it, but she'd slipped back several times for respite from his parishioner problems, of which she now owned fifty percent. For better or worse.

The sixth ball rolled down the chute, almost smiling as it scooted into place. Fran looked at the paper in her lap, looked at the screen, looked at her lap, took a deep breath, and squinted.

Then, she looked again. Shock sucked her breath. I'll be go to hell and back! Did that just happen? Is this a dream, a fairytale, or a nightmare come to life?

Bonnie's, er Carl's, numbers were winners! Fran's heart felt as skittish as the numbered balls had looked inside the tumbler that assured their mix. Her sleeves fluttered like monarch wings while she flapped her arms in a wild chicken dance. She'd never pranced with abandon at wedding receptions, not even her own. She grabbed a table lamp before it toppled, then twirled it for good measure.

She longed to scream. She was a former school administrator, used to being in control, and a newlywed mindful of her husband's rest, not a frivolous teen. Yet unbridled joy surged through her arms to the ceiling to accompany a silent "Hip! Hip! Hooray!" No high kick, her knees still aggravated by the beside-the-bed crouch to answer the cell call.

When she realized the size of the lottery win, she gasped and slid to the floor. Her mind flip-flopped like the ponytails of the cheerleaders whose moves she'd emulated. The ones whose skirts grew shorter every year—as did Fran's fuse, fueling her retirement at the end of the last school year.

Should she call Bonnie back? She'd said something about being on Illinois time, an hour earlier than Michigan, but not whether she and Carl would be driving or sleeping at this hour. Perhaps Bonnie and Carl were as *involved* as Fran and her new husband, Pastor Paul, had been an hour ago.

She couldn't tell Paul. She heard her snoring giant, sawing logs as if cutting away the sins of the world, perhaps beseeching God on His heavenly throne to fix all of the church problems overnight.

She couldn't call Jackie Breeden. It wouldn't be copacetic, as her husband, Steve, would say. Fran knew the farm couple awakened earlier than early for chores.

"Bonnie, how are you? Are you sitting down?"

"I'm fine. Carl's doing 80 mph on I-80 so, of course, I'm sitting. I'm seat belted and squeezing the handle above the truck cab door, gluing my tongue to the roof of my mouth to improve my balance, like you told me from yoga class. I've only driven small town roads, never been accelerated as a passenger to this speed. Carl said the sky's the limit on the Interstates, so I'm hoping to not go airborne."

"You won."

"Of course, I won. I won the man, took that church secretary job and shoved it. Did I tell you we're headed to Vegas to marry in the Little White Wedding Chapel near the Strip? Elvis will officiate."

"You won the Boffo Lotto." Fran kept her voice flat. Mention of a *strip* flustered her all the more. *Was the former church secretary wayward already?* She held her tongue, willing Bonnie to comprehend soon. Fran longed to end the call and return to bed.

"I did, er, Carl, my intended, did? What's the total?

"$536 million."

Fran clicked off the TV. The lottery win was the only news needed, and her tolerance for noise not what it used to be. Perhaps that's why she disliked football, that *roar of the crowd* bullshit.

Along with the silly frilly cheers.

Then Fran realized that the phone echoed the silence in her home. Bonnie said nothing. No sounds. Not even road noise broke the silence. Eerie.

Fran shook her phone, pulled it back from her ear to see if it had gone dead. "Are you there?" Still silent. Fran wondered about tunnels on I-80 that might block cell reception. She'd never been west of Chicago.

Fran clicked off the call and sent a text, which took longer than it should because her fingers kept hitting the wrong keys. That many zeros after a dollar sign seemed inconceivable. The spacing back to erase and then re-enter the correct numbers took several seconds. Her phone rang, startling her into additional errors. Bonnie's name appeared at the top of her screen, but she ignored the call until she completed the text.

She didn't bother with the voice mail she received in the interim. She suspected it would be a resounding yelp. Instead she hit the callback feature.

"Yes... Yes... Yes... Bonnie, calm down. You won. Yes, you won. Or did Carl? Where did you buy the ticket?"

"I bought the ticket in Tinley Park, Illinois. At a Speedway station while Carl gassed up. It was a whim. I was bored riding shotgun in a truck. Carl didn't even need me to read maps! I had to pee and the kiosk in the station enticed me as much as the snacks, so I bought one of each!"

"A ticket and a Twinkie! You're a two-fisted wonder woman!" Fran doubled over with laughter, almost peeing her pajama bottoms. Fran thought, but she didn't admonish Bonnie not to pee the leather seats in Carl's new truck—nor did she ask if the dog was along for the ride. She held her tongue and remained patient. Bonnie's giggling seemed out of control, but she'd come around to finish the call. Midwestern manners called for it.

Bonnie calmed to talk, her voice stronger now. "The station and neighborhood looked safe, not likely harboring Chicago's high crime, so I won't mind going back to claim the money. $536 million, really?! Wow-oh-wow-oh-wow!"

"Well, as I recall, you don't get the cash at the ticket seller's. It's not like an ATM. Think about it, woman. Give your brain a spin."

"You shouldn't insult me now that I'm a millionaire, Fran."

"I'd say sorry, but it's near midnight, Bonnie. I'm trying to help. Anyway, come home. You have to lawyer up, hire an accountant, and a financial planner. Maybe a publicist. I'll call my brother—remember he's a judge—tomorrow to see who he recommends."

"Well, I hadn't thought of coming back to Michigan—" Bonnie said.

"Where else would you go?" Fran interjected.

"I guess you're right. There's no place like home, among people we trust. Thanks. Thanks a multi-million!" said Bonnie, her excitement building to a shriek.

Despite the distance, Fran heard a loud "Woot! Woot!

Whoopee!" The news must be sinking in. Fran could almost hear the phone tossed over Bonnie's shoulder into the back of the truck cab. How sweet the sound, indeed!

Two | Bonnie

BONNIE RAN HER HANDS down her thighs, hoping to compose her body, her self. She wanted to shudder, shake, and shout. Instead, she frowned. The fresh contact with her cellulite caused her to miss the compression of pantyhose, the virginity constraints of her youth.

She turned toward Carl, who'd taken his hands off the wheel to cover his ears. Uh-oh, she *had* shouted. The Dodge Ram cab was like a triple wide phone booth. While road noise didn't intrude the super plush space, enthusiasm swelled.

To cover her gaffe, and to stop herself from shrieking "Put your hands back!", Bonnie put her palm to her lips as mea culpa, then kissed two fingers to his cheek. "Want an Advil, honey?"

Carl shook her off, eyes glued to the road. He wasn't giving an inch, but at least both hands returned to the wheel.

Suddenly she pointed, nearly stabbing Carl with a nail. "Honey, see the Holiday Inn up the road? Let's pull in there for the night." She shifted to touch his forearm, to soothe and to align him. "You may have heard, but I want to tell you in style. I'm now a girlfriend—soon to be your wife—with more benefits than before. Let's celebrate with a chocolate from Jackie's gift box. Maybe a martini or ten!"

She clicked open the glove box, ripped the shrink-wrap from the candy, crinkled it into a ball, and tossed it into the back seat, Twinkies eclipsed. She paused to inhale the heady scent of chocolate and stuffed a cream in her mouth. She was about to offer a chocolate to Carl when she noticed his jaw clench and unclench, illuminated by the business signs along the road. Carl couldn't be annoyed at the news, could he?

"I heard. There's cause to celebrate and not. I hope you don't mind, but our marriage plans are off." Carl, eyes on the road, death-gripped the leather-wrapped wheel and kept his foot steady on the gas. He resembled Reagan, even in profile. As if to negate his dismay, his single stud earring winked at her as it caught the neon lights' glow. The Holiday Inn sign fuzzed as the truck sped by.

Though stated matter-of-factly, Bonnie didn't take it that way. She considered unwrapping the Twinkies to stuff into Carl's mouth, but she refused to waste her favorite snack on the turd. "What do you mean we won't get married, Carl? I'm a former church secretary, a servant of the Lord. While I admit we are not virginal—I think He accepts that in this day and at our age—I hadn't planned on being a long-term whore."

That remark shut him up. Bonnie could see Carl was stunned. "Since I'm the one who bought the ticket while you pumped gas, I'm the wealthy one, and I'll just command a wedding. Acting like the Widow Braghorn may suit me. I listened to her harangues, as buffer for my boss, so I know a thing or three about bluster, making people flinch due to one's omniscient amount of cash."

"Bonnie, you don't understand—" he began.

"You've got that right." Bonnie clutched her shoulder harness to entrench. "Maybe for the first and last time tonight. We are about to have our first fight, Carl Edwards." She swept away the chocolate cream she held near Carl's mouth and replaced it in its paper ruff. "I'm not sharing my chocolate—or *my* money—with you."

She thought about Forrest Gump. Life was not like a box of chocolates. You did know what you'd get. Hurt. Again.

"Let's not fight. Let me tell you about California's community property laws." Though Bonnie could sense Carl taking his eyes off his road concentration, she refused to turn back to him. No way would she meet him halfway on this matter. Men always expected their woman to relent.

She'd seen it a million times as couples entered and exited the office for pastoral counseling. Male body language was always strong, go-ahead, while women appeared wholeheartedly subservient. She intended to eat this entire box of chocolates, then collect and spend her cash by herself.

"Remember we're headed to visit my three adult kids in California? They are married, and they have kids of their own. California's an expensive state. If we're married, half of the winnings we receive will be mine, regardless of who bought the ticket."

Bonnie gasped. *What? What? What?* She winced, whipped a sidelong look at his mask-like silhouette, and grabbed another chocolate. She clamped the lid and returned the chocolates to the glove box, slamming the door shut. She crossed her arms in front of her sweatered chest. Case closed.

"And." Carl paused for emphasis and reached over to tap her forearm. "You were aware the winner only receives half of the lottery cash, weren't you? *If* there's only one."

"Ha!" barked Bonnie, tossing her head for emphasis. Her long, loose-curled blonde tresses entwined the raised headrest, forcing a pause to solve this problem rather than forge ahead with math.

Bonnie refused to be embarrassed. She began to work her fingers through the snarls, new to the hair extensions as well as nervous with angst. She'd paid a fortune for the new hair color with special premium blowout. Summer highlights had been added to ready her for her debut with Carl's California kids. She resolutely worked to preserve the style, as important to her upper hand.

Finally, her golden strands released their stranglehold on the headrest. She forced *cool,* like a steel blade, into her voice as she continued, daring Carl not to laugh. "Go on. I'm not seeing the upside of winning half-of-half while I'm losing a husband."

"My kids came from a gnarly ex-wife." Carl spoke softly, his words articulated with precision. "She'll sic them on me, sure as hell. May even come after an alimony increase."

"You pay alimony? To a woman who left you for another man, a woman whose kids are grown, a woman I'll hate on sight?"

"Let's not get bogged in that mess," Carl said. "Let's consider how we claim the winnings as well as how we can preserve and shelter our $536 million."

"I don't know." Bonnie shook her head. Shook it again, enjoying the heft of the loose curls, to amplify her authority. "I just don't know anything anymore. I don't feel like *we* should claim *our* winnings, since *I* bought the ticket."

"Well, how about we circle back to the Holiday Inn like you suggested. *Dear.*"

Bonnie recognized that tone, used daily by her former boss, the pastor, attempting to *disarm with charm.* Bonnie could tell

Carl hoped for the final word, but his mere presence in the cab aggravated her. *First item I buy will be a long limo with a driver in black tights, tuxedo shirt cuffs, and bowtie.*

Bonnie smiled broadly as the vision expanded. A young dude with a chiseled physique. Who can dance. Joined by a passel of buddies in the trunk.

"No-o-o!" she shouted, thrusting clenched fists aloft. This adamant move caused her to bop Carl's nose and the passenger window simultaneously. Her shout reverberated while she checked her knuckles for bruises. When Bonnie gathered her spirits to voice her thoughts, a bump in the road warbled the tone, but not her resolve. "If I'm rich, I demand a better bed than a Holiday Inn. Let's use Siri to find a Radisson or a Wynn."

"The Wynn's in Vegas." Carl's tone, so like a funeral director's feigned tenderness, exasperated Bonnie. She might be blonde, but she recognized patronization. His voice practically patted her on the head.

Well, he was not the boss of her. She'd shed that circumstance when she resigned. "I know. That's where I'm spending my wedding night."

Thus began the war of the winnings.

Three | *Jackie*

SUNRISE, FLASHING THE GAP in the bedroom drapes, bolted Jackie upright. Despite its fresh promise, she felt cranky and forlorn. One of her best friends gone, maybe forever, road-tripping with her husband's *favorite* brother, with whom friend Bonnie was in love. Though a half-brother, and a Californian to boot, Carl had wedged himself into everyone's hearts with the force of the freight trains that hurried Midwestern grains to food preparation plants. Hubby Steve was bereft too, but shoveled his feelings into working his dairy farm.

Edgy that she'd missed the alarm, Jackie flung on her robe and stepped into slippers to descend the stairs, ritually kissing the 8x10 color photos of her only child, framed to align with each of the sixteen steps. Brandon's birth, first fish, first school day photos as long as he would allow them—through fifth grade—followed by high school and college graduation portraits, and every stud shot of his glorious football career. His brief marriage had failed, so she removed that portrait. Today its empty spot triggered reminiscence of Carl.

Virtual snapshots shuffled, blackjack fast, and whizzed past Jackie's visual field. Her first glimpse of Carl Edwards, mildly drunk and seated at her kitchen table as if he belonged. The day Carl bounded into the Koffee Kup Kafe to announce he'd purchased a nearby farm and a decrepit old bull to start a stud service.

The next unexpected step was Carl's instant outlandish wealth. A Canadian energy consortium swooped in with a mineral rights lease on Carl's land, but the fracking venture quickly contaminated his well.

Jackie's eyes teared up. The image of Steve, her still handsome six-footer, diminished with protracted grief over the simultaneous deaths of his dog and the favored cow in his micro-dairy operation, renewed her guilt over not being able to bring him to peace. His mustache bushed and his hair clumped and, when he washed it, she saw the grey streaks had paled to opaline.

Steve, typically a temperate man who walked with his hands in his jean pockets, accosted Carl and banished him from their lives. The attack was stridently verbal, also atypical of Steve. He leaned on a broad smile and tucked in behind her social butterfly wings, ready to stalwartly back her up, but seldom to provoke. His community moniker was Even Steven, because he was—in temperament, aptitude, and style.

It was another time in her life when Jackie didn't know where to stand. She gripped the handrail, willfully moving forward to recall when her sweet friend, Bonnie, who rapidly attached herself to the new man in town, scooped up a replacement pup to mend family fences. Sadly, the new dog failed to live up to the loyalty or the legend of their beloved Sparty. Dalmatian heritage didn't help.

Perhaps propelled by grief as well as guilt, Carl had negotiated a sizable settlement with NOEBBLE Energy, its millions divvied—repentance by cash—and deposited in the local bank.

Well, a little siphoned off to pay for a van, a washer and

dryer, and two splashy diamond rings. Jackie considered it *wages* for living an obedient, God-serving, good wife life. She felt as entitled as Steve, who planned to expand his micro-dairy herd and renovate their milking parlor. She'd purchased several pairs of Levi's and light plaid flannel shirts from Sears to outfit him appropriately, leaving his stockpile of rock & roll tee shirts untouched. He cherished each hole, rip, and tatter. It was a boundary the good wife didn't cross.

Since meeting Steve at age seventeen, whenever he smiled, his eyes crinkled in sync with his grin. In those hyper-happy days, Steve's eyes practically laughed. Lots of friends, lots of shared effort, and a beloved son shaped their good life. Zip replenished with the advent of Carl as they eased toward retirement age.

But, in the flash of a few months, Bonnie and Carl departed and tedium returned. Now Steve's eyes appeared as flat as their farmland.

Jackie mirrored her man. Her life reminded her of the children's verse, "There was an old lady who swallowed a fly." Feelings wiggled and jiggled inside her, but her body and soul remained numb.

The close of the school year loomed, just days away. Jackie needed to make a decision: to retire or not. Although no longer needed to make ends meet, her salary had been a longtime safety net. Jackie didn't know if she could forego its crutch, the all-mighty enabler of her occasional independent thought.

Further, she didn't feel ready to witness the tango of her dairy co-workers, her husband and only son, the latter now a strapping thirty-one-year-old. She also wasn't ready to watch soap operas and talk shows all day. The notion of filling empty hours with household tasks like making new drapes or random crafts or benefitting the church made her knees ache. Since her other best friend had married the pastor, Jackie definitely wasn't ready for Fran's long arms to nail her to church projects.

She filled her tall Michigan State mug with tap water, plopped in two teabags, and thrust the whole kit-and-kaboodle into the microwave. No slow-brewed specialty tea this morning because she was running behind.

A bird trilled outside the kitchen window, as if to say, "Plop in your club chair and prop up your feet to read." How long had it been since she'd read a book besides Betty Crocker's?

Bing! She retrieved the mug and gulped hot water, caring less if the tea was fully brewed. Ah, a caffeine hit! All would be copacetic soon, husband Steve would say. She gulped again. Sweet, spicy fragrances filled her nose. She gazed out the window as she swallowed, willing the bird to sing more.

Bonnie's ringtone jarred her reverie, causing her to splash the countertop with tea. She reflexively grabbed the sponge to wipe the counter, rotating to snag her phone from her purse on her kitchen desk. See what a pop of caffeine accomplished?

"How sweet the sound," Jackie said automatically. Now she reached to twist a curl, but there were none in place. Holy crap! She hadn't run a brush through her hair yet—or washed her face. She gasped as she looked at the clock. A hundred potatoes needed to be peeled by 9:00 at the high school cafeteria.

"You bet your sweet bippie," Bonnie exclaimed. "Can you hear Cha-ching, cha-ching? Make that 536 million cha-chings."

"Whatever are you talking about? Why are you calling at this hour?" Jackie asked. "Where are you? In Locotown, USA?"

"Carl and I are in the middle of nowhere, but that's not

what matters. I won the Boffo Lotto last night, haven't slept a wink, and," Bonnie paused to inhale and soften her voice, "Carl proposed."

"Proposed what?" Jackie cut in. She had no time for whispered riddles; she needed to get ready for work.

"We are on our way to Las Vegas to get married in the Little White Wedding Chapel with Elvis presiding. We want you and Steve to be our witnesses."

"What? Pastor Paul will be mad if Elvis takes his place." Jackie fumbled for her kitchen desk chair and sat. "Are you sure? Bonnie, what's gotten into you? One week you're a careful, *safe in the secretary's chair* person, and the next you're on the road with Carl. Now you're rich! Is a Vegas wedding really what you want?" Jackie slurped her tea. She needed to wake up and back Bonnie out of this odd dream. She regretted not reheating a cup of the coffee Steve brewed at o-dark thirty. She needed its higher caffeine count, *stat.*

"Jackie, I won the $536 million lottery. I can be and do anything I want. You can, too. You can retire. You and Steve can resume your Charles Kuralt road trip dreams. Carl wants you and I want you and I'm certain the Lord wants you to travel."

"But what about the farm?" Jackie asked, unable to shed her hyper-responsible self. It was always in place, even mere moments beyond dreamland. A dreamland in which Bonnie appeared to be planted.

Bonnie tsk-tsked, jarring Jackie's still fuzzy brain. "Don't you think Brandon's talent and knowledge have grown? Let him take over the farm. The young man's thirty-one and engaged. He needs to fully assume the position of Adult. He can. He's a former Michigan State All Star. *He's the man!* Has been since I've known him. Even when his baby boy antics drove you and Steve nuts, he was quick to say, 'Sorry.' He even ate the humble pie you served. It's just you who won't let him grow up."

Jackie let the slight slide. She could almost see the fist pumps, the wiggle of Bonnie's behind, and exhilaration swirling within Carl's truck. It was almost as if Bonnie had Face Timed her to announce the news.

Bonnie's hyper-enthusiasm seemed to stall the possibility of hers, to disallow a boogie around the kitchen island. Jackie's inclination—as well as her butt—super-glued to the chair. How could a simple secretary like Bonnie, her forever friend, win the Boffo Lotto? It was surreal. Was it merely a lack of sufficient caffeine, or was she jealous? Well, I'd better rid myself of potential unChristian envy. Didn't half the Commandments basically instruct, "Thou shalt not covet?"

Jackie yanked a pencil from her purse. "Let me take down a few facts, Bonnie. I'll talk to Steve tonight at supper. You know he's not settled until he's completed his chores. Keep it succinct. I have to get to work."

"Not for long!" Bonnie shrieked. "You can be free, like me, Jackie. But first, you truly must sit."

Jackie didn't waste time to argue that she was already seated. She readied the pencil to take notes. She clicked off with a faint, "Bye." She stared at the phone as if Bonnie's voice lingered within, ready to take back the news.

Jackie nervously tapped the pencil on the desk blotter, a glut of papers masking any sound until... until she gasped and nearly fell off the chair. $536 million?! Won with a dollar ticket purchased on a whim at a Speedway Gas Station? There was a God.

For now, Jackie needed to focus, so she said a quick prayer of thanks. She hastily resumed her work prep tasks, glad she had frozen scones, leery because they freezer-resided next to marijuana-laced treats she'd baked in secret, stored for moments of need. This might seem like a moment, but she didn't want to peel potatoes stoned. She'd seen that woozy look in the eyes of students and the uncertain stumble when she scooped their mashed potato serving onto their cafeteria tray. Good gravy!

Zoom to the garage and return, relieved she didn't trip in her scuffy fluffies. Grab-and-go! She needed more caffeine, not mild tea or canna-products, to bolster her resolve.

She dumped coffee in a cup and placed it in the microwave, zapping it along with a paper towel-wrapped scone. Holy of Holies Crap! She'd kick up her heels if she could.

While the microwave whirred, Jackie recalled that Bonnie had a bridal gown on lay-away. She reckoned she'd be tapped to retrieve it, maybe make the final payment.

The microwave bleeped. Jackie flashed to memories of her slot machine win. She'd already been to Vegas. Why wasn't someplace exotic, like the Hawaii evoked by Carl's wardrobe, the destination for their wedding?

Hmmm. There'd be a persuasive chat. Jackie retrieved the coffee and scone from the microwave, wishing she'd selected a low-cal breakfast. She prayed her luscious mother-in-law dress, with its lace and flounce, still fit, so she could properly stand up for her friend. Then hula in Hawaii.

Jackie bounded upstairs to increase her calorie count,

energized for her morning ablutions. She twirled as she chose among her identical pair of khakis and array of Spartan green tops. She deep-knee bent as she pulled on socks and nearly capsized with a twinge of pain.

She'd be glad for the heavy foam pad under her scullery path today. She'd been warned not to pound her feet when she walked, but she knew she'd forget throughout this special day. How to share this world-tilting news with Steve would come to her while she peeled potatoes.

A spud-bred plan for my stud.

Four | *Fran*

FRAN AWAKENED EARLY AND stared at the ceiling. Maybe she shouldn't have encouraged Bonnie and Carl to return. Should she buy a megaphone to cheer Bonnie or a rifle to defend her?

Carl could defend himself. As he already had when Paul complained about the loss of his longtime secretary, Bonnie, whisked away to California unwed. He'd stared Paul into a corner, a sight Bonnie witnessed and touted around town. Oh, to be a fly on that wall, to witness God Almighty apparently switching sides.

Fran glanced sideways. Paul, her husband for thirty-five days, remained swaddled in covers, despite it being the first day of summer. Hell's bells. The prospect of telling Paul, the ever-eager-for-cash pastor, made her want to burrow under the covers and never emerge.

She knew Paul's eyes would glaze with ego-driven schemes, spurred by Carl and Bonnie's anticipated ten percent tithe. He'd be the first in line, garbed in his best vestments, disguising his request as the blessing required of their good fortune.

His good fortune. She already wanted to stuff Paul's ears with cotton, blindfold, and handcuff him. Not to the bedposts—he might consider that amorous. Fran giggled at the thought.

Visions of a new church with a steeple, followed by a school named in his honor, er His honor, would burgeon mightily. Hell, the steeple would likely stretch to heaven's pearly gates, like the beanstalk that grew overnight from Jack's magic beans.

But this was no fairy tale. This miraculous happenstance might push Paul away from Martin Luther's path, back to the Indulgences of the Pope. Dammit to hell or holy crap, as Jackie would say.

Fran admitted, here in the cave of her covers, that she personally welcomed the prospect of a monumental tithe. Her anticipated promotion to fundraiser-in-chief, the fine print of her passion for a pastor, made her blood chill. Not her good fortune at all.

The short-lived Silly Hats and Caps Society—the triumvirate of her, Bonnie, and Jackie—had infused the church lady chores with humor, but she cringed at Paul's tacit expectation that cash-amassing duties would continue to be her domain. Almost as much as she dreaded the inevitable entanglements with the Widow Braghorn.

When her husband alluded that the two women were alike, Fran smacked down the absurd notion. She wouldn't be compared to a woman who'd likely screwed her way into Big Braghorn's fortune as well as his heart. Hell, he'd probably died so his insurance would pay off her American Express bills.

Ha! Her insights, spoken only among her friends, cracked her up. Fran's body reminded her she needed to pee. Pronto.

After she washed her hands and face, she took a moment to feather her lengthening bangs. Without a stretch, they parted nicely and latched behind each ear. Her forehead looked like a blank stage with silver-shimmered brown curtains parted, ready for the really big show that this news was. Proper wardrobe was required.

Fran hustled into her closet. She changed into her silken

cornflower blue robe, deciding it was too early for a bra. She stepped into moose slippers and finger-combed her hair, pinching her cheeks for color despite the mirror's report that she didn't need blush. She got down on her knees and prayed. She'd already thought very un-Christian thoughts, and said, "hell" more times than the devil should tally. She rose with renewed resolve to reform her penchant to curse.

There would be hell to pay if her honey found out about the Mother Lode through the inevitable gossip channels that spread faster than a prairie wildfire. Maybe faster in this small community. She blushed again at the prospect of the town's loud speaker, hairdresser and wife of still-fully employed and legendary high school football coach, Maybelline, semi-softly whispering the news while she shampooed Fran's hair. Coach Uhrig would probably help march the news around town just to spite her former administrative authority over him. Paybacks could be hell.

Yup, she couldn't release that dandy word to the Lord just yet.

She swept down to the kitchen to prepare French toast, to be slathered in creamery butter, real maple syrup, and super-thick bacon. The way to a preacher man's heart.

Her plan worked perfectly. Paul smiled more than he'd smiled in about a million years as the smell of oven-cooked bacon warmed the air. His nostrils quivered like the pony Fran once adored in her teens. She knew cereal was his habitual breakfast, a choice among several open boxes in the cupboards.

As she flipped the final French toast slice onto two plates, she looked over her shoulder to catch him carefully tucking a linen napkin in his collar, to prevent sullying his pastoral garb.

Widows, orphans, and church members were often hungry. He couldn't flaunt his good fortune via a dollop of maple syrup mid-chest.

Good fortune. The refrain constantly crept to mind this morning, nearing the frequency of "hell."

"Back in a moment, dear."

Fran zipped upstairs to her laptop and accessed the Boffo Lotto site to affirm Bonnie's win. Hmm. A second winner. No worries, however. Half of a half-billion remained a hefty sum. She skipped downstairs, smiling wide, and slipped into place at their cherry wood table. "Did you notice the textured swank of your bib napkin? I used my fine china, too. I hope you like the pattern. It's Lenox Eternal. Appropriate for our pastoral home, right?"

Paul winked, then beamed as he piled his plate with bacon. He blew her a kiss before he cut into his French toast, swirled the quarter-slice in its syrupy puddle, and stuffed it into his mouth. He attempted to blow a second kiss, but his puffy cheeks were stretched to the max.

"I guess you must have said a silent prayer." Fran found herself unable to contain comment. She never suspected he'd brush aside prayer. Her man's hunger for breakfast astonished her as much as his sexual appetite.

"My taste buds pray for me, dear," Paul said. "In truth, I'm not used to a breakfast partner other than the Lord, and I know He hears me, words uttered aloud or not. Would you like to say grace before or after you pass the butter?"

Fran bowed her head in reply. She recited the prayer of her youth, with an unspoken request to forgive her for using *hell* as a constant refrain. She continued aloud, "Bless you, dear Lord, for the gift Bonnie and Carl have received. Amen."

A slip of drama to get his blood pressure primed, to suss if his listening skills had succumbed to the husbandly habit Jackie constantly ascribed to Steve. Fran cocked an eyebrow and paused, willing Paul to ask about Bonnie and Carl's gifts.

"Speaking of gifts," Paul said, "Susan Carrigan stopped by the office and offered to fill in as church secretary while we search for a replacement. She's already worked a half-day, helping me update the member data base."

Hell's bells! Uncle Walt's Feel Good Forever Farmacy, for whom Susan home-delivered products under Avon Lady cover, probably already possessed the entire membership file. Uploaded to its server in a jiff, what better way to mine prospects for Walt's marijuana products? Wait'll Jackie heard this!

"In other news," Fran mimed the nightly news correspondent, who wore short dresses with tiny belts that threatened to meet her cleavage. "Bonnie, your former secretary, has won the Boffo Lotto."

"What lotto?" Paul stuffed an entire strip of bacon into his mouth, then swiveled toward Fran. His face wore the shock she felt, though her source differed: shock at his obliviousness. He, the great sin-chaser, unaware of this preeminent source for the root of all evil?

"What rock have you been hiding under? Saint Peter, the one on whom Christ built his church? Surely not the one the wise man built his house upon! The $536 million, multi-state lottery, the one with trillions-to-one odds, a share of which will fund your new steeple if you cuddle up to Carl, like you have for years with the Widow Braghorn."

Oops! Fran knew from his scalding look that she'd stepped out of line, over the line, whatever. "Well, Bonnie actually won half the lottery amount." She stuffed a piece of bacon into her mouth, almost gagging as it nudged her tonsils. An omen.

Paul bowed his head in silent prayer. Probably praying for the Lord's guidance to deal with me.

The bow was more like a bob. Paul lifted his head and darted to his desk for pen and paper. He raced back to the table. He bent his head again, French toast forgotten, as he doodled the steeple. Food may be the way to a man's heart, but money fueled its avarice.

Like a hooker fueled desire with a tiny waist and belted-up breasts.

Fran surprised herself with that thought. She wouldn't voice that comparison. She'd already said enough for one day. She was surely going to hell. Would being a proper wife to a pastor earn her entry in Heaven's gates? She resolved to try harder.

Fran yoga-breathed, mentally configuring her body in an asana. When she opened her eyes, Paul was still drawing his dreams. She began to collect the dishes, pack the dishwasher, and scrub the stove and counter as if they were her mind. When she stepped back to admire her handiwork, she was as clear as the kitchen.

Practicality won over morality. She'd have to fire Susan, offering herself as temp secretary. Wait 'til Jackie heard that! Hell had surely boiled over, bubbled up to taint this town, and Fran was in the middle of it, right where she belonged.

Five | Bonnie

"YOUR NOSE IS GROWING," Carl said.

Bonnie stretched into the back seat to retrieve her phone, hoping her sweater rode up to reveal flesh. Enough smooth skin to distract Carl from tweaking with her truth, yet not distract him from driving. This highway bustled with more vehicles than she was used to in the middle of Michigan, the automaker state.

As Bonnie groped, she wiggled for emphasis, so her breasts skimmed Carl's ear when she clutched the phone. She slid back into place, rearranged her sweater, languidly smoothing wrinkles gathered by the shoulder strap. After she returned the phone to her purse, Bonnie straightened in the bucket seat, attempting to sit taller than she felt. She looked out the passenger window, daring neither to acknowledge nor comment. Whatever she thought or said, Carl was going the wrong way. At 50 mph in a 40 mph zone.

"I said your nose is growing, my love." His voice carried its teasing lilt. Bonnie vowed not to succumb now that she was rich.

Dang, what a snare his mockery was. She had to get this man to the altar, to recite marital vows, so she tossed her mini-war out the window. She clasped her hands atop her knees, hoping she effectively emulated an Egyptian goddess on her throne.

Bonnie side-glanced at Carl. Dammit, he looked terrific, smiling eyes apparent, aglow like the roadside lights. How did men look that good without make-up and artful hair combing, just some dumb baseball cap tossed backwards onto their heads?

"Jackie's a nice lady. Steve's my brother. You ought not lie to them."

"Maybe I'm not lying," Bonnie said. "You will marry me. It was our plan, so we could meet your kids as a couple. Remember? Maybe I'll just grab Elvis by his white suit lapels, marry him in your place, Carl Edwards. I'm rich. I can do anything I want."

Bonnie repositioned her arms, to skim her shoulders and left-flick her hair. Why had she let Maybelline talk her into extensions? The temperature in the truck cab had risen in the past ten minutes, no matter what the dashboard said. Perhaps the loose curls would go limp, like her pride at losing a husband before she had one.

"May I remind you, Cinderella, that you are not rich yet, and you are riding in my truck? Now, darling, where's our hotel to bed down for the night?"

"I forgot what Siri said." Gosh darn, Bonnie'd been the brains of the office, able to recite every fact, figure, and fiction of the church. The lottery win had truly blown her mind. "Oh, just pull in here," said Bonnie as a Best Western sign hovered ahead on the right. "I think it's an omen that we'd best be heading west, to marry soon in Vegas."

"I'll book us two rooms, adjoining if that suits," said Carl. "That ought to serve the pastor's protocol as well as our peace. We can sleep on this matter and proceed in the morning—in the correct manner as well as the correct direction." Carl flipped his ball cap around to emphasize his point. "The advice of our true friends would be prudent, don't you think?"

Bonnie agreed, but she didn't feel compelled to admit it. Didn't the money give her permission to rule? She turned to stare out the window when Carl continued. "There is that small detail that we need to produce the winning ticket to the Boffo Lotto authorities to claim the prize. Look at me, my love. You realize the rules."

Carl flipped the truck's blinker and turned into the motel parking lot. *Don't confuse me with the facts* echoed in Bonnie's head. Her chin quivered. Involuntarily, of course. She'd get her queen on soon enough. After rest and a romp. She'd find a way to breech their adjoining rooms. Sanctity was bullshit in these circumstances.

After he parked, Carl continued, "I propose that we return home and lawyer up. Judge and Paul and Harold Prince at the bank, even Coach, would provide better counsel than that scumbag attorney I had in California, the only brush I've had so far. Hometown loyalty trumps a Yellow Pages lawyer any day."

Bonnie chuckled. She couldn't remain miffed at her prince. "Great. You include Coach in your counsel, and I'll include his wife, Maybelline. I need her to yank these extensions before they strangle me." *Or perhaps she can show me how to use them to strangle Carl.*

Bonnie grinned and regrouped. With the authority of experience, she said, "You might want to reconsider conferring with my former boss, Pastor Paul. Not only is he pissed at me, but I also suspect we'll be targeted for his steeple building dreams. That man is a righteous fund stalker for the Lord."

Six | *Jackie*

"STEVE, YOUR BROTHER'S RICH."

"I was hoping not to hear that ass mentioned before Thanksgiving when the obligatory family gathering occurs. I know David's rich. That damn pastor guilted us into providing for him and his family. For life. We'll hear how he once again squandered his share of our family farm soon enough, and *never* would be good for me." Steve rubbed his biceps with Miracle Ice. The vigor of his massage shouted rage.

Jeepers creepers, brother's keepers they were. Now there was potentially more money to divvy and plunder. Holy cash! No one who grew up in a small town was skilled at secrets. What if she or Steve revealed the settlement details over turkey and dressing? The prospect of prolonging the destination wedding plans so that they'd miss that family meeting appealed.

The oven timer dinged. No sense worrying about the future when a problem loomed in the present. Jackie needed to inform Steve of Carl and Bonnie's recent Boffo Lotto win. How she told the news mattered. Carl had already been enriched twice without much effort, and she didn't want Steve's ego to sag.

Thank goodness his mind didn't attach meaning to her previous false start. A certain sign that he was tired and sore. She didn't want to make him pained in spirit as well as in body.

Jackie stuck her head into the oven, further than necessary, to mutter "no more white lies." She retrieved the casserole and nudged the oven door shut with her hip. As she neared their supper table, she could hold her breath in no more.

"Steve, that stinks! How many times have I asked you not to bring that obnoxious salve to the table?" Jackie couldn't pinch her nose. She had both hands, encased in padded mitts, committed to a piping hot casserole. She twirled and set it on the stovetop, deftly avoiding the Corian counter. While swank, it wasn't burning-hot safe.

Not safe. The significance of Steve's minty massaging set in. He'd done all of the early morning milking and sanitation tasks—delivery, too? The evening shift remained. "Where's Brandon? He's been scarcer than hen's teeth for days. Are you pulling double shifts, like in your GM factory days?"

Jackie shushed. Her mother's scolding tone avalanched her brain, threatening the slippery slope of her self-esteem. Worse, MaMa Bree's vision agreed.

Steve hefted his chest to begin defending his son. When a cramp zapped his leg, he winced and rolled up his pant leg to massage his calf.

"Did that lovesick boy drive down to Purdue to check on his beloved, Julie?"

Steve looked up and nodded. One of his sun-bleached locks wiggled on his forehead when he did so, an ever-alluring gesture for Jackie. Sigh.

Jackie mellowed. She was in love with the idea of a daughter-in-law once again. It was a bonus that Julie Watson was sweet, a homegrown honey with long legs, and enrolled in Pharmacy School. Jackie would have grandchildren to spoil and a pharmacist on call. She wouldn't mind babysitting in exchange for no copay on their meds.

Steve ignored her and continued massaging Miracle Ice, now on his haunches after he'd dropped trou. Ordinarily, Jackie would protest nudity in her kitchen, but she was on a mission to divulge spectacular news.

Besides, she was struggling not to grab the Miracle Ice jar for her own knees. She'd walked a couple of miles, peeling, boiling, mincing, and mashing potatoes in the high school kitchen, then what seemed like a half-mile in her own. She longed to retire from one of those kitchens, knowing the other was forever a farmwife's lot.

But back to the matter at hand. If she couldn't share soon, she'd burst.

"Steve, pull up your pants! Put away the salve and focus, like you're always chastising me. You know I'd never willingly bring up David's name, though I do feel for his wife, Claire, and his children, Tessa and Kenny."

Jackie brought her forefinger to the dimple in her chin. She waited until Steve met her eyes. Mentioning his brazen brother David's name always did it.

When Steve complied, she brought her finger to her lip to shush his snarky remark. "I wonder if I could get Julie to befriend Tessa, to encourage that girl in school? Do you think a cyber pen pal arrangement could work?"

"You can't be Tessa's savior." Steve returned to his rubdown—finished in three seconds—capped and stowed the Miracle Ice in the bathroom medicine chest, and pulled a beer from the fridge.

Jackie admired the speed of his moves. As swift as his change of moods sometimes. After he near-drained the can,

Steve sported an anticipatory smile. "Would a cold one help you get your story going again? You can't be referring to Carl, can you?"

Jackie shrugged off the beer, kept her eyes on her slicing tomatoes task. She'd recently sharpened her knives and didn't want to guillotine her fingertips.

Steve swigged. "By-the-by, you can tell how much Bonnie loves my brother. She agreed to travel 2000 miles in a truck."

"You mean you couldn't tell when the former church secretary agreed to travel without a wedding band? Sit, husband." Jackie shook her head as she carried the plated tomatoes to the table. "What exactly did you men ponder?" Over her shoulder she could see Steve's leer.

She returned for the casserole, now steaming its glass cover. She admired the table she'd set: Fiesta Ware plates with the matching salt-and-pepper shakers and sugar bowl to sprinkle the tomatoes, the utensils parked pertly atop paper napkins. As she nestled the Corning Ware onto a trivet, she opened the lid and shoveled the scent toward Steve.

His attention secured, she looked him in the eye. "Steve, Carl and Bonnie won the Boffo Lotto last night. He's asked her to marry him in Vegas. They're returning to Michigan to retrieve us, and take us to witness their Elvis-officiated wedding."

Steve launched from his chair, whacking his knees on the table and nearly colliding with the casserole lid hovering near his head. "Are you joking? They won the $536 million I heard about on the radio? The cows bellowed when the announcer shouted it. The guy said the winner might be a single ticket! Doesn't that beat all?"

"Here's what really beats all." Jackie set the lid down to twist one of her errant curls. "Bonnie and Carl invited us to consider world travel, too. The sky's the limit, I think, were Bonnie's exact words."

"What did Carl say?" Steve sounded suspicious of the offer. Jackie knew Steve was neither used to manna from heaven nor lightning striking twice, three times, as it now had to build Carl's wealth.

"He misses you." Jackie winked and then clasped Steve's hand. "Now let's sit down and pray before the casserole cools."

Her mind drifted during Steve's prayer, considering how to make Bonnie and Carl's good fortune palatable. Steve had labored throughout his life to earn a living, including a paper route to earn money for clothing in his teens. Predictably, he hadn't considered any claim to a portion of windfall cash. New Levi's and plaid flannel shirts didn't amount to much—and Jackie had purchased them.

So far, her personal desires had raked the top, and they'd loaned Brandon money for Julie Watson's engagement ring. They'd tithed to the church, and their new dog received an engraved leather collar. Yet Steve hadn't spent a frivolous dime on himself. She felt badly that Steve's turn to wish-and-receive was last. The way his life went, the dog would learn to speak for himself before Steve did.

"Jackie, have you already left on the trip?" Steve dropped her hand to wave his in front of her face. "Again, what did Carl say? Did you talk to him?"

"Not exactly. Let me serve up the casserole." She paused to shake the serving spoon under his nose. "I can't believe you prefer details before food."

Steve surveyed his farm table, laden with a chicken casserole, sliced garden tomatoes, and fresh buttermilk biscuits. A beer in his hand and more in the fridge. His ice blue eyes smiled into Jackie's greens, sparked with loving concern.

She wiggled her ring finger so the diamond flirted for her, then squeezed his hand. "Remember your commitment to eat as many tomato slices as biscuits. I'll be keeping tabs."

Thank goodness hunger conquered Steve's questions. Thank goodness he ate as many tomatoes as biscuits and beer. Thank goodness half the casserole remained for Brandon to inhale, if and when he showed up for dinner.

Jackie deep-breathed again, folded her hands above her clean plate. Before Steve repeated his question, she answered it. "I think it's your call. Carl would love to hear from you, receive your congratulations."

Steve grimaced slightly. "Geesh—"

Jackie grabbed his hand and spoke before he could cuss. "Just like it's your turn to spend cash. And, remember your *good* brother shares."

"O'Katie." Steve withdrew his hand.

Jackie scooped something from under her placemat and plunked it beside Steve's.

"I've already snagged one of your tablets to begin a trip to-do list, and I suggest you start a spend-the-dough list."

Steve stared, then leaned to peek at Jackie's paper.

"Don't you go cheating off me like you did in high school." Jackie tapped the corner of the tablet and handed a pen to Steve. "Begin your list."

"Woman, you sound like that Capitol One credit card *What's in your wallet?* ad. We do have a comfortable amount in the bank, so I was considering upgrading the milking equipment." Steve made a rueful face. "If we leave the farm in his care, do you think Brandon can handle it? I love our son, but his learning curve is not fast and firm."

"Fast and firm?" Brandon near-shouted as he entered the house. "Just like my truck rides."

Jackie held Steve's gaze as they gauged if he'd heard the full remark.

"Hope I'm not too late for supper."

No, he hadn't. Or, if he had, he didn't let the slight undermine his appetite.

"Did you know I made a quick trip to Purdue?"

Jackie lifted her fork, left it suspended in front of her mouth. "Spare us the details, Mr. Impulse. You have some explaining to do. Wash your hands first."

Brandon scurried to obey. When he returned, Jackie restrained her notion to inspect under his fingernails. The kid might pout.

"You didn't ask your dad if you could cut out on chores. You didn't even leave a note. I don't think you've earned supper tonight."

Steve reached over and pulled out a chair. "Sit down. We have much to discuss."

Jackie knew he'd refrain from dubious lecturing. It seldom worked, anyway. Steve had Brandon over a barrel, and the kid knew it. She'd set the stage.

She moved the casserole in front of Brandon. No sense dirtying a plate. The kid probably hadn't eaten in the last twenty-four hours.

Jackie cleared the rest of the table and started kitchen

clean-up. She'd witnessed this act many times before, on the other side of the island, Steve's slam-dunk. She hummed while she wiped and mentally packed her suitcases. Yada-yada-yada. Bam-bam-bam. She and Steve would escape, and Brandon would be down with the plan.

"Shut the front door!" Brandon spouted repeatedly, as well as, "H. E. double hockey sticks!" Jackie wondered why Brandon didn't pepper his enthusiasm with football-speak.

She chanced a glance as she wiped her hands on her apron, untied it, and hung it up for the day. Beer cans littered the table and her guys' heads were bent over the yellow pad, Steve scribbling, occasionally stabbing the paper, and Brandon nodding along. Just like the old days when they devised football plays. She sidled over to the table, peeked, and then smiled. She could see *things* were settled. *Neat.*

She re-entered their conversation. "When I heard about the wedding, I remembered Bonnie put a wedding dress on layaway—"

"Excuse me, but I think your rich friend can retrieve it from hock herself." Brandon paused to butter the final biscuit. He shoved half into his mouth, not looking at his mom.

Steve nodded. "You don't have to fix everything, Jackie."

Brandon tag-teamed. "Besides a white wedding dress may not be right for a Vegas wedding. Wouldn't she want something sequined, low-cut, and slinky?"

Jackie looked down her nose at her men. "You handle your lists, and I'll handle mine." She crossed her arms. A boundary. "I've mentally packed, so I'll have plenty of time." She uncrossed her arms and pointed behind her. "See that apron? It's already hung. I'll give notice to the principal tomorrow... I can't wait! There's only a month of school left. I feel like I have Senior-itis!"

"Don't you think you ought to wait to see the whites of Bonnie's eyes and the green of her cash?" Steve, ever the measured plodder. "Theirs might not be the only winning ticket. All is not copacetic yet, Jackie. You are wheeling out of control, and I'm not willing to join you."

"Besides," he said as he elbowed Brandon to share the buttered biscuit, "what if hers isn't the winning ticket?"

Jackie glared. "Are you suggesting Fran got the Boffo Lotto numbers wrong?"

Steve chewed the biscuit as if it was the only thing in his world. Brandon wisely stared at his plate.

"Speaking of Fran. I'll call her after supper. We've got to lunch when Bonnie arrives, convene a secret conclave." Jackie winked at Steve and then gushed, "Maybe you can call Carl to confirm his take on things and find out when they plan to arrive. I've got to freshen the guest room sheets."

Just then the puppy slithered in the doggie door and approached the table to beg. Jackie would add his name—if he ever earned one— to her list of problems to solve. Brandon could subsist on junk food, but the dumb dog couldn't. Steve was right. She needed to let go of caretaking peripherals and confine her fixing to her own home.

So that she could be gone. Jackie ran to her apron to retrieve a mildly crumpled tissue from a pocket, to dab her eyes and then blow her nose.

Seven | *Fran*

"I'M MIFFED THAT YOU got to watch the lottery balls fall into place. Why didn't you call?"

"Jackie, don't get that pinched look around your eyes." Fran reached to gently touch the crow's feet threatening Jackie's youth. "We've been friends since second grade. You can't hide your feelings from me. Everyone in this community knows you and Steve go to bed early. You'd have been mighty peeved if Bonnie had called you at 10:30!"

Jackie began to titter, and her hat shimmied and shook. "I wish I'd been in the room to see you taking orders from anyone, let alone Bonnie, Paul's former secretary."

"Well, be that as it may, Bonnie won 268 million dollars, and she's invited you to witness her wedding in Vegas and maybe travel beyond. Do you see me pouting for being excluded?" Fran shook her head *no,* willing Jackie to acknowledge her good grace. "Let me tell you who *is* pouting though. Paul." She didn't add he was compensating by drawing plans and rehearsing his cash request.

Jackie swallowed firmly and looked Fran in the eye. "Speaking of travel, I was wondering, er, we were wondering, uhm you don't suppose that, uhm, some local newlyweds might have time and inclination to *adopt* a kid?"

"You mean Brandon?"

Jackie nodded, raising her cup to her lips, and took a

languid sip. She peered over the cup, eyes fixed on Fran's face, leveraging her thirst to assess the sometimes prickly moods of her friend.

Fran had witnessed this stall before, the cup as a shield to deflect Fran's well-considered input and opinions for which Jackie had no retort. Such as the fact that she was over-mired in her men's well-being, to the fault of subrogating her self. While Steve did speak for himself in the community, it was a strange circumstance that Brandon didn't when he towered over almost everyone in town, in stature and status. Stranger still because he was no longer a kid. Fran accused Jackie of *smotherhood,* a role for which Jackie seemed born.

"Jackie, you don't have to complete a requisition form, like when I was your boss. Paul is a firm friend of Steve's, as well as an enabler of the Lord. Of course, we'll monitor your son's management." Fran leaned forward and winked. "You know we're up to the task. I personally paddled Brandon's backside to help shape the man he's become, while Paul prayed you through every mess. You have earthly partners and the Godly One. We'll police the young man."

"I'm afraid it might be necessary." Jackie shook her grape-hatted head, then looked around. She'd miss the Koffee Kup. Its picture window into the lives of the town's hustlers-and-bustlers supplied priceless fodder for conjecture and I-told-you-so's.

Today, the two friends were sequestered to a corner, causing Sally the waitress to fidget. Fran knew she and Jackie were running against type. While they'd dined and dished, they'd never dallied before. No matter, it was a new era.

Sally scuttled forward, her generous bosom threatening to

burst the buttons of her uniform, to refresh their hot water pots and pluck two more teabags from her apron pocket. Neither friend acknowledged her presence. They didn't want her to linger and listen. Neither did they want her bosoms to spill out and smother their scones.

After Sally eased away, Jackie cleared invisible crumbs from the corners of her mouth, leaned in closer, and then peered side-to-side in a panoramic sweep of the restaurant. The next words tumbled over each other as if to disclaim their truth.

"Steve had to do double duty yesterday. Brandon abandoned responsibility, again, to spontaneously visit his betrothed. He apparently worked his after-supper milking shift and drove directly to Purdue. A five-hour trip—four hours if he was in heat—and you know he hadn't slept a wink before he arrived late for supper last night."

Fran bit her tongue and Crazy Glued her lips to suppress her quip. "At least he didn't miss supper." For Jackie to complain about her entitled child was new. She hoped that her and Paul's relationship would retain such passion, not settle into a rut. Abrupt home sharing with a relative called *husband* still jarred. Better not to think, just listen to her friend.

Fran nibbled fervently on a scone while maintaining eye contact, willing Jackie to affirm that Brandon had completed last night's milk shift after his tryst.

"Brandon agreed to do the dairying while we travel, but Steve's in the midst of overhauling the dairy barn and equipment. Tens of thousands of dollars have already been invested in a Trans-Iowa Milk Parlor with a robotic milking system. I heartily approved because I got my bling—new washer and dryer and a righteous diamond ring. He figured to foster Brandon's fledgling interest with modern gadgets and shiny equipment, but ours can't match Julie Watson's. The kid seems to have even cut back on gaming in order to text. Sweet nothings in the new age."

Her big diamond winked as it caught sunlight when Jackie reached for her tea. Its flash didn't deter tears, nor did the tea's sweet-and-spicy tang. "Steve's been contemplating doubling the herd. While it'd remain a one-man operation, the research indicates cows sometimes choose to be milked four-five times a day, so buns would have to be hustled. It seems a dubious time to leave a dilettante in charge."

Fran gasped, Jackie echoing her surprise, because the word *dilettante* slid from her lips. Jackie'd taken issue, her husband over her son. She'd never done that before, always the go-between between the men of her household. She enjoyed the role, Fran suspected.

So, she drew them both away from this precipice by bringing up another household male. "What about the dog?" Fran scratched at a sudden itch under her cuff. "Has he gained a name yet?"

Jackie managed a laugh. Bark-like, Fran thought. "No, but Steve has uttered 'damn dog' enough times for it to become his name."

Jackie sighed. A frown squelched further laughter. "The pup still puddles freely, and he hasn't made himself indispensable to Steve yet. Maybe never." She shook her curly head, lifted her double chin. "Brandon will be the alpha while we're gone, and the dog will remain the zeta. They'll get along."

Fran smiled ruefully. There wasn't supposed to be a hierarchy among family and friends, but some animals were more equal than others. Fran knew she would ever be the alpha, ever in command, even when Bonnie and Jackie vagabonded. Even when clad in yoga pants. Fran clung to the notion she had more clout when wearing a hat. Her thinking cap.

Fran pursed her lips. Her friend's perky one-liners—shields to deflect feelings—frustrated her, so her words surged forth, almost gagging her before they got out. "Wait just a minute!" Fran plopped her teacup back in the saucer and pulled herself erect. Her hat almost catapulted into the sweetener packets with the sudden jerk. "Brandon's engaged to sweet Julie? Why don't you have a chat with her? The way to a man's brain is sex. The problem's going to be keeping his nose to the dairying tasks and her lectures and inducements could hold sway."

Jackie looked dubious, despite the cherry-studded scone she'd just chomped, her favorite flavor on earth. She tucked a curl, chewed, swallowed, and took another bite. Better to avoid a divergent view in the moment. Fran could be decidedly fixated.

"Conceivably, the dog can assist when you leave him with Bran. As I recall, Sparty was integral to Steve's farm work."

Before Fran could settle her cup in its saucer and cross her arms over her chest to end the argument, Jackie piped in, "The dog's best skill seems to be marking his territory, and I don't think Brandon needs help with that."

Fran laughed, but not overlong. Jackie mustn't entertain notions about bunking the dumb dog with her and Paul. They were still circling each other's deeply ingrained habits. Trying to acclimate and compromise would become a tad harder with a third wheel in their home, one who peed all over the place.

"Back to urgent business, something which we can

accomplish," said Fran. "When are Bonnie and Carl expected back? We've got to get them lawyered up, financial-advised, and safe from predator relatives and friends." She neglected to cite that Bonnie and Carl needed shelter from her husband's already-schemed church expansion.

She hadn't yet considered where her brother, Judge Blackstone, would side. Hell, every other citizen of the locale... for God's sake, the town would splinter... and not merely between university loyalties of Michigan vs. Michigan State. This news needed to be contained. Note to self.

"They didn't say—"

"Well, call and ask them, Mrs. Fluffy Head."

"Good idea! My desire is to resign my job, but millionaire house guest prep must prevail." Jackie's eyes shifted to the upper left, a certain sign she was in planning mode. "I'll check the larder, maybe bake some festive Lemon Bars."

"Say no more." Fran drained her teacup for emphasis. "I'll write the letter and present it to the School Board myself. Then we can bake the bars. I need the recipe if you're leaving town."

Jackie's turn to laugh aloud. Thank goodness her recipe files were sacred, and people seldom asked for copies. She could never, ever divulge the marijuana Lemon Bar recipe, especially to Fran. What a hash of many lives that would make. On the other hand, collection plate receipts might double if patio donuts were replaced with Mari-Bars.

She sealed her lips and hustled out of the Koffee Kup booth. Fran had offered to pay, and she had a house to whip into shape, groceries to buy, and a freezer to fill with meals that Brandon and his sidekick would share while she and Steve traveled.

Caretaking 201.

Eight | *Bonnie*

"HOW SWEET THE SOUND." Bonnie began with a tone characteristic of the nouveau riche, but softened to remove the cliché. "Did you know that I only won half the Boffo Lotto?"

"No, Jackie. I don't know who the other person is, nor do I care. Let them eat cake!" Bonnie went for a flippant tone to camouflage her indignity. "Half of a half-billion, halved again for Uncle Sam's share, should still gain a heck of a lot of respect for a country girl who's remained single too long, and endured twenty years of servitude to an egomaniac who quoted the Bible, but often took the credit. It's my turn to shine, and I'm inviting you into the glow!"

Bonnie pulled the motel room drapes aside to check the weather for what to wear. Rather than disturb the numerous bags she'd brought, stuffed with all sorts of outfits to impress Carl's ex-wife, she settled on the clothing strewn all over the floor. Apparently she and Carl had had a wild night.

"I've got my priorities straight. Yes, I do. I've got to look glorious for a wedding. I've already inquired with Maybelline, who promised to learn how to do a Vampire Facial. I'm gonna have that after she yanks these extensions. Like you said, I look fab, but I'm thinking a dozen wigs would be better, more versatility to match my audiences and moods. Maybelline's sourcing Hollywood's stars' preferences, too."

Bonnie flicked her nails, one-by-one, as if flicking away

allure that might be greater than hers.

"Oh, what's a Vampire Facial? It uses your own blood. Totally revitalizing, recapturing the fountain of youth. Shall I book one for you, too?" Bonnie looked toward the mirror, gathering clothing along the way. She turned to capture each side profile and then stretched her chin forward to see if her neck wrinkles would disappear.

She also righted her posture. Years of secretary duty seemed to have permanently rounded her shoulders. That and the various church members' demands. Of which the Widow Braghorn's ranked number one. Bonnie so looked forward to peering down her nose at that woman. In her new five-inch heels.

"Don't you be stopping me with your fainting spells at the sight of blood. You can sit this one out, but I'm going to go for it. Kim Kardashian popularized it, and she looks mighty good." Bonnie arched her back to emulate one of the richest bitches in the world.

"Oh, only $1500, but so worth it. Let's face it, Jackie, good looks will fade, but not as fast with this bundle of cash. I've already researched the Korean and Saudi women's beauty secrets. Ever heard of Argan Oil and Marula Oil? I know you've heard of Oil of Olay? I ordered a case of each on Amazon."

"Why, to your home, of course. I'm a Prime Member, so the products may arrive before we do."

"Well, Carl's thinking we'll highball it and arrive tonight around suppertime. You don't mind us staying do you, since Carl sold his farm and I long-term leased my townhouse when the prospect of traveling to California presented itself."

Bonnie reflexively scrunched her eyes, in case Jackie's tone sounded tinged with regret. How bad would it be to be rejected by the nicest lady on the planet? Not until she heard 'Yes' did she breathe.

"Well, thanks. We are mighty beholden. Hey, I tried to order 350 gallons of Evian water to replicate the $5000 bath of Miami's famed Hotel Victor spa, but I lost my nerve when I thought that the only plausible container was the cow's water trough."

Laughter erupted on both sides of the phone call.

"I know. I know. Steve *would* have a cow. You're funny, my friend. How I've missed you, and I've only been gone a day."

A beat went by as both friends processed that, feeling an empty place in the remark. Bonnie wished touch was included in calls. "I've missed supercilious Fran, too."

Bonnie ran a hand across her neck and lifted her hair. "Think of it, Jackie, we were formerly a band of middle-aged women, log-jammed by other people's *stuff.* In the prior chapters of our known lives, we merely craved margaritas, a million bucks, and magic wands to resolve all the problems, and that combo had seemed out of reach."

"I know. I know. We had prayer. But God didn't answer promptly and properly, according to my mind, and I know you agree."

Bonnie almost dropped the phone with Jackie's newsflash about leaving her Lunch Lady job. How could she have been so insular overnight? You'd have thought sex cleansed such self-absorption.

"You retired? I never thought I'd live to see the day—"

"You're right, I didn't physically see you do it, but I'll be there soon. Woot! Woot! Hey, I read online that there's a world famous spa in Phuket. We'll go there!"

"Thailand, babe. With $134 million bucks, the sky's the limit. We can nap on massage tables there. There'll be no time in the interim, what with the hectic pace of packing, marrying, and honeymooning in Hawaii."

"Yes, it'll be great to escape the issues and personalities of this tiny town. Heck, the interest from $134 million would buy enough margaritas for everyone in town to remain mildly loaded—problems solved."

Nine | *Jackie*

AMPED FOR BONNIE AND Carl's return, Jackie left the lights on in the stairwell and the upstairs guest room. The couple might arrive before she got off work. Wasting a day's electricity seemed called for, so they'd know where to settle. She'd briefly considered the propriety of the double bed versus Brandon's twin beds, but holy crap, none of them were sixteen. Even Brandon was close to doubling that age. Crap, she was getting old.

She knew she'd wrestle with Steve later over the increased bill, like she did when the outdoor Christmas display ticked up their electricity use. Steve scrooged each January, questioning every Master Card charge, even for his gifts.

The porch light was turned on, too, as beacon to the UPS driver, who'd never delivered to their farm home before. Steve wouldn't allow interruption of his dairy duties to sign for anything. Jackie fervently hoped he wouldn't feel compelled to carry Bonnie's numerous Amazon boxes up the stairs.

At least Steve agreed that Bonnie and Carl's bunking with them, for an indeterminate amount of time, was a blessing. Jackie welcomed another female into her home, a partner for homemaking chores. She'd long buddied with the Barefoot Contessa on TV, though she snickered at the name's pretense. There had been the ex-daughter-in-law, but she was good-riddance forgotten. Bonnie was better, though Jackie sensed her friend had already changed. Jackie hoped she didn't offend the freshly minted millionaires. And vice versa.

She also hoped that Bonnie and Carl didn't expect to be served.

Jackie paused to peek at her lap, where a creased apron lay over her khakis, stained and limp as if it hadn't been meticulously washed and ironed a few days ago. *I'm feeling flustered in my own home, where I'm supposed to be at peace. Lord, keep envy at bay and subdue my sarcastic streak.*

She'd forced Brandon to help her refresh the guest room linens. While he hadn't grumbled, neither had he looked his mama in the eye. She hadn't confronted him about the overnight foray to visit his betrothed. She figured the task belonged to Steve, since the farm heir apparent had forsaken his share of the chores.

Jackie smiled ruefully. Brandon was long past requiring a lecture about birth control. Besides, Julie probably supplied their condoms, direct from the shelves of her father's drug store.

Jackie checked her veggie supply and retrieved steaks from the freezer in the barn. Her own mother's recipe for potatoes would be served, along with green beans and salad. She texted Steve to barter Breeden Dairy milk for California wine, nix the champagne. Jackie almost swooned at the prospect of how her home would smell. Rafter-to-rafter love.

The heirloom linens, china, and sterling were hauled from storage in the wee hours of the morning to celebrate Bonnie and Carl's return. The boomerang, wrapped in unimagined wealth, lent an odd air to rituals that were formerly confined to holidays. She prayed that she, Steve, and Brandon would behave appropriately. Brandon always hiccup-burped when excited or embarrassed. It was a wonder that the habit hadn't interfered with his All-American football play.

Late for work, her thoughts caused Jackie to fret a nail as she sped to the high school. The guest prep was accomplished by awakening with Steve's uber-early alarm. Thank goodness she knew where to nap in peace at school. She smiled, revived by thoughts of her imminent retirement.

Jackie's home-sweet-home, Steve's family heirloom, glowed with sun-blessed welcome at the end of their long, undulating lane. The accelerator seemed to lean into the van's floor of its own accord, rooster-tailing dust in the van's wake. Jackie spotted Carl's road-sullied truck parked near the kitchen door. She pulled in beside it, foregoing her ritual parking routine with the tennis ball suspended from the garage ceiling, her marker for being safe in place.

She hoisted the bundle of sweet peas whose fragrance had danced her home, glimpsing her coarse, calloused hands. She'd forgotten to lotion up. Again. Thank the Lord she was a hugger, so her hands would be behind her friends.

Before Jackie was fully out of the van, Carl rushed to sweep her into his arms. To carry her across the threshold! Even her husband hadn't done that thirty-seven years ago.

Or was it thirty-eight?

Accuracy didn't matter now, because Bonnie nearly upended Jackie and Carl when she barreled out of the mud room to group hug. Perhaps Steve saved the trio when he bounded from the barn to join in, enacting a mini rugby scrum.

Everyone jumped when Brandon shouted, "This looks like

a huddle! Mind if I join?"

Jackie wriggled out of Carl's grasp, quickly surveying the flowers to assure they weren't smushed, and led the parade into the house. Bonnie joined Jackie at the sink while she plunked them in the only cut crystal vase she possessed. Bonnie drew the water, leaning in to whisper in Jackie's ear, "Just so you know, I'm the winner."

"Show me the money," Brandon near-shouted. Thank goodness he stood a head taller than everyone else, even Carl, so his exuberance didn't zap anyone's hearing

Jackie interceded before Brandon began to burp. "Forgive my son, the one who'll have to eat his meals elsewhere if he doesn't mind his manners." She whirled to glower at the kid who would never grow up. "At least shake hands before you put your hands into their pockets. Crimeny, who raised you?" Jackie snapped, looking askance at Steve.

Steve embraced Carl, and then pulled beers from his jacket pockets. Carl didn't waste time with more greetings. He glugged. Then, turning to Jackie, he said, "May we take you out for steaks? Someplace posh and spectacular."

Jackie's face clouded and her shoulders sagged. "Well, I already have supper planned—"

"Besides," Brandon threw in, "the Boffo Lotto win is the talk of the county. I doubt there's anyplace where you won't be included in speculation about who the winner is. People are adept at reading faces around here."

Jackie vigorously nodded, pleased that her Julie-and-self-absorbed son noticed other people, as well as reading their expressions. "There's likely to be lots of questions about why you came back, too. People might already have connected dots."

Steve took over, his forehead wrinkling in earnestness. "I think we should have a quiet meal here and let the blessings sink in. Have a good think as well as a good night's sleep. We figured you might want to assemble a financial management team before you step into the public mess."

"Fran personally unplugged her husband's office phone, pretending a billing snafu, and confiscated his cell, so he can't call you two." Jackie winked. "Her brother, however, is prepared for your call, with a roster of financial advisors and plans."

Carl looked up from his beer, mildly shocked. Bonnie shushed him with a look.

"I warned you about Pastor Rankin's need to out-holy the Catholics across the street." Bonnie smiled—like an anxious rabbit eyeing a dog, Jackie thought— and turned away, to slip into the apron Jackie had placed atop the counter. Jackie could see her face appeared as red as Brandon's fancy truck.

Jackie scooted to her side, put her arm around Bonnie and gave her a sideways hug. "Our mouths sometimes don't mind our manners, do they? Welcome back, thanks for taking over my regular role." Jackie released Bonnie and turned her to look into her eyes. "Everything cool between you and Carl?"

Bonnie winked. "We'll work it out." She side bent her head to Jackie's as they began to spiral off the Idahos' skins. After several beats, she whispered, "Who's secretarying for the pastor?"

When Jackie whispered back, Bonnie nearly peed her pants. "Fran?! Lord, let me be a witness when the Widow Braghorn blusters in!"

To which Jackie replied, "That may be another reason Fran

unplugged the phone. " She wiggled her eyebrows to emulate Groucho Marx.

Bonnie cackled. "Reason three: remember that she and Paul are fairly new to romance."

Jackie's turn to double over. As she did, she gestured toward the men, bringing her finger to her lips. She whispered directly into Bonnie's ear, "Hunker down to the supper tasks, though there are few. We can talk later. We've got to listen in to the menfolk's chat. It's intel time."

"So, have you got the winning ticket in your wallet? Can we see it?" Brandon asked.

"No, it's in Bonnie's purse. She's the one who bought it, signed it, and deserves to be the prime beneficiary."

Jackie nudged Bonnie, who nearly dropped the peeler. Both women smiled at their reflections in the window above the sink. Bonnie flicked her hair like a pony who'd won a blue ribbon at the rodeo. Jackie twirled a curl in reply.

"She said she slid it under my picture, though she won't let me see."

Bonnie winked at Jackie to affirm this truth.

Though Carl was older, Steve went all Big Brother now. "I've checked on the Internet. You need to take the winning lottery ticket to the state commission for validation, and the office happens to be close by in Lansing. You won't receive any cash—full lump sum payout or an annuity spread across many years, which I personally wouldn't do, given your age—for fifteen days," Steve said. "Plenty of time to surround yourself with a proper financial team. Have you thought who you'd pick?"

"Thanks for reminding me I'm old, Steve." Carl elbowed his half-brother. "I was wondering more how to keep the genie in the bottle, so to speak. Got an underground bomb shelter where we can hide?"

"I'm mighty concerned about my weasel brother, David, racing to bask in the cash flow. Jackie told me something about you wanting us to travel with you some, and I think it'd be a good idea to skedaddle fast. Fifteen days until the funds are released is a stretch for keeping a secret. If Bonnie starts running up charges, people will ponder the source. Best to get out of Dodge."

"Are you leaving me to babysit the farm? Again!" Brandon yelled, setting down his beer so hard that beer splashed the TV screen a yard away.

"Son, have you seen the Trans-Iowa Automatic Milking System literature I left on my desk? The computerized system is right up your gaming alley. All it takes is one person to release the stall gates, cleanup, and sterilize, the whole shebang."

"Dad, with the calves we doubled the herd. That's going to extend the home delivery time. There'll be more driving, accounting, more cleaning cow teats to control the odor. More feeding and tending and cleaning stalls. You can't fool me. I'm not twenty anymore... And, I'm your only begotten former football star son!"

Before her son skulked to his Winnebago abode, to game or text or to speed to Purdue, Jackie announced supper, signaling Bonnie to wash her hands in advance of the men. A trio who'd trash the fresh hand towels.

Bonnie, in the middle of arranging the sweet peas in a vase, bent in to a deep whiff of the flowers. She picked up the arrangement and carried it to the table. In a bride's cadenced step. Then, she waltzed to wash her hands.

Steve and Carl rushed to pull Brandon back into the meal. Jackie relaxed, heartened that it wasn't up to her to unruffle Brandon's feathers. Carl had a good effect on Steve. Steve and Carl sat on either side of Brandon, each holding one of his hands. The prayer was uttered with the men in this pose. Jackie knew because she peeked.

Before anyone could spread napkins over their lap and dig in, Bonnie spoke. "Guys, hold your horses. Though I'm newly blonde—" She paused to shake her locks.

The room paused. Everyone watched and held their breath, unused to Bonnie's demand for attention. "I'm not a helpless dim bulb. I may have purchased the ticket by chance, but I won. I signed the ticket, without Carl's direction, and secreted it in my purse." She paused to reach for Carl's hand.

"With great love, I will add. I don't need everyone climbing all over me on how to handle the win. You may recall I was a church secretary for twenty years, so I know my way around a computer. I've learned that, while Michigan requires a lottery winner to publicly claim their prize, Illinois doesn't. I've already talked to Judge and he's going to create an LLC."

"Like the micro-dairy—" Steve began, planting his elbows on the tabletop.

Bonnie shushed him with a look, which Carl seconded. It may have been Steve's home, but it was not his place to override his lady millionaire.

"The LLC will claim the ticket on *our* behalf," Bonnie said, turning to bat her eyelashes at Carl. "Judge will see to everything, so that we can go to Vegas and get hitched."

Bonnie sat taller in her chair and turned her attention to Brandon.

"Yes, Brandon, you *will* babysit the farm, but you will receive a generous allowance from the corporation as long as you remain silent about our win. I'm planning to beseech the pastor to convince Fran to claim she made a mistake ..."

Everyone's eyes rolled at the chances of that happening. Pastor Paul asking his wife to lie? Could Fran even admit she'd made a mistake?

"If word gets out, I'll rely on them to squelch rumors by spreading word that my ticket was one number off. I need all of you to collude. Agreed?"

Everyone did, and then everyone ate, though doubting the success of Bonnie's plan. Especially Brandon, who had already texted Julie, the new love of his life. How could it matter since she was far removed from the local community, studying hard at Purdue?

Julie texted back. Gossip about the wigs and expensive facial had already drifted down to Purdue. She planned a trip home to meet the new Kardashian. Oops!

Brandon gulped and return-texted, "Mistake. My bad. Eating supper. Talk later with details."

As soon as I digest food as well as the facts. I'm not getting jammed again.

Ten | *Fran*

FRAN ALREADY PLANNED TO suggest surveillance cameras be installed in the Breeden milk barn, with live feed direct to her computer, before the lotto spenders left. She took her role as chider-in-chief seriously. She'd been given a sacred duty, to keep everything down on the farm copacetic until Jackie and Steve's return.

She didn't consider the indecency of Winnebago cams. She did not want to see the condition of Jackie and Steve's sweet retirement ride, now given to the adult child as his bachelor abode. A hundred yards from his parents' home but secluded between the barns. Brandon's slovenly dress guaranteed the interior would be unkempt, and she didn't need to voyeur his bedroom moves. She and Paul had moves of their own.

She felt joyful but wistful that her friends were about to vagabond again. As soon as the payout arrived in the various LLC accounts and the school year ended. Fran adored the glint in Jackie's eyes, similar to the reflection in her own mirror when she retired. That woman was itching for freedom, to be no longer bound to kitchen detail. Fleeing to travel assured that.

It was Steve who was tepid to travel although Carl's brotherly allure was strong. Brandon? No vote. Again. She almost felt sorry for him.

Fran was a list maker, a taskmaster supreme. The arm's

length list for Bonnie was lush with methods to protect her wealth. Her own name—Fran Blackstone Rankin—was in the mix. As the pastor's wife, the first lady of the congregation, she possessed the influence to keep the predators at bay, though she didn't know what kind of chains could keep her husband's claims on the money bags as religious conveyor belt. He, too, was adept at lists.

Fran had already alerted her brother, the Judge, to cut back on the booze and bone up on trust and estate planning. His eyes glistened, maybe brimmed with tears, as he considered limited liability company creation. His leather law books could use a good thumb through. Perhaps release a few moths into the rarified air of the law office. He'd likely have to wear a mask to not succumb to dust-induced coughing.

She'd even done research on suitable fees for his expertise. Hers, as well. Perhaps she wouldn't need to sell her beloved cottage after all. She'd still live with Paul in the parsonage, of course, but have her own home as a refuge... to write her memoir or to escape the thunder of the parishioner's demands, er needs, would be a boon.

She could leave her hair in curlers, buff her nails, leave an egg white facial on her face for hours. She wouldn't have to wait 'til the afterlife to have a great body. Her exterior would be as beautiful as her assuredly saved soul.

The countdown was two weeks to get it all done. Fran felt familiar with, even emboldened, by deadlines. The thrill of beating the clock, holding back the throngs of money-grabbers, packing the travelers' bags, and expediting battening down the Breeden dairy farm made her heart race. She hadn't felt this exhilarated since lottery night.

Wait, about last night...

Her phone blared "Amazing Grace", shepherding away her salacious daydreams. She picked it up and replied, "How sweet the sound."

"Do you think Judge can expedite passports?"

"I reckon he can do anything. He's bright, and he's my big brother. Must be your resignation papers are in order." Fran already knew this, of course, because she'd attended the School Board meeting last night and strong-armed four out of five votes and signatures on the dotted lines. An acceptance letter she'd prepared prior to the meeting suited all.

She bypassed protocol to scan it in the school offices, pausing to caress her oak desk and spit on the current principal's leather chair. She emailed the scan to Jackie and the Board members, blind-copied herself. She jogged back into the new boss's office and spun the chair, slammed the door, and jogged to her car. The finality of Jackie's retirement made her feel frisky. Her management skills remained intact.

A thud of the phone hitting a hard surface served as Jackie's response to Fran's inquiry. That wasn't the expected reply. Fran ran to her refrigerator to fetch a Coke.

Fran sipped the Coke, her migraine mitigater, until Jackie came back on the line. "Jackie, were you multi-tasking, crimping the phone to your shoulder again? Hope your chiropractor isn't booked, because your body is going to require adjustments."

"Well, our travel discussions have advanced, you might say. Instead of merely flying to Vegas to witness Bonnie and Carl's wedding, then accompanying them on a Hawaiian honeymoon, we are leapfrogging the Pacific Ocean to Australia. After that

Bonnie wants us to lounge in a famous spa in Phuket."

"Hell, I didn't know you knew where Phuket and Australia were, Jackie."

"You insulting me again? Actually, I might not have known except Steve has a globe in his office. This morning, he strong-armed the globe like a Wheel of Fortune contestant. Downed a few with Carl after milking, I think. The new equipment install is going great, by the way."

Fran frowned while clenching her jaw. Jackie tended to digress.

"Anyways, Carl's finger landed on Australia. Did you know it looks like the United States upside down? Without Florida, of course."

Fran crinkled her nose and quipped, "Some say we'd be better off without Florida. All those raisins down there filling the waterways with errant golf balls. No income taxes, no goals, snaggle-toothed alligators lurking about."

"Didn't your honeymoon cruise depart from Ft. Lauderdale?" Jackie rushed on—Fran felt her embarrassment—for referencing their shared secret. Fran and Pastor Paul had seemingly pre-marital cruised, causing congregational lips to flap, and church coffers to burgeon when church members lost bets. The Pastor's sermon topics after the cruise hadn't flinched. He and Fran never told his flock the ship's captain had married them prior to the cruise departure.

"That was quite an audacious move we pulled off, wasn't it?" Fran mused, then laughed aloud. "As I recall, we returned to Paul's flock with tans juxtaposed with the church members' red faces." She scratched her cheek as if to remove a final layer of peeling skin.

Fran was done with this subject, so she veered back to Jackie's kitchen tasks. "What are you so fuss-budgety in the kitchen for, Jackie? Why are you cooking rather than packing your bags?"

"I'm busy preparing freezer meals for Brandon to eat for many weeks, not one."

"Well, I gotta say you're foolish to have not taught Brandon to make scrambled eggs and toast. Thank heaven the kid knows how to use a Keurig machine and water comes in bottles. At least you aren't asking me to feed him and the dog. I won't have time. Did I tell you I've decided to write my memoir?"

The phone thudded again. Soon, Jackie returned to tease, "Do I get to fact check your story?"

"Don't worry, Jackie, I won't tell about the time you took the dare to use play money to pay for a PayDay candy bar at the senior canteen."

Jackie squeaked, "Oh!"

Fran cut her off. "But I'm considering revealing your hayride make-out sessions, though. For gracious sakes, you two nearly set fire to the hay."

"Oh, there's Call Waiting," Jackie said and hung up.

Judge came through with passports for all and documents to shield the lottery funds. Inviting Fran to his office for celebratory slugs of Maker's Mark, he broke lawyerly tradition by revealing Bonnie as the sole owner of the ticket, though not the sole winner. $134 million remained a lofty amount. Both wondered how it would effect Bonnie and Carl's relationship?

Her relationship with Jackie and Steve, too? Her relationship with the town? Would she ever return?

After several refills, Judge told Fran of the fiction with which she needed to agree: she'd erred with Bonnie's lottery pick numbers, which would be the only plausible means for shushing rumors that Bonnie had won. Fran considered glugging the rest of her glass' contents and, rather than swallowing, spraying Judge's face. Oh, the cruelty, the ignobility of his request. She never made mistakes!

But her brother held her gaze, as only a big brother could, and she relented. It dawned on her that her husband, the Pastor, would have to comply with the subterfuge, too. They'd be partners in crime. This wasn't an example of bearing false witness against a neighbor, was it? How *technical* did Ten Commandments interpretation get in their faith?

Well, Fran decided to do what she could for her friend's cause. She raised her right hand and pledged. Later, she'd make Paul swear on a Bible. What the hell? He wasn't Catholic, where every lie was a sin, and his cause, his church, would benefit.

However, Fran knew Bonnie intended to take Jackie shopping for a suitable wardrobe, stating Spartan green tees and sweatshirts wouldn't play well in a country dedicated to rugby and where soccer was football. Something about vampires and facials and wigs. Fran would be appalled if/when the two women arrived at the Koffee Kup for their final Silly Hats and Caps Society meeting garbed in matching minks.

Hell, her friends had gotten more bosomy and giggly, regressing to their teens, the scamps. And for Jackie to bring up her honeymoon cruise! Fran contemplated including Jackie and Steve's pre-marital shenanigans under the old comforter on the hay fresh from the Breeden's barn loft, in the corner in the back of the truck in her memoir. They were fortunate the church youth leader was unfamiliar with a stick shift, so he stayed busy with driving, his eyes on the road. They were fortunate there weren't cell phones with video capability in the '70s. They were fortunate everyone writhed equally beneath blankets.

Except for Fran, who secretly swilled whiskey stolen from her dad's bar. Time to tell all. Ensconced behind a larger desk, Fran decided. With a large monitor iMac to complete the ensemble, paid for by her minder fee.

Eleven | *Bonnie*

"AMAZING GRACIOUS IS AT hand, Jackie!" Bonnie entered with her arm extended, Lady-Liberty-like. "Let's go shopping with my new Capitol One card. The sky's the limit!"

Jackie's gasp was not what Bonnie expected to hear. She expected glee. Then, she spied a piece of paper parachuting to the floor. Jackie looked ruffled, yet calm. In the midst of an out-of-body experience, perhaps.

Sort of like I felt when my Boffo Lotto win settled in.

Knowing that Jackie had a bad back and knees, Bonnie bent to retrieve the letter. "May I read it?"

Jackie nodded, wild eyes flitting around. "It's my official School Board letter. Steve must have printed it this morning after he settled into post-breakfast emails. He taped it to the fridge for me to see when I got home."

Jackie sighed. Bonnie knew that sigh and agreed. Men! She was barely getting used to Carl's moods and attitudes, and she knew Steve's well as per Jackie's reports. Conversations of the Silly Hats and Caps Society had often not been silly.

She contemplated their lunchtime sessions of the past. It was a wonder Jackie accepted marital counseling from two same-aged, yet single friends. Fran was now married, and soon she would be, too. Wonder which way the advice would flow now?

"I drudged through an awful day at the school cafeteria,"

Jackie said as she kicked off her shoes, sat down and rubbed her feet. "Wish he'd texted me. There'd have been more spring in my step as I slung hash. How did I live with a teenager all those years?"

Bonnie didn't know, and she cared even less. She wanted to pump up the room's mood. "Yoo-hoo!" She plunked the letter on the counter and pulled Jackie to her feet. "Don't you see? It's God's perfect timing. An official resignation begs for a fur. We have time to hustle to the Love and Lace Shoppe at the Flint Mall. I was headed there to retrieve my wedding dress from layaway. Let's go!"

"God's perfect timing may be fur-fabulous, but I have meal-making chores." Jackie scooped up her shoes and trudged to the hall closet, returning to the kitchen in tennies. "What are you doing in the kitchen, a room from which you've been scarce until suppertime each day?"

"Jackie, you're just grumpy because your feet hurt. Too much change marshaled across your countertops. The hard part is decided, because the *fur-chase* is on me." Bonnie paused to hugely wink, to underscore her pun and push it past Jackie's mixed mood. "Your only decision is shall we go today or tomorrow, though I'm ready now. I want my wedding dress in my arms, to have and to hold from this day forward. Let the men fend for themselves. Mama Bree isn't here, shaking her finger at you."

Jackie put her hands on her hips and then transferred them to the counter. "Seriously, Bonnie. You haven't gotten your first deposit in the bank yet. I know, because Harold Prince, the bank manager, hasn't done parade laps around the town square yet, seated atop the back ledge of his new Cadillac convertible like it was the Fourth of July."

"That's the benefits of plastic. Buy now, pay later. You didn't dump your Master Card after your road trip last year, did you?" She giggled at Jackie's arched eyebrows, then slapped her knee. "Of course, you did. And Steve paid cash for your diamond, washer, and dryer, didn't he?" Before Jackie turned away, busying herself with something in an upper cupboard, Bonnie saw her flush.

"It doesn't matter, Jackie." Bonnie backed off poking fun. "I've got an auto bill pay system as well as auto deposit into the LLC account, which may be in the Caribbean for all we know. Harold Prince has nothing to celebrate, because he'll receive a plausible dribble of cash, maybe for Brandon's farm management draw. Remember, this is all going to be secret, hush-hush. That's why we're shopping far away, in Flint."

Jackie turned back toward Bonnie at that notion. She put her hands on her hips, in control again. "I wondered about buying fur, a rarity here despite winter's extreme chill. That's flashy advertising of a boost in financial circumstances, as well as pandering to the flesh. If Fran were here, she'd smack our hands for our lust."

Bonnie threw her head back into full-bodied laughter. "We can fix that by inviting her to shop, too. She's probably mighty bored with retirement by now."

When Jackie's face maintained its disapproving frown, Bonnie stopped. She shifted her tactics. "Did you read the church bulletin, and the small ad in the back page of the paper, announcing Fran made a mistake with the numbers, as rumor control. Thank God, Pastor Paul has the Lord on his side to convince her to fictionalize a fact."

"Actually, Fran told me her brother got her smashed and gave her the news." Jackie smirked. "So, how are you managing a straight face when people offer their condolences?"

"I was grateful my head was in the beauty shop wash bowl, with the water on full blast, when Maybelline asked me if I wanted the Vampire Facial. She bought what I murmured, and the moment passed. All the more reason to go shopping!"

Jackie pantomimed sealing her lips with one hand and crossed her fingers on the other. "Good grief. Keeping this secret isn't going to be much fun, is it?"

"But shopping *is* fun." Bonnie spun Jackie around and untied the apron, to metaphorically unleash Jackie from her chores. She walked to the laundry room and stashed the apron in the hamper. "See, you're *unhampered,*" she said. Bonnie withheld laughter, even at her own quickly crafted joke. She desperately wanted Jackie to get it, and then let go.

Jackie remained standing, limp-armed, so Bonnie pushed more vigorously. "Straighten that posture. You'll survive without your kitchen *uniform,* but I may not be able to walk beside you in Australia in constant Spartan green, your other uniform. Look at your bland-colored slacks. I've only been staying here a few days, and I'm bored."

She paused, but didn't allow Jackie to object. "Let's get that fur for Fran. That'll ease the pain of being publicly wrong. And wouldn't that just roast the Widow's tits when the new pastor's wife sits in the front row of church in a longer, fuller, lusher mink than hers? Think I can bribe a choir member to snap a photo to send to us?"

Jackie closed the cabinet door and marched back to the closet to don her shoes. Bonnie had her in tow now, aka a

Capital One card in her wallet.

"Let me write a note for Steve that we'll bring tacos home for supper. It's Tuesday, isn't it!"

"As I said. Jackie, you no longer have to bargain-think. We've got dough to go, cash to dash anywhere at any price we want!"

Bonnie's Jaguar growled to life, almost before Jackie swung her purse inside and closed the car door. What a resounding closure the door made, unlike Bonnie's old Camry or Jackie's vans, old or new.

"We'll go to the furrier beside the Love and Lace Shoppe. I'll pay my layaway bill and convince the clerk to ship my wedding gown directly to the Wynn Las Vegas. You'll help me with that, won't you, my matron of honor?"

Holy crap! The topic came up fast. There was nothing to do but proceed, so Jackie did, hand ready to steady the wheel if Bonnie wilted in her seat. "Steve shared that Carl isn't going to marry you in Vegas, Bonnie, Elvis or not. Something about his ex-wife snatching half of his half of the cash due to California's tax laws."

"That's a dodge bigger than Judge's tax-shelter plans." Bonnie tossed her loose-curled hair and toed the accelerator further to the floor. "That man's in love with me, and he fears the Lord more than he surmises. He's gonna marry me, or I'll unleash Pastor Rankin on him. He'll put the holy screws to Carl when I suggest a cash donation to my former boss, the steeple chaser."

"Well, that's a fate worse than death. He's called Steve

several times to insist he be invited to supper, so he can lean on your compassion. Fran said she practically has to nail him to the chair at the office. Again when she feeds him supper each night. He's even badgered her to make a butter cake to bring over. And Fran doesn't bake."

"That man is so transparent. He forgets I worked for him for twenty years."

Jackie gasped. "No one's made butter cake since Mama Bree retired her recipe after her final bake sale." She fished her iPhone from her purse.

"Look at whose Googling with her phone!" Bonnie snickered. "You really have been spending too much time with teens."

"Gag it, Ms. High-faluting. I just thought about fact-checking that community property law b.s. Sounds like another load of California crap, now that I've said it aloud."

It took a few minutes before a Wi-Fi signal popped along country roads, but Jackie soon had an answer. "Bonnie, Google's top entry encapsulates the law. Looks like community property only applies to items acquired after a couple is married."

"Why didn't Judge figure that out?" Bonnie frowned. "I certainly paid him a fine sum and everything I needed to know should have been included." She checked her look in the mirror, puzzling over that. Jackie kept her mouth shut.

"Men are mizzly weasels. Judge is such a boozehound. I hope my trust wasn't misplaced."

"You know that your bestie, Fran, watched over his shoulder to assure that it was all copacetic." Jackie used Steve's favorite term on purpose, pulling his Christian aura into play.

Bonnie steamed on. "Carl is twisting the truth on me, thinking he can bamfoozle a blonde. Well, he's got a thing or two coming. Like my fists in his gut." Bonnie smacked the steering wheel with her palm to emphasize her point.

"Hold on, Bonnie, hold on. Don't throw the baby out with the bath water. You didn't let go of your solo claim on the ticket, so if he wants to travel with his cash to dash idea, of which Steve and I highly approve, you've got him where you want him. And I don't mean in your wallet with your Capital One card."

Bonnie drummed her thumbs on the wheel, to join Jackie, the lover of school bands, who thumped her hands on her thighs in drum cadence. Several seconds passed, then Jackie giggled and clapped her hands like cymbals. She gulped air to exclaim, "You're on top, in control of your man."

Bonnie yea-hawwed, then yelped, "Having control over Carl is going to be better than the cruise control on my new car." She pushed the button to lower the Jag's convertible top, and they glided to the Flint Mall, laughing all the way.

Both women knew, as women do, that sex was the best control overall.

Twelve | *Jackie*

AFTER BONNIE DUMPED TWO paper bags, already greasy and enticingly odored, Jackie eased an enormous cardboard box onto the kitchen island, gently, as if it were a wedding cake. Steve's eyebrows raised.

And raised even higher when, with a brazen smirk, Jackie teased off the lid and tossed it over her head. The lid landed in the sink and bumped the faucet, pushing it on to drench one of the box's corners before Bonnie stepped over to nudge the faucet off. This was a *waste not, want not* house.

Jackie turned her smirk on Bonnie. "Who's the one who's completely forgotten that she's a millionaire, able to afford all the water in the world? Talk about habits, Bonnie."

Bonnie ignored Jackie's appropriation of her chide. She launched into a cheesy stripper tune, purposely over-loud and off-key, bending notes as only a seasoned singer could.

Steve's eyebrows relaxed, his creased forehead moving to a frown, so Jackie paused to inhale deep with a prolonged exhale before she slithered a fur from its tissue paper. She ignored the tacos' scent, hoping her bosom showed to good effect. Midway through the protracted process, she fluttered a coat sleeve and lofted an air kiss.

Bonnie sent a volley of air kisses for Carl, too. Both winked extravagantly at their guys—Bonnie with alternate eyes—ordered to set down their beers, and they keep their hands clamped to their knees. Attention.

The dog didn't obey. His head pendulumed like the grandfather clock in the entry, now chiming six o'clock.

Jackie stopped, confused for a moment, too. *My, it's late and... and why is the dog inside?* Oh yeah, the tacit agreement of the household. The dog used his own door, and remained inside when tacos were the meal. Popcorn, too, because he lapped up the mess, playing fetch without bidding, to clear the floor. His body language looked expectant, miming his master, his Dalmatian markings a-dance. What distinguished the men was that they did not pant. Their faces looked befuddled and tinged with alarm.

Jackie slinked into the coat, lifted the collar to her ears, and twirled like Marilyn Monroe. She bowed, in part to assure that the dog didn't consider her aggressive, though she hoped Steve thought she was, in a sexy, fashion forward way.

Bonnie continued the bump-and-grind song. Who knew she knew more than a few bars? The dog's tail metronomed against Steve's wooden chair, back beats to Bonnie's sleazy croon. Occasionally, he let out a howl, which might have been interpreted, under the circumstances, as a whistle.

The women paraded around the island, and then sat on each man's lap. Concerns about the furs' cost evaporated with caresses and kisses on the neck.

There were three furs, but Jackie had insisted on this teasing approach to appraise, er influence, Steve's acceptance. Two more resided in the Jag's trunk, awaiting permission to be donned by Bonnie and gifted to Fran, if the men agreed that furs weren't too *spendy.* Bonnie regarded a fur as entry level for a millionaire. Multiplied, the furs represented solidarity among good friends.

Brandon shuffled into the room just as his mom planted a big one on his dad's lips. "Shut the front door! It's either too hot or too cold in here, and I can't figure out which."

Jackie jerked, unknowingly streaking a line of lipstick across Steve's cheek. Brandon may have been an adult, but it wasn't a habit to *carry on* in front of him. She snatched her apron from its hook and dabbed at Steve's cheek, busy to cover her embarrassment.

Brandon chuckled. "Must be too cold, because my mom's wearing a mink." Then his neck swiveled to take in the entire room. He whistled, causing the dog to bound to his side. "Did you buy a fur for me?" Brandon jerked a chair from the table and swiveled to sit. With his arms propped on the chair back, he seemed to be willing the show to go on.

Eager to exit, but willing to stay, Steve and Carl stood to avert a response. The reflexive move dumped the women to the floor. The dog ambled over to lick at the fur. Jackie was glad that she wore slacks, so her son didn't glimpse her underwear.

"Something amiss?" Brandon's arms flew up in feigned wonder while the women clambered up, using the counter top as leverage and wishing for a pulley. Brandon leered at his mom and dad in turn, enjoying their awkwardness and his seldom-gained upper hand.

Moments passed. Everyone avoided eye contact and no one spoke. All except Brandon wanted the incident to vaporize. Only the dog took a neutral stance.

Hunger intervened. Carl and Steve made eye contact. If the flustered women weren't going to release the tacos from the bags, they would, with or without plates. The better to ignore

Brandon, who likely *would* wear a fur, not even knowing another football star, Joe Namath, already had. In the '70s, long before history began for his generation.

When Steve rose abruptly, Jackie's hands jammed into her coat pockets and gouged a hole in one seam. Yikes, could she take the coat back? Not up to 4-H sewing standards.

That's it! A plan hatched, the better to drown Brandon's teasing banter. For cripes' sakes, the kid usually ignored her, so she could ignore him.

This was a sign that God wanted her to take her secret stash on the trip. She'd impulsively attempted to abandon such kicks when she'd thrust the canna-candies in Bonnie's hand as a goodbye gift, a little something to stoke the mega-miles drive. Now, Bonnie confessed her desire for more treats.

They *needed* a stash. But cookies would crumble, chocolates would melt, and gooey lemon bars would attract ants. Jackie blushed as she recalled the padded hangers she'd religiously stuffed for the Winnebago trip. So much precision, so much work for a few months travel. So 2010.

This time, the travel plans were open-ended, fueled by bounteous cash. So much more could be stuffed in a pocketed pouch, encased in fur coats. Four bags to fuel a dash or a dawdle, whichever pace they preferred.

Just then the dog spurted from behind Steve's chair. He went straight for her crotch – no, her hand in her pocket, perhaps surmising a doggie treat in residence and ready to be dispensed. Oh no, that stash-in-the-coat-lining plan wouldn't work. The DEA had drug-sniffing dogs at the airport for reals. Going international might be hazardous, might lead to charges, maybe even incarceration. Would God mitigate that crime?

Too much to think about on an empty stomach. Before the men gobbled all the tacos, Jackie re-boxed her coat and went to the cupboard for plates and glasses. Just because those gathered were rich didn't mean they could abandon manners.

The next afternoon, as she drove away from her final day at school, Jackie called Uncle Walt at the Feel Good Forever Farmacy. He merrily sold her a hollow cane, with the weed pre-stuffed with single-pop bags. Did she want ZigZag papers stuffed inside as well or would she be baking abroad?

"Abroad?" Jackie croaked. "How did you know I was going abroad?"

To which, Walt replied, "I am your Uncle. I know everything, Mrs. Breeden," in his slithery snake oil voice.

Uh, er, gulp. Jackie ached to get away from the cloister of a close-knit community. "We'll pay extra for you to swallow this secret, Uncle Walt. Put it on Bonnie's Capitol One card, please. Consider it a tip."

Jackie hurried home, mindful that she'd accomplished her final errand in her known world, *for an indeterminate time.* With each repeat of Carl's phrase, she acclimated. She put the pedal to the metal to avert tears and then eased back. It wouldn't do to leave town with a ticket for their friend, Judge, to fix.

Jackie parked the van in the garage, hefted the plump plastic bags from the back, and trudged carefully into the house. She dumped the bags on the counter, stashed her keys in her purse, and then tossed it to her kitchen desk. She shrugged out of her hoodie, allowing it to slump to the floor, then paused. *Holy crap, I'm starting to act as slovenly as my carefully-brought-up-but-clueless adult child.*

Double pause. And, I like it.

In seconds, she climbed the stairs to Brandon's boyhood room. She'd been sorting and re-sorting clothes for their trip, the patterned squares on the quilted twin bedspreads providing a nice grid. Early summer's chilly sunshine warmed the room and, almost against her will, Jackie warmed, too. Adventure was going to be good, all good, and cure the doldrums that clogged her mind.

Despite Bonnie's insistence that there were stores in the places they'd travel, she enjoyed this review of her wardrobe. Jackie knew her friend preferred not to see her uniformly clothed in Michigan State green, but leaving the array would be like leaving her community of friends, which was tough. Not packing fan wear would undermine the familiar.

It wasn't the finances of new clothes purchases that daunted her. Bonnie, the new half-of-a-half-billionaire, would fund anything and everything. It was the near-lifetime habits betrayed. Her entire safety net severed, like the basketball hoop's net dismantled by the winners of final tournament games.

Jackie grimaced, as she knew Steve, her sports authority husband, would. Her comparison was off. Brandon would mock her endlessly. One act was victory, the other was not.

An hour later, Jackie's bags were packed. Three suitcases and a plastic garment was not. Thank goodness she'd be *in a posse,* as Brandon now termed *a team,* as they ventured forth.

Everything else would be new.

Nope. All new was not all good. That Jackie couldn't, wouldn't contemplate total uprooting. She looked down at her posture, fists to her hips. It reinforced her resolve. She wouldn't acquiesce. She plucked two of her Spartan green shirts and plunked them back into the to-go pile. She'd pay extra if the luggage poundage went over the airline allotment.

She fingered her single pearl necklace, an item she wore constantly in homage to her mom. Then, she sighed a repentant sigh. Perhaps because they lived in the Breeden homestead and were entrenched in a community in which Pa and Mama Bree towered, she hadn't thought of her own mother in a long, long time. It was time to visit her grave, time to say good-bye yet again and shed a few tears. Australia was a gigantic leap away.

An hour later, Jackie finished packing her bags. Three suitcases and a plastic garment bag filled with her friend-of-the-bride gown and new full-length fur. She played with the zippers a few moments, feeling like a carefree, but quizzical kid. An adult about to go truant on an adventure extraordinaire.

The garage and kitchen freezers were full, pantry snacks stockpiled, and the farmer who cash-rented their land had brought in five-pound bags of popcorn. Her thirty-something son would not miss a meal. No one could challenge her Great Mother cred.

The utility bills were six months pre-paid, guaranteed by overdraft protection from one of Bonnie's LLC accounts. Even their monthly tithe to the church benefitted from an over-generous donation on the entourage's behalf. That much money ensured Fran and Paul's lottery win silence, if not their bond with the Lord. The vetting of steeple builders had already begun.

All the potential loose ends tied as properly as feasible, sans fanfare and forget-me-nots. While she'd been incensed with the high school staff's lapse of a decent send-off several years ago, when their travel had been a mere US gallivant, now she didn't care. Fran had retired as principal and half the personnel differed from their heydays. Let the high school children bring their own food or starve. Jackie had peeled enough potatoes to line the Equator.

The dog howled as if admonition for her snark. He howled and wailed and barked. What had gotten into that idiot dog? He should be with Steve. Was he pre-complaining about their departure?

She trundled down the stairs—it was time to prepare the last supper, anyway—massaging the banister with one hand. The action gave her the handle on events she didn't feel she had. She winced as the familiar board on the third step creaked, an occurrence no matter which way she zigged or zagged.

Was that scratching on the back door? Damn that animal. She abbreviated her habitual kisses to each gilt-framed Brandon portrait in the stairwell, wondering if the dog would grow up any more than Brandon. Brandon wouldn't consider repairing a damaged door, and Steve wouldn't leave a tattered door behind.

Carl would defend the pup and then insist on helping with repairs. The Dalmatian pup restored him to Steve's heart, so Carl idealized it. Jackie wondered why they'd never gotten around to properly naming him? They'd had him six months.

Yelp, whimper, scratch-scratch. This was incomprehensible. Why didn't the dog enter via his special door? She half-ran past the entry and through the kitchen, at last arriving at the mudroom door. She attempted to cover her ears and jerk open the door simultaneously.

The dog squirted past her. He streaked toward the kitchen, followed a second later by a stench. Unmistakable, that odor. The dog had been skunked.

Jackie slammed the door and raced after him. The dog rounded the kitchen island, galloped through the house, and leapt over an ottoman into Steve's chair. Dear God, not there!

Jackie grabbed an apron and tied it around her girth. She retrieved the vanilla food flavoring from the cooking supplies cupboard, soaked the bib and long strings of the apron, ready for the occasional inhale of the scent in case she forgot to mouth breathe.

Thus prepared, Jackie set out across the space, clicking her tongue soothingly, a sound she hoped would calm and lure the dog for capture. She drew closer, but as she got within an arm's length of the still-whimpering pup, he bounded out of the chair and headed toward the bathroom just off the kitchen.

Jackie arrived at the bathroom in seconds and slammed the door. "Good dog!" she yelled before she ran to Steve's computer where she Googled 'How to de-skunk your dog.' She was already dizzy and out of breath. A sit for research would do her good.

The Humane Society website's No. 1 suggestion: Keep Fido Outside. Ha! As usual, the best solution was outside the parameters a farmwife was given.

No. 2 looked more promising. A mixture of peroxide, baking soda, and Dial dishwashing liquid while the animal was still wet.

Jackie smiled. She'd found a reason to appreciate Amy, Brandon's former wife. The bad-ass chicka had been a fake blonde and had left behind a bottle of peroxide. Jackie knew exactly where it was. In the back of the pantry. She blessed her sweet mother's advice to never purge anything.

Jackie sped to the barn to grab Steve's neoprene gloves, thinking sadly that her favorite Spartan shirt would need to be burned. She quickly surveyed the area, knowing that, as usual, the men were scarce. She spotted a small, galvanized tub and appropriated it to mix the potion that would quell the stench.

"Amazing Grace"... Holy crap, even from the barn, Jackie could hear Bonnie's ringtone, though it was stuffed in her purse. A shrill command, rather than a comfort, it made the calamity worse.

Thank goodness the distance back to the kitchen was short. Thank goodness the door was ajar, so she could enter easily with her hands full. Finally, the phone stopped ringing. A blessing because Jackie hadn't time or inclination to hear whatever demand Bonnie was insisting upon now. Her dance card of chores was more than full.

Jackie shook her head to refocus on her own agenda and to dismiss the inevitable bitchy voicemail from Bonnie. She assembled the ingredients, donned the gloves, and stuffed her hair up into one of Steve's baseball caps. She snatched a couple of pairs of sunglasses, too. One for her and one for the dog. Might be a barrier to eye sting.

Wait! Jackie closed her eyes to recall the bold print item at the end of the article. Milk may be another way to treat your pet's eyes and face. She drenched two kitchen towels with milk. She didn't concern herself with economy. Plenty more milk where that came from in the milk barn. She wanted to do best by the dog and herself. Eyes were needed to obey.

Jackie took a deep breath, entered the bathroom quickly, tackled the animal, and blindfolded him with one of the milk-soaked towels. She placed the other towel atop the small sink counter, after a quick dab at her own eyes. Insurance. She edged through the door, picked up the galvanized tub, not caring if she sloshed.

Thank goodness the skunked mutt opted to hide in the shower tub, the normal bathing location. She hefted the galvanized tub to her hip, mouth-breathed deep, and dumped the contents. The dog didn't balk or bark or budge throughout. Glory be! *Their discipline-challenged dog trusted her love.* This would work out.

The dog shampoo, step No. 3, perched nearby, a squeeze bottle quickly flipped open with a thumbnail. Thank goodness the shower was fitted with a handheld spray. Thank goodness a mountain of towels lay stowed under the sink. Thank goodness the dog obeyed one training aspect: to not shake himself dry inside their home. Stay!

The dog hunkered down. Ashamed? Wish Brandon would absorb some of that sentiment. Would his hyper-huge ego ever abate?

Jackie drew a milk-soaked towel edge to her nose, treasuring the familiar scent, their income stream for six years, and now the savior of eyes. Refreshed, she bent over the sink to wash her own face and hair with shampoo, and then wriggled out of her clothes. In her hustle, she forgot to mouth-breathe and almost passed out.

Eyes closed, she fumbled for her damp towel and wrapped herself. She grabbed the mouthwash, unscrewed the safety cap with effort, and held it under her nose for several protracted yoga breaths. Pranah, purification, near-peace in a bottle. Her towel turban fell. Naked and mildly chilled, Jackie didn't care. She lofted the mouthwash and chugged.

Jackie's eyes widened. A reflexive glance in the mirror shocked her as much as the inadvertent shot of minty alcohol. Her disheveled image reminded her of Jack Nicholson's look in the movie posters for *The Shining*.

She needed renewal, a soak in her tub, but that was upstairs, and Jackie knew she must deodorize their home. Before the aroma asphyxiated her and her family. Before an asthma attack hit. She snatched up her towel and wrapped it snug.

No longer longing to vaporize the dog, Jackie grabbed air freshener to spray throughout the house—with one hand firmly clamped on her damp towel shroud. She'd slammed the door on the dog, ignoring his whimpers for sympathy, glad that he had no words to explain. She didn't want to hear it. She didn't want to hate.

Jackie loaded her clothes and towels into the washer, knowing she might end up tossing them despite the power of detergent. God knew what could/would be done with Steve's favorite chair. Goodwill wouldn't take it. Even downtrodden people had noses.

She'd made it to the base of the stairs—she didn't want to be The Naked Chef, even though she admired the man—when Bonnie slammed into her home.

"What the heck, Jackie? Were you born in a barn? You left the back door open! Is something wrong? I called about a half-hour ago and you didn't answer your phone. Are you weirding out on me?"

Bonnie shouted her way through the mudroom and into the kitchen, then stopped. Her mouth was open wide enough to catch an army of flies. "What's up, Jackie? Have you packed all you own?" Bonnie's laughter was loud, and it hollowed Jackie to the core.

"Don't ask—" Jackie began.

"Eww-w! What's that smell? Has the Widow Braghorn come a-calling?" Bonnie's mood swung from rant to sarcasm, bypassing concern.

Feelings shifts as physical as a hot flash, Jackie bet. Bonnie already seemed oblivious to other people's issues and needs.

"Don't ask, don't ask, don't ask!" Jackie yelled as she ran upstairs, slammed into the master bedroom, and sank onto the bed in tears.

A few moments later, Bonnie peered in, abashed. "I just figured it out, Jackie. The dog got skunked. I heard him whimpering in the shower—"

Jackie looked up quickly, alarmed. Bonnie smiled, placed her hand on Jackie's forearm, and softened her voice, "I didn't open the bathroom door."

Jackie, swathed in a blanket, nodded. She ran a hand through her still-wet hair, now forming ringlets, and then massaged her wrinkled fingertips with her thumbs. Tears pelted her lap.

Bonnie engulfed her in a hug. "I'm here. I'm here." After a moment Bonnie leaned back and lifted Jackie's chin. "That does it. The dog doesn't go."

"But." Jackie's chest heaved. Words wouldn't warble out. She lifted a corner of her shirt to dab at her eyes. She attempted a grin to reshape the incident, but Bonnie's reaction told her that it was a grimace. Jackie took a deep breath, let it out in a long sigh. "You don't understand," she wailed. She tugged at the blanket, which mildly toppled Bonnie, and then lifted her head to look Bonnie in the eye. "*I* don't want to go."

Bonnie held Jackie through a cry of several minutes. Neither had any experience with a departure of this magnitude, except for the death of their moms.

Bonnie spoke first. "This feels like the death of something."

Jackie's forehead creased...but she brought forth a cosmic quip. "Yeah, the trip is the death of housework. Now, I'm ready to go."

Thirteen | *Fran*

"COME INTO MY OFFICE for a minute." The hair on Fran's arms bristled to attention. Her husband's tone of voice resembled her father's when she'd transgressed.

Her eyes instantly searched out the clock on the discretely green wall: 9:14. That was quick. Her husband was onto something, and it might not go well for her. Fran grimaced and decided to slide interior paint refresh for the office and sanctuary into the steeple budget. To bolster her nerve.

"Yes, dear," Fran chirped, by her tally too many times a day. Paul, a brilliant, yet needy man, over-relied on his secretary as much as he did his wife. She felt as if she lived inside a squeezebox, making holy music with him in the office, keeping house, shopping, and preparing real meals. It'd be hell without the nightly reprieve of unholy music in bed.

A super-size Sleep Number bed. She felt as if her number selection was the only place where she had true control in this house. She needed the sanctuary of *her* home and resolved to not sell. Perhaps she could leverage a discount from a painter who would paint her home in addition to the church.

Daytime relief proved forthcoming. Two women called about the ad in the church newsletter and interviews loomed. Fran was generating the interview questions when the Widow Braghorn bustled in with her directives and dubiously generated to-do lists.

Fran peered at the computer clock. 9:20 a.m. It was ritual. The thrust of the Widow's over-powdered jaw revealed that she assumed to encumber the pastor's entire day. Her eyes revealed her savor. If punctuality and dedication were the sole requirements for the job, The Widow could step in, er, sit in the secretarial chair.

As usual, The Widow hovered in front of the desk, shoving her list near Fran's nose. She wore so much perfume, she almost didn't require clothes.

Fran contained herself, never minding the throat clearing and sighs. She fielded the typed to-do list without a glance and placed it on the desk blotter. She didn't bother to offer coffee and donuts because of past ditherings and demands. She knew the Widow craved a *Tah Dah* and *much ado,* but Fran considered it useless to reinforce a pig.

The Widow was no match for the "High School Principal of the Year" eight years in a row, the Finesse-ess of the Hiawassee County School System. Hers was the only Blue Ribbon High School in the county. Hell, it was the only high school in the county, key to the sports teams' prowess, truth be told. Coach Uhrig, of course, thought it was all him, not the talent he was handed, the corn-fed young lads who stumbled into his corral, eager for football success to help them score with sweet-faced high school girls.

Ability was one thing, but motivation was everything. Fran was motivated to assure a competent, kindly, matronly new hire. One who dressed like *Whistler's Mother.*

The Widow stomped her expensively shoed foot. Her jewelry rattled, along for the ride. Fran looked up and offered the smile patented for interfering School Board members. No entry to the Pastor's closed door office, no tea, no crumpets, no place to rest, though the French Provincial furniture in there had come from the Widow's home. She remarked on the Widow's fine suit and thanked her, holding her tongue to not say, "Don't let the door hit you in the ass."

As soon as the outer door closed, Fran grabbed a Sharpie, boldly checked each item, and slipped the list under her husband's office door.

He flew out of his office, hugged Fran, and kissed her on the cheek. "Remind me to take you out to lunch." Paul pivoted, then paused, with his hand on the doorframe, as if to stabilize his soul.

"By the way, I handled the crisis that I called you for a half-hour ago. It seems that few people believed the bulletin, because Maybelline had already provoked phenomenal gossip by broadcasting Bonnie's order of a dozen wigs. You're going to have to glue Bonnie's lips shut and shut down the rumor mill until our friends get out of town."

"A set of requests right up my alley, my dear man." Fran tapped keys to access the church's directory and reached for the phone. When the door closed behind Paul, Fran laughed. "Perhaps I should take the Jag off Bonnie's hands."

At 11:45, Fran had drummed her fingers long enough waiting for Paul to remember his promise. She'd placed the church phones on take-a-message mode, aligned all the pens, and checked the in-and-out boxes, patting the papers flat. There were no emails requiring response.

She'd called eighty people, counted and recounted the

collection plate cash, resisting the itch to palm the Illinois quarter, the last needed for her coin book. She twiddled and fiddled her thumbs, plucked out several gray hairs, and booked an appointment with Maybelline to explore the option of dyed hair, praying the woman's discretion could be bought. Knowing that she'd be able to second her husband's efforts to plug this leak in the lottery non-win story with one stop in that shop.

Now, she contemplated what she believed to be a monetary *sweetener* for the secret-keepers, her and Paul. She'd stuffed a file with suggestions and research. Its bulk splayed it open, reminding her of an oyster pried open to reveal its pearl.

Fran rubbed her right ear and then replaced the earring she routinely removed because it pinched a lobe. She shook her head to assure that all the deplorable facts fell out of her head and locked all the good ones in her heart. She rose and smoothed her skirt, then knocked lightly on the office doorframe. "I've already reserved the back booth at the Koffee Kup."

"Oh, it's time?"

"Yes, dear. Isn't your stomach compelling your taste buds anymore?" Fran crossed the distance and gently closed his laptop's lid. "Come away with me."

Now it was Paul's turn to say, "Yes, dear," though he undermined obedience with a smirk. "What's the hurry? It's early and only a short walk to the Koffee Kup. The trouble with being punctual is that nobody's there to appreciate the effort."

As soon as Fran slid into place in the booth, she sensed something was up. Paul grabbed the menu, despite the fact that he knew it by heart, and always ordered a half grilled cheese sandwich and tomato soup. He held the open menu in front of his face as if it were a fort.

Fran went along with the charade for several minutes. If the dude could abide, she could, too. After Sally placed chilled water glasses in front of them, she asked, "Did you enjoy your morning, including tweaking May's gossip among the church council members? I've made an appointment to achieve that among the gossip squad." Fran's hand involuntarily moved to tuck her growing bangs behind her ear. "What's your sermon topic this week?"

Paul let go of the menu and looked at Fran. He smiled before he drew his small Testament from his inner coat pocket, thumbed through a few pages, and then looked up and into her eyes. He cleared his throat, which prompted Fran to push his glass of water closer, but he waved her off. "The greedy stir up conflict, but those who trust in the Lord will prosper."

"What a great sermon topic! You've been researching Proverbs again, haven't you?" Fran beamed, relishing the opportunity to demonstrate her Bible knowledge. "I thought how I handled the Widow's daily list this morning was brilliant, didn't you? I'm going to blaze new trails as I handle the community rumor mill."

Fran plunged her head into her menu so she wouldn't see if he agreed. She needed to think he'd agree. From behind the cardboard, she continued, "That woman knows greed like the back of her hand. Though we'll be hiring Bonnie's replacement soon, you have nothing to fear as long as I am at the front desk."

"Actually, Fran, the Lord took me to my knees this morning, regarding my overt and shabby plans to grab a righteous portion of my friends' bounty."

Fran lowered her menu to agree, yet disagree. "Uh-huh, you were riding a wild horse to steeplechase, without regard to holy hurdles in your path." She winked and smiled broadly, reaching for the affinity of his hand. "The Lord knew your intent was to honor Him."

Paul refused to acknowledge her humor. Fran froze. There was more, more conviction to come.

"God also passed along your mindset, Fran. Seems you've been planning to glom onto some cash. You plan to re-decorate your home? The one you vowed to sell?"

"How do you know?" Fran sputtered. Love could reduce you to your essence, especially when your beloved had the ear of God.

"You talk in your sleep." Paul picked up the napkin-encased utensils, shook them out, and laid the napkin in his lap.

"Oh" formed on Fran's lips, but she willed herself to seal them and listen with intent. There was something more to this, something more. Had to think.

Sideways, backwards, and forwards. She was learning the wedding dance steps as fast as she could, but Paul often stepped on her toes.

Whew! Saved by Sally, who took their orders, stuck the pencil back in her wisp-spoiled bun, and sashayed away. Fran hoped she wouldn't choke on the soup and grilled cheese sandwich she ordered to align with Paul. There'd be thunder later due to her lactose intolerance, but she needed to soothe her anxiety now. Replication of his order filled the bill.

Fran decided on diversion. She folded her hands, placed them on the table, and leaned forward. "That mysterious envelope I found in the Suggestion Box this morning. One of the small envelopes provided for church members, the ones the Widow won't stoop to use. It was double-wrapped in duct tape."

Paul looked around the restaurant, picked at his fingernails, and sipped his water.

"Bonnie dedicated a ginormous sum, didn't she, Paul? Your steeple aspirations have been over-matched."

He tried to play poker, but his good nature betrayed him. "Yes, the Lord works in mysterious ways. She pledged an amount and requested the bank's routing numbers. I've spent the morning schmoozing the Council and contacting builders. I've even drafted a letter to ask the Widow to match the sum in return for naming rights for a new hall."

"You haven't?"

"I have." Paul smiled. Their food arrived. He reached for his knife. "Back to your intentions, Fran. Why are you keeping your home?"

"Well, it *is* paid for—" Fran paused to reshape, to magnify her need. Two could play the noble game. She crossed her fingers in her lap, under the napkin that suddenly reminded her of a nun's veil. "In anticipation of being replaced as your temp, I've decided to write my memoir."

Paul nearly choked on his grilled cheese, and then reached over the table to high-five his wife.

Fran beamed. She'd slip her suggestion file for the church into his hands later.

Fourteen | *Bonnie*

LATE, LATE, LATE. LATER than she'd ever crept in from a date, Bonnie stepped into the high pile of the church office carpet. She'd been sneaking in after hours to use the computer for a week, using the key she'd failed to relinquish, for God knew what reason back when she resigned. Wasn't He wise?

The operation was delicate, given the high use of the church. Choir practice, youth group, Bible Study, ESL classes, and meetings of various cliques, er groups. Such as the children's ministry, the Bible-cloaked babysitting the church provided to spur Sunday attendance. The teachers prepared Bible-based lessons with crafts to charm the parents and grands. That group giggled over-much.

Tonight was special, so it was worth the risks. Her purpose and timing were precise and spiked with champagne. Bonnie sought a glimpse of her cash, whizzing through the system to fund her future, her lottery lump sum wired directly from the lottery's Swiss Bank into her LLC. She'd waited the promised two weeks and two days beyond.

Bonnie slid into the chair, surprised that it hadn't been replaced since her departure. Her butt settled in. She swung her feet under the desk and willed her heartbeat to slow. She put the computer on private browser mode, so there'd be no history of her Internet trek. This was not information to land in others' hands.

Bonnie click-clicked. She accessed the LLC site with her password, hoping that patience wouldn't be her sole reward. Again. A fortnight. Geesh, a lesser woman would have pouted and beat her breast. Two weeks had been a long, long time to wait. To bide time when she longed to leave. Especially when shopping was banned.

Packed, anxious, and ready to get out of town. She and Jackie had left most of the lying to their men. Paul and Fran ran interference, too. Brandon's silence had been bought and his dairy farm tutelage was proceeding well. Jackie was tired of cooking, though, and Bonnie was tired of buying so much beer.

A screen appeared, brilliant in the low light she'd allowed herself to turn on. Woosh! While the intellectual component of Bonnie's blonde mind understood that there'd been no sound, no lightning and thunder, no comet streaking the screen, she felt emotionally sha-zammed.

"Zippety-doo-dah, whoopee!" Bonnie rocked back in the armed office chair. "Holy-moly!" Her hands shook first. Then her entire body joined. Jubilation, justice, joy!

She gripped the chair as an orgasm flamed. Dear God, an unexpected consequence, for which she was unashamed. It was a bonus, not to be confessed to Carl. She doubted any man would like to be *out-sexed* by cash.

Bonnie blinked at the sum. Wow! She hadn't bothered to calculate her share of the Boffo Lotto prize. $134 million, moving faster than the instant she fell for Carl. Love at first sight, a second time in life.

Besides Uncle Sam, no one knew. No one in their entire community, the county, the state, the nation, the world knew. Except for Carl, Jackie and Steve, their son and their dog.

Maybelline had been effectively shushed.

Fran and Paul, too. And Judge, whom she assumed was reliable. He was Fran's brother and, in this small community, the only man who habitually wore three-piece suits. His silk-on-silk ties were legendary, as was his explanation that he wore them to evoke vomit if matters didn't seem to be going his way. So far, no one claimed to have witnessed. Since there was nothing to do and she felt glued to the chair, Bonnie sat back, put up her feet, and recalled her encounter with Judge.

Judge's expansive office, all walls lined floor to ceiling with vanity certificates and framed photos of him posed with other professional men, served as a shrine to the power of intelligence and craft. Bonnie noted that all of the other men's ties looked bland. Judge was a peacock. An over-priced peacock, but magic flowed from his brain. Gosh, she relished every detail of that meeting, just as she would this night.

The bemused look in Judge's eye told her she'd been gaping at his office accouterments, but he had all day for a multi-millionaire. Bonnie shook his hand.

Dang, it was cold. Sort of firm, stolid, yet dead, as if he'd already made himself into a monument. Is that where calculation began? Crapola. Could she, should she trust him?

She didn't know where else to go. She had no patience for Internet research and/or vetting, anything that would stall getting her show on the road to a Vegas wedding, placating Carl's kids, and then moving beyond these milestones to vacation forever.

What a voice Judge had. Deep, ardent, eyes focused directly on yours. A voice that could leave a jury in tears. The voice of a reasonable and savvy man. A man who'd give you his word, then bend or break any rules that got in the way. Never mind the rumors he was a drunk. Heck, maybe that was how he achieved that persuasive baritone.

Bingo, the salvation of savvy, sizing up people skills assured her. Twenty years of separating the wheat from the chaff, the faithful from the flakes. Bonnie relaxed.

Shock and awe over, she'd regained her upper hand. She recalled the knowledge, anointed by interaction with many small town church members and their hands, summer, fall, winter, and spring. *Cold hands meant he had a warm heart.*

A Lions heart, because when she'd surveyed his trophy photo wall, she noted he was a valued and integral member of the international service club. Like her dad. Any man with qualities like her dad was sincere, solid, and held especially close. He could be trusted to know as much as Carl and Jackie and Steve, an exclusive circle of no-harm-friends and confidantes.

Not Coach or Maybelline, not the Widow, not Harold Prince. Not the grocer, Santa, or Sally at the Koffee Kup. Not her dentist, gynecologist, or any charity thief. She already had enough friends, and she didn't need the entanglements of pseudos.

Or psychos whom she suspected would troll. Her thoughts turned to Brandon. It was his generation that invented trolling the Internet.

Cool Stud Brandon. His close-clipped crew cut made him look like a Marine, American's best image of solid. While not overly smart, she hoped he'd be stalwart. His mother and father—his controllers—would be traveling with her, not in proximity with their man-child. A superstitious incentive to Julie Watson, the pharmacist-and-Mrs.-to-be, might be required. Would a case of nail polish seal a deal? Perhaps a hula skirt, bikini, and flip-flops from Waikiki?

Thank God she'd purchased the ticket where lottery winner anonymity was assured, unlike Michigan where the public clamored with the right to know. Thank God's stars she'd signed the ticket, slid it into her wallet, and zipped up her purse. Thank God she'd determined the true nature of California community property laws.

Carl should thank God that she was a good forgiver, too, for trying to dissuade her from her most important purpose—to be his lawful wedded wife—with a fabrication that seemed true.

She was about to travel to Vegas to marry Carl, who was induced—she resolutely refused to consider the term seduced—only with a new vehicle to drive during their two weeks in town. With a promise to purchase identical others so that all of his kids would cleave to and love him. That man had been influenced by Even Steven, who'd purchased a spirited, tricked-out truck for Brandon as college graduation gift.

Though Carl had not asked, Bonnie had already arranged for the Jag to be shipped to the gnarly ex-wife when she'd been encouraged to not flash cash about their locale. No attribution or return address. Being a Santa Millionaire was fun.

Fifteen | *Jackie*

THOUGH STEVE WAS A lapsed member, Jackie called the VFW post in Lodenberg to remove Steve's club chair. She'd scrubbed as much as she was willing and able to do, which was nada, none. She believed hauling it outside, single-handedly, and dousing it with a 54 oz. bottle of Febreeze was mission fait accompli. She left it to bake in the summer sun. In the back yard.

The pick-up was scheduled during the period when Steve made his late day home deliveries. Jackie hoped the two vehicles' paths wouldn't cross when the chair went directly to the dump. Thank goodness the driver was prompt. She tucked two twenty dollar bills in his shirt pocket, one to honor Steve's service, one to honor his chair's. Incentive for the guy to stick his nose in a few beers after the dirty drive's completion.

She hurried into the house to slice and then microwave three pounds of Florida lemons to place throughout the house. It was a hand-me-down tip from Mama Bree to remove odors. Her own Momma Clay had not raised boys on a farm.

Lemons were meant to sanitize the air but, since it was summer, Jackie *real*-breezed their home by opening it to the outdoors, trying to abbreviate her frustration with a fresh point of view. She limited the window and door opening to those with intact screens. Although not mosquito season, it was June, a month with its own namesake bugs.

Yet it was time to get out as reprieve for her spirit. She grabbed the dog's leash and affixed it, thankful she'd not tossed the pound puppy collar after Steve bought him the embossed leather one, now in the trash. She'd thought it frivolous—until she got her diamond and a fur.

The dog looked so dejected, she reached out. Jackie ruffled the dog's still-damp coat, lightly with index fingertips only. He quivered, leaning into her affection, deeply abject. She readily forgave him, something she'd been doing with the other men in the household for years. They gave her much practice to perfect this Jesus-ordained trait, year after year after year.

The dog bounded out as soon as sunshine slivered the doorway, as ready to escape as Jackie. He didn't know this was her final day in the homestead nor that Brandon would be his primary caretaker. His wild abandon was uplifting.

He pranced ahead of Jackie's final stroll down the lane. The lane lined with trees towering above the fence, some of which Steve's dad had planted. Lupine and milkweed clustered the fence, nothing that would offend an already-accosted sense of smell.

When the dog paused to sniff and/or spray—didn't he ever give up the game?—she classified the array of trees that populated their land, wondering what species would grow in Australia. She looked forward to being re-introduced to the palms she'd adored during their brief foray to California two years earlier. Further, she envisioned rows of tall, swaying palms as Hawaii's welcoming arms. She wondered if the wind shimmered through them as it did Michigan trees.

Jackie glanced at her watch. Time to return home. She wondered how long before she'd return from places further than the end of their lane.

Back at the farmhouse Jackie grabbed a Febreeze spray bottle, spritzed the dog again, and released him, urging him to join the men in the barn. She gathered the lemons and ground them in the garbage disposal. The house smelled like a lemonade stand.

Jackie inhaled, but not too deeply, more like a sigh of release. She didn't want to ignite an asthma attack now. She washed her hands, slowly and deliberately, imagining herself as a famous heart surgeon rather than a beleaguered farmwife. The tears she'd held throughout the debacle surged. So much for the makeup she seldom wore.

Jackie closed all the windows, searching each room carefully to assure that no one languished in bed. All seemed in place. She latched the packed suitcases. Time to douse the frenzied dog's path, and she could use some help. Where was that Bonnie, anyway? She assumed Carl was helping Steve with the chores, safely away from the fray she hoped not to confess.

She sprayed and sprayed and sprayed. Another 54 oz. plastic bottle emptied. She feared she'd cause carpal tunnel as well as permanent damage. No time for a chiropractic visit or a trip to the allergist or otolaryngologist, although there might be an extra visit to the dump. Holy crap. Cleanup accumulated as much trash as one of their gang's football parties. Bye-bye to her rag stash.

She slid her phone from her ever-present apron, suddenly mindful that she'd stash her longtime uniform in a drawer tomorrow. Would she feel naked and unarmed?

"Steve, where would you like to eat tonight?"

"Why are you calling me? I'm in the barn, giving Brandon

final instructions for the new milking parlor. The kid is making me proud. You shoulda walked out to witness."

"I'm tuckered and sitting in my chair." Jackie clapped a hand over her mouth. Best not to reprise the skunk incident, a disaster that resulted in forfeit of his easy chair. She envisioned his eyes narrowing, his mouth setting hard. "I've done a lot of work and have more before our house is prepared for vacation spree, and I need something to look forward to besides another meal to prepare."

"Take a load off and have a beer," said Steve. "That's what I plan to do soon."

Jackie was glad that they hadn't Facetimed, so he couldn't see her wince. "It's a little early to treat myself, but I get that I'm bothering you. Bonnie and I will figure it out, as soon as I find her. Is she perchance with you guys, clinging to Carl like she does?"

"I'm glad she's not," Steve stage-whispered. "I'm already dreading their lustful public displays."

Jackie chuckled. "Me, too. Not to change the subject, but let's do." She paused to accept Steve's applause, because she co-opted his ploy, the one he'd invented for whenever she tended toward gossip or rant. "Have fun on your final milk delivery." She softened her voice with optimism, "You'll probably return with your pockets filled with well-wishes, cash, and treats, rendering you unable to sit in a chair. No worries, though. There's always room on the couch because Bonnie and Carl sit closer-than-close."

"Hello, did I hear my name?" Jackie flinched, jammed the phone off, and slid it in her apron pocket.

Bonnie smiled. "Are you all packed? The washer and dryer

tuckered by now?"

Jackie turned to face Bonnie, hoping a stare would remind the millionaire that she could have used housecleaning help. She looked down to her reddened palms to avoid eye contact and complaint.

"I take it, since you're not gagging or holding your nose, the stench is clear. As part of prepping our home for Brandon's bachelor tender, I've fumigated every corner, closet and cupboard with lemon. I'm tuckered. I hoped a beer would walk its way into my hands, but since you're here, perhaps you can bring me one." She held up her hands. "Would you fetch me the hand lotion, too?"

Jackie monitored Bonnie's walk to the fridge, but said nothing until she held the open beer in her hand. Ah-h, she glugged. "Welcome back. Where did you vanish to, when I could have used some help?"

"I promised Fran I'd hold down the fort while she helped Paul pick my replacement." Bonnie surveyed the room, then level-eyed Jackie. "You might say we were both cleaning up, er, stuff."

Jackie declined to agree or disagree. The dog disaster had mandated hyper house cleaning, which she'd done by ritual in Spring, though not in such a compressed into such a tight time frame. Her perpetual spunk was petered out, and she felt too tired to converse.

"You may have noticed that Steve's chair is gone." Her voice was just above a whisper. "It finally broke." She hoped that Bonnie wouldn't call her on her white lie, the version Steve received. "The good news is that Steve is unhurt, because he wasn't reclining when it went down. VFW already removed the evidence. You know, before Steve could explode."

"Want me to take your empty?" Bonnie easily extended her hand because she still stood. It had only taken a few minutes for Jackie to drain the beer. "Must have been some whirlwind cleaning session. Too bad I missed it."

Thank goodness Bonnie had already turned on her heel to dump the beer in the trash, so she didn't see Jackie mime a hangman's noose, yanking Bonnie's uppity neck to the ceiling before she began lotioning her hands.

If Bonnie noticed the trash overfilled with rags, she didn't say a word. Instead she hummed, "It's a Nice Day for a White Wedding." She filled two mugs with tap water, put a teabag in each, and started the microwave. She didn't return to the family room for several minutes, allowing the tea to brew as well as to allow whatever had transpired in this home to become a forgotten episode. Soon enough she settled onto the couch, lifting her feet to the coffee table. "It's time to review our plans."

"But, but—" Jackie sputtered. She hoped she'd re-screwed the lid tightly, so the lotion didn't splash when she plunked it down. She pulled a clump of tissues to her face, now as red as her chore-chapped hands. The tea remained on the table, which looked like an orphan without Steve's chair.

"What have we done? What have we done?" Bonnie's eyes grew wider with each heave of Jackie's chest. "What have I done, my fair friend? I longed to escape, but I already want to come back. I admit it'll be nice to see you lovebirds married, visit Vegas again, and then head to Hawaii, but flying eighteen hours to Australia where we know no one? What kind of crazy commitment have we made?"

"Are you missing your laundry warriors already, Jackie? Don't worry. Brandon will never use them, so they won't wear out. His jeans and jerseys will likely be able to walk by themselves by the time we return."

"How long do you suppose we'll be gone?" Jackie hiccupped and pulled another clump of tissues.

"We don't have definite plans," Bonnie said. "What does it matter? You're retired and rich." She flung the remark into the air and then picked up her tea. She sipped loudly, willing Jackie to join her in the soothing ritual, but settled for allowing Jackie to cry herself out.

"I realize I was richly blessed before," Jackie said. "Friends, family, respect, routine." She suddenly felt restive. She scooped up her mug and walked to the stairwell to gaze at the portraits of Brandon, her pride-and-joy boy.

She removed Brandon's baby picture, shocked to see the wallpaper behind it stronger-colored and sharper-detailed than outside the perimeter of its imprint. How long since she and young Steve braved the task of wallpapering the stairwell? She could almost feel the pressure of holding her arms aloft while Steve aligned each segment.

Her sides instantly ached. No wonder wallpaper was no longer fashionable, like the mauve and blue plaid of the wing-armed couch. She wondered why she'd not re-covered it with Spartan green plaid, especially when all their friends congregated in this room to watch ball games. Especially when Brandon was an All-American whose number was retired by Michigan State.

Especially when the couch arms were threadbare.

Sometimes, she felt as frumpy as the couch looked in

summer's light, but at least she and her couch were comfortable. Airline seats were reportedly not, and who knew what the numerous hotel beds, chairs, and couches portended for everyone's backs.

She returned to the empty space no longer occupied by Steve's club chair. Not bothering to retrieve a coaster, she set her mug down on the table. Blatant disregard of one's own rules was a baby step to freedom.

Then she noticed the carpet that had been under the chair appeared several shades lighter than where Steve's feet had parked for many years. Abashed, she fetched the vacuum to clean the errant bits of popcorn strewn about. Was that a dime?

Before she plugged in the vacuum, Bonnie grabbed her arm. "Get out of your private pity party, Jackie. I hadn't expected a relapse." Without waiting for reply, she turned on the TV—timed perfectly to hear Ellen DeGeneres cackle. "Saved by a laugh," Bonnie said. "Let's sit a spell and vacuum later. We'll eat out tonight. Where would you like to go?"

Jackie's whimpering couldn't turn on the dime that remained on the floor. "But, what about our packing review?"

Bonnie pointed to her purse, perched beside Jackie's on the kitchen desk. "My gown should already be in the vault at the Wynn. We're all packed. For any other needs we have charge cards. Let it go, Jackie, let it go. You're retired and your metaphoric gold watch is the trip. Leave that dang dime on the floor."

Bonnie was truly rich and retired. To model that mode for Jackie, she placed an imaginary football on an imaginary tee and kicked it. "Picking up trinket cash is another habit to release into the atmosphere."

Bonnie reached over to swat Jackie's butt. "Hey, new jeans, Jackie?"

Jackie bent toward her toes to show Bonnie the lacey pocket embellishments, emphasized by the dark wash, on her new jeans. "I got these to wear when we revisit Disneyland. Whaddayathink? Too Tinkerbell?"

"Don't plan to wear them on the lengthy plane ride," Bonnie quipped. "The pockets are low, and the designs might forever stipple your butt."

Jackie stomped her foot. "Stop giving me advice I don't want, Bonnie." Then, she winked to soften her remark. "I feel a mom quote coming on." Jackie fervently hoped Bonnie's new habit of advice and commands wasn't foreshadowing conversation on the trip. "Where was I? Oh, yeah. Life is like a pair of jeans. Some are sturdy. Others seem perfect but never quite fit. Some get shrunk, fade overmuch, or just lose their appeal. Some you get rid of, and then wish you hadn't. Others you keep and wonder why.

Bonnie clapped. "My mother had scads of aphorisms, too. I sometimes used them in the office. They were a lot easier than actual answers to inane or politically-charged questions. Sorta sounded like the pastor's frequent quotes of Proverbs or the letters of the apostle Paul. Caught people off-guard."

Jackie plopped back into her chair and scowled. "The store clerk proclaimed these Mom Jeans and then sneered."

"Time to get out of here!" Bonnie said and reached to clink her mug to Jackie's.

Just then the van used for small church field trips glided into view via the dining room windows. "Oops. Hope the dairy chores are done. Corral our guys and our luggage. Our taxi to the airport is here." She raced to the kitchen, deliberately dumping both mugs in the sink.

"Didn't your mom used to say *Life isn't a journey. It's many trips?*"

Jackie knew Bonnie was serious, because that was the first chore she'd voluntarily done in her two-week guest stay. Jackie knew she was in for a journey all around, allowing Brandon to clean up, work the farm, and manage the dog as well as his love life, as well as dealing with Bonnie's imperialism on the road. Thank goodness Carl and Steve were strong, capable grown-ups. People she could rely upon to carry her through this trip.

Sixteen | *Fran*

FRAN REMOVED HER GLASSES, rubbed the lenses with the hem of her cotton shirt, and shook her head nay-nay throughout. There had to be a plausible explanation for what she saw. A glance at the time stamp—6:45—didn't offer a clue. Hmmm. Brief thought reminded her that Jackie and Steve had only been gone four days.

The glasses seemed heftier when she replaced them on her nose. Life on the Breeden farm might not be right. What was Steve's word? *Copacetic.* Not quite.

She leaned into the computer monitor, squinting to determine what she saw. She was certain Brandon was well over six feet, had been for half his life. If the male figure working the automatic equipment in the milk parlor was him, he'd shrunk half-a-foot and whittled his girth. The nervous energy of a gifted athlete anticipating a surprise play, like Brandon used to be, but was no more. Hmm.

She grabbed her mug, stared within, and then swirled the contents for traces of hallucinogen. Improbable, but she had switched to a new brand of tea.

Hell, this was crazy, down right impossible. In the weeks before departure, Jackie had been caught preparing copious amounts of freezer meals, so how could Brandon have lost weight? The dog looked fit. The animal seemed always afoot, nudging cows into place in the milking stations of the Iowa System.

Fran gasped. The dog was acting like an Australian sheepherder, channeling the continent that was her friends' eventual destination. As if he existed in a parallel state with his true master. Fran chuckled. She wasn't the only one babysitting Brandon. *If* this person was the young man.

Fran took a slug of her tea, slammed the mug on its coaster, and mindfully switched gears to explore the adventure of her friends' travels while she studied the screen. She twiddled her thumbs while her mind multi-tasked.

Fran waved a wand like Harry, Hermoine, and Ron. Gosh, she missed Harry and gang, their collective antics and magic spells—and the series' amazing ability to induce kids to read. Clearing space for the series had spurred her to gift numerous issues of *National Geographic* magazine to Carl when he moved into the community, an impulse she now regretted. Carl left the trove in the house when it sold. Hell's bells, that entire episode hurt. Grrr.

Fran feared she was losing her battle with mind control. Crabby suspicions invaded as quickly as a summer squall. Her computer monitor reflected a deeply wrinkled brow.

So, she abandoned the surveillance cam to survey her friends' road trip emails. Brimming with juicy tidbits and goofy snapshots, Jackie's enjoyment leapt from every page. She wrote like a schoolgirl, focused on scenery and facts, a report for a favorite teacher—or friend. Yet, she hadn't littered the wedding details with a string of cringe-worthy emojis.

The wedding was a fat Elvis fest. On a sorry note, a drunk suffered a stab while they waited on the sidewalk bench for their turn in the Little White Wedding Chapel off the Strip.

The good news—a police car and an ambulance arrived within seconds. Since none of them truly witnessed the skirmish, their names and numbers weren't recorded in cop notebooks, so they weren't detained for a court date.

The better news—the man seemed all right. The best news, Bonnie and Carl's wedding went well. *Hitched without a glitch,* Jackie wrote, which sounded like a Carl remark.

The foursome's win-loss record at Las Vegas slots was upside down, but Jackie reported Bonnie said "no matter"—so sorrow didn't counterbalance their bliss.

Bliss. Hiss. Fran removed her glasses, rubbed her eyes, and inhaled happy thoughts. Relieved that Jackie shared few pictures, because she wanted neither to feel jealous of their good fortune nor dismayed at any absence of her own. While she cherished her Craftsman's privacy, it was dark due to its surround of tall pines. Her fervor to refresh the interior remained undiminished. Now was the time. Her creative juices flowed with the portent of Bonnie's cash. Yes, she'd carve a chunk for personal use, a tithe for her Brandon sitting job, from Jackie and Steve. Never mind what Paul decreed. He was guilty of sin, so why not? Didn't they serve a God who forgave all?

She toyed with a visit to her Pinterest page, where she'd amassed a collection of wanna-be rooms, many now dated by fashion's new palate. Her focus quivered, her intentions see-sawed. She drained the mug and decided. Better to submerge her creative spirit in writing her memoir, though she felt wistful.

She'd spur herself to write a bestseller. Garner her share of fortune and fame.

She returned to Jackie's email. Fran was heartened to re-read that the reconcile of Carl and his kids had eluded the ex-wife and her potential for money-grabbing mayhem. No mention of the new vehicles, so Fran didn't ask in her reply. If Carl's adult children were of Brandon's mindset—millennial, one and all—so be it. Fran didn't need extra aggravations. Brandon's antics and attitudes were enough.

This thought reminded her she was procrastinating her surveillance as well as her memoir. Fran checked the digital time in the upper corner of the computer, calculated with a pen on the pad, and beamed at her instincts. The Breedens and Edwards had landed in Honolulu. Sydney would be next, but days away, so the dog's movements had not presaged. She reset her glasses and clicked to the surveillance camera feed.

Wait! Did the dog just back up to the kid and pee on his pants? An audacious and unfriendly act. Her incredulous stare at the screen, hoping for a rewind, caused Fran to notice the guy wasn't wearing a Spartan jersey and was younger than Brandon by half. What the hell? Was that Seth Thomas, the quarterback of the Hiawassee Hasslebacks?

"What did you say?" demanded an imperious voice, one that could only be the Widow Braghorn.

Fran slammed the laptop closed and flashed on the wall clock before mustering the well-mannered attitude required. She willed her pulse to slow before greeting her nemesis on earth. "How may we serve you today, Mrs. Braghorn?"

"Please. Call me Charlene. I've counted the days until a true secretary sat behind the desk, and I know that today is your last. I've come by to invite you and the Pastor to dine at my club."

While Paul was familiar—even the bartender waved from across the space—Fran had never before entered the country club. Well-heeled golfers rarely attended School Board meetings or ran for PTA. They also rarely attended church.

Fran glanced around the room, hoping that her tailored pants suit fit in. She hadn't had to court public funding like Paul.

It did. It's mild green color would fit in anywhere among Michigan State fans, the abiding predominance of citizens who populated the county.

Her suit fit in with the crowd better than it fit her. It certainly fit more snugly than Fran's usual yoga togs. Thank God she'd invested in Spanx. In addition to squishing her middle into the suit, she felt as if the garment pulled at her double chin, sculpting her profile to a trim middle age.

The Spanx and the heels shortened her stride, so that Fran discreetly trailed the pastor and his rich parishioner. In this manner, Fran averted the conversational niceties she couldn't call forth.

All seated, all ordered, all settled in. Fran earnestly hoped her face didn't match her ennui as Charlene Braghorn droned on. *Sharing brags via horn.* Fran's brain bitching was in fine form. Too bad she couldn't wisecrack out loud.

On and on, interminably on. The woman loved the sound of her own voice as much as she loved her money.

Fran pushed the Chicken Kiev around her plate to occupy herself while her companions discussed church particulars. She attempted to chew softly, to allow her well-honed listening to sift for pertinent tidbits. She was literally soaking up the haute gravy while her husband was metaphorically achieving the same.

"Yada, yada, yada...saw the steeple schematics on the table in the narthex. You ought to move it. One could stumble before worship...yada, yada...I anticipate the second group of stained glass windows to match the ones my original donation installed. The sanctuary will look balanced at last."

"Of course, the final six windows are prioritized—" Paul ventured.

When he paused for a breath, the Widow interjected, "I do affirm the need for a steeple, but a neon cross visible on the Interstate? One questions whose values we are serving, Reverend Rankin. Yours or the Lord's?"

The Widow—Fran felt she couldn't properly digest her food if she switched to the woman's first name— punctuated her opinions with thrust chin and eyebrows plucked in Gothic arch. The former like a pulpit and the latter like the windows she'd demanded and paid for. Fran witnessed the facial expression each morning when the Widow swept into the office... and gladly, albeit silently, celebrated the end of her tenure.

Once Fran cleared her plate, she softly hummed *Amazing Grace* to occupy her mouth and remain above the fray—all glory to her man, whose turn it was to handle a tasteless and entrenched ego. She knew the stained glass window contract was already bid, and work had begun, so she mentally began to arc her memoir rather than enjoin.

"Yada...what is the benchmark for naming rights of an education building and community hall?"

"Son of a Baptist preacher, it's uncanny, dear woman, you are ahead of the game." Paul reached across the table to enfold Charlene's hand. Fran turned to gaze out the wide windows so as not to witness *the son of a Baptist preacher's* gambit. It was one of her husband's preferred cuss terms. She dared not upstage his ploy with ill regard.

Paul bent forward. The Widow matched his move. Fran felt like more of a fifth wheel with each lean. Soon their bodies would form a gothic arch. Fran's back ached.

"Your communication is more direct with the Lord than mine, Mrs. Big Heart. We hadn't considered such a building project, although it would most certainly serve God's purpose to become a magnet to the community. What a mission for our flock to serve the unchurched. What goals may you have in mind?"

Fran was glad she'd chewed the chicken thoroughly and had water glass in hand. She nearly choked as Paul replied falsely and with semi-concealed smarm. Mrs. Busybody B. had thrown down a gauntlet, a possibility to align with his desire for more.

Fran didn't have to see Paul's eyes to know they resembled the neon of his coveted cross by the interstate fence. She could feel his body generate heat from where she sat. His dream to quadruple the congregation, ignited with the initial lottery news, outsized the country club membership. From 200 to 800, nearly half the town's population.. Was Charlene that gullible? Lonely? That rich?

None of it mattered to Fran as she awaited dessert, trying not to squint. The big squeeze was no longer limited to her Spanx. Soon enough, she'd be home with the garment on her closet floor.

And she'd find a way to get rid of that widow woman's encroachment, too.

Paul possessed enough ambition for all three of them. While Fran didn't know the terms and amount of Bonnie's tithe, she knew the scope of the church projects had expanded. She now contented herself with catch-up to do the mental math. The steeple, new roof, and interstate signage she estimated at a half-million bucks. Paul penned an equal amount for cost overruns and reserves, as well as his salary increase. Fran was aghast.

Bonnie's donation likely covered that and more, as a large lottery tithe should do, but Fran had to deal with Paul's burgeoning ego. One could only hope his sexual appetite increased proportionally.

Fran blushed and refocused her mind. The Ladies Aid Society, with her as vanguard, hadn't even rattled the Council's cage, though she'd filed her suggestions with Paul. She ticked off the list now: the church interior needed painting, new pews, new flooring, maybe statues and fountains and art installations. Fran certainly intended that the popular dove gray wouldn't be chosen. Given the age of the members, a church service would appear as *Fifty Shades of Grey*, the book improbably atop the bestseller list.

Fran vowed not to read the trash, though many women in the small farming community indulged. Penning her memoir suited her goals. Her mental capacities were suitably challenged—and her sex life couldn't be finer. She swallowed a chortle.

Fran tuned back in to the table topics. "Certainly the land is available. I disagree with others, who've suggested that the three-acre lot which sides the church be utilized to bury our aging congregation as they pass. I ceased to be interested with disposal of the dead after my late husband, Big, was cremated. Let that procedure suffice for everyone. It's less costly and takes up less space."

Paul merely ah-hmed and smiled. He re-reached across the table to clasp both the Widow's ring-adorned hands. Based on inflation, of which there was little during these still-sad economic times, a reasonable estimate of $15,000.00 each for the windows was a large chunk of cash. Did the Widow want to match her original tribute to her sainted husband? Could she cough up a million for the building she proposed?

Ah, Paul had turned Charlene's suggestions back to her pocket book. *Deft sleight of hand.*

Fran folded her hands in her lap and watched her thumbs twiddle. Her Spanx itched. She was afraid if she scratched, they'd explode. She dared not breathe to encourage this potential explosion. She dared not breathe due to her husband's gamble, recalling the familiar saying, *If you chase two bunnies, both would escape.*

Fran exhaled. She applauded under the table when the Widow folded, just as anticipated. Mrs. Big wrote a check for the additional windows and slid it across the table.

The pastor pocketed it pronto. He finger-snapped the waiter's attention and ordered coffee and pie all around. Fran, delighted to witness the transaction, imbibed both, willing her flab not to splay.

She admired her husband's polished technique. How sweet the sound of his words. The boon to her was obvious. Her dig-up-the-donation duties were over if this deal went down. She could devote herself to her memoir. *Crafting in a Craftsman home. Her present perfect and her past recast.* Fluid and flush with freedom, Fran felt content.

Wonder if *Fifty Shades of Grey* was checked out of the library?

Seventeen | *Bonnie*

BONNIE SNUGGLED HER RHINESTONE-STUDDED sunglasses against the fluorescent sunlight and stretched her arms high. She longed to downward-dog yoga stretch, but felt it'd be impolite to hoist her butt in Honolulu's face. She longed for a mirror, yet not. Assuredly her perfect blonde locks, now stripped of the confounding extensions, no longer perfect, and her comb remained lost in her over-large purse. Her arms would cramp before she found it.

Already, she wasn't sure world travel was her best millionaire's plan. How could she have known? She'd never traveled beyond the Flint Mall and, recently, Illinois. Now, she'd been to Vegas, all high rises and glitzed, and California. This was a new state entirely.

Jet lag pummeled her body, yet Bonnie focused on the lurching baggage carousel, desperately searching for her fur. Dang, dammit, darn. Why had she run to the local travel agent to book flights, never considering purchase of her own private jet? Not even first class seats?

Oh, that's right. Her team had advised full clamp down, so to not turn the entire community into fevered millionaire-chasers. Lots of effort had been expended to amend people's points of view after she'd gone wild when she first got the news. The disappearance of Carl's truck and the Jag had solidified the impression. Most town folk thought them re-possessed.

Carl rubbed her back, and Bonnie leaned into the caress. "Carl, I love you. I feel blessed." Bonnie mentally beseeched the common church vernacular to overlay her mood.

She could feel Carl's thick wedding band against her backbone. Ahhh. Real. Just as real as the diamond they'd purchased together in Beverly Hills, *after* they'd met the ex-wife and Carl's kids. The twinkle, twinkle, twinkle rallied her millionaire spirits.

Carl's back rub ended when their luggage bypassed them on the airline carousel due to their jet lagged trances. Crapola! Bonnie still felt as tossed as her new luggage looked, so she planted after she snagged her fur. Carl and Steve sped after while Jackie fetched two carts.

Alone, Bonnie reminisced.

The Elvis impersonator wore white. His onesie had more bling than her wedding gown. But at least she was everlastingly married to Carl.

Jackie looked lovely, and Steve looked proud. And all of them won and lost at slots themed with Sponge Bob Square Pants, a goofy cartoon character Jackie recalled from Brandon's TV-hogging days. The casino-topping honeymoon suite made up for this jarring detail with satin and velvet and swank. The blinking lights of the Strip sparkled and flashed. The sex transcended the splendor of the room.

They'd departed the next day, eager for adventures in the happiest place on earth before they tackled the family reunion. They arrived in time for dinner—not 'supper' here—in the Napa Rose restaurant of the Grand California Hotel.

Again, the honeymoon suites were grand, replete with room service of ten kinds of caviar, prefab wedges of various high-fat cheeses, and buckets of chilled champagne. Swoon and sign the tab. Bonnie tucked two extra bottles of champagne into their dirty laundry and then locked the bag.

The Storytellers Café provided breakfast like back home, the same fare but far higher prices than the Koffee Kup. When Carl asked how far Disneyland was, the waiter beamed and said it was a short stroll, just follow the path. Bonnie felt like Dorothy and gang following the yellow brick road to Oz.

What a day! California's unclouded blue skies affirmed the sky had no limits, Bonnie's favorite phrase. Jackie and Steve acted as guides, glad to revisit Disneyland, the happiest place on Earth. The entire entourage felt certain the 9:30 fireworks shot overhead for celebration of their good fortune.

Bonnie purchased two suitcases, named them Mickey and Minnie, and loaded them with souvenirs for Carl's kids, never-minding that they were adults. She was girded to meet the relatives, win them over, happily honeymoon in Hawaii, and then escape to Australia and beyond.

The visits went well. With Yosemite sandwiched between, the two couples survived the onslaught. Jackie and Steve walked backcountry nature trails while Bonnie and Carl trekked back and forth to the kids' homes.

The flashy trucks, fresh off the line at the Dodge factory, arrived. Carl beamed. Bonnie beamed, too, as she watched the bitch ex-wife's face when she signed for the Jag. The document addendum forever ended alimony. Carl could relax and feel even richer. Relief by hook, crook, or Jag.

Bonnie returned to the present when the cart bumped her leg as Jackie struggled to load luggage. It didn't seem the time to laugh at her maid of honor's choice of head gear. "Your

Minnie hat becomes you, Jackie," Bonnie said with all the dignity of a Disney Princess-crowned millionaire. "You look as fresh as when I first met you."

Jackie rolled her eyes and quipped, "Your Cinderella crown suits your circumstances, Bonnie. Think of it. Two members of the former Silly Hats & Caps Society have replaced their chapeaus. Do you suppose Fran has recruited new members?"

Bonnie winked and pulled Jackie close to whisper in her ear. Jackie's eyes widened, and she nearly shed a tear. Fran wouldn't have to fundraise without them, now that the church was flush with Bonnie's donation. Praise the Lord, but with whom would she gossip, er, problem-solve human nature? Bonnie had more than shed her former shadow woman persona with an outsized presence, bound to gain status and respect via bitch.

The men were suddenly in a taxi van. Bonnie witnessed the twinkle in Carl's eye as he toyed with blowing the horn. Wouldn't that reverberate under the terminal's canopy and blow out a few eardrums? So she leaned over and jabbed the steering wheel. "That's your applause, Carl. We conquered alimony and established rapport with your kids."

Carl pulled her to him, testing the taxi van's shocks with his enthusiastic hug. "You da man!"

Bonnie leaned back to look him in the eye. "Bestowing cash with panache, I'd say. And, in case you don't recall, I'm most certainly not a man."

Money was not the root of all evil. Money was the *route to love.* Short-term, anyway, which was all that Bonnie cared about in the moment. She was a millionaire forever, no matter what. For now, she was determined to achieve an even Hawaiian tan.

Eighteen | *Jackie*

ELVIS, WHOM SHE'D FALLEN in love with when she was eight, evaporated as Steve snapped his fingers in front of Jackie's face. Her eyelashes fluttered. Steve smiled at her flirt. Despite her half-century-plus age, it was nice to know she still had it, had him. When she hugged him, she didn't envision Elvis. Not the dimpled crooner in *Blue Hawaii*, the first movie she saw. Not the spangled-and-bloated Vegas version. Not anyone but Steve.

Jackie smiled. She'd already forgotten her imperial majesty's slight with the luggage handling. She suspected it might not be long before she snapped at the Attitude. Jackie had already trashed her Minnie Mouse hat, determined not to follow Bonnie's slide into childishness.

When Jackie moved out their hug, she glimpsed her wrist, wrapped around Steve's neck. Her pulse thumped, bringing her notice to her watch. "I wonder why I wore a watch? Holy crap! I'm retired. I don't have to mind time."

"Or consequences, since Fran and Paul agreed to oversee Brandon's management of the farm, and Julie, our future daughter-in-law, will mind the other essentials." Steve's eyebrows boogied, but the look in his eyes disavowed his chuckle. Jackie could see he hadn't unwound from habits of work ethic, either. She gave his cheek a pinch before he turned and ducked his head into a multi-colored floral necklace. Jackie was shocked he accepted it.

A moment later, Steve encircled Jackie's neck with plumeria and kissed her longer than he had in years. Hawaiian music and the sultry air of the Honolulu airport's outdoor walkways lulled as well as siren-called. They were ready to wheel away from the airport to their hotel, further away from their home and farm with their humdrum and routines. Thank goodness the luggage cart wheels didn't squeak to interfere with their serene.

All senses registered that this was truly different. Jackie guessed if you were born and raised in Michigan like her and Steve, you basically breathed your own breath nine months a year, mouth wrapped in a scarf during cold weather outdoors and breathing recycled heat or air conditioned air inside. Some day, she'd ask Carl about growing up in smog.

Ah. Mmmm. Breathe deep and begin to vacation, now that wedding duties were done. Cut loose and relax on Hawaiian soil, not home ground.

Jackie felt a wifely duty to model this for Steve. Despite his floral surprise and smooch, he'd need guidance to get in sync with vacation's nondemands. Despite protestations, men were like cell phones. They liked being held and talked to, held close—though if you pushed the wrong button, you'd get disconnected, in Steve's case. She couldn't push him too far or too fast.

She fondled her iPhone in its purse pocket, pulled it out and took a selfie, her face framed in her lei, hiked a little in front to cover emergent neck wrinkles. Before Jackie turned to include Steve in a photo, she frowned. No, men were *not* like cell phones, because it wasn't prudent to trade them in every couple of years. Men didn't have automated updates and apps. Men required mucho maintenance, no matter how much they ascribed this attribute to women.

Jackie danced with her wheeled bag, but soon stopped. The air's humidity reminded her of Michigan in August, and she felt heavy instead of light. Asthma symptoms sucked at her chest.

"Steve—" she began, but rather than squelch the collective excitement, Jackie shelved her issues and clutched Steve's arm. Her fingers grazed his firm biceps. She nearly swooned at the reminder of his work day chores. She realized she'd focused too long on his worn-out knees and crunched spine.

Carl whistled a taxi van to transport them to the Royal Hawaiian and its pre-reserved honeymoon suites. The driver shooed the men away from helping to stow the bags. Steve and Carl stifled laughter as the guy grimaced and shoved, packed and unpacked the luggage, finally abandoning voyeurism when Bonnie yelled from within the vehicle. Waikiki beach beckoned, so they stepped into the van. Steve acquiesced to Carl to sit in front with the driver, to enjoy the legroom and view.

There was little conversation as they traversed the city, which seemed to be wall-to-wall condos, buildings, markets, and hotels. Many cars, horns honking beep-beep. Grim-faced pedestrians waiting on curbs for lights to change. Not much more scenic than Flint.

The hubbub vanished when the taxi entered the Royal Hawaiian property, sequestered and movie-set lush, a rain forest of palms wedged near Waikiki Beach. Jackie felt welcomed to heaven, grounded in green. The hotel grounds smelled better than the fragrance aisle of Watson's Drug Store with more flowers than any funeral she'd attended, including Big Braghorn's.

Jackie languidly mounted the steps, the heat hypnotic, clutching the handrail for balance, she looked all around. She almost toppled when the tile surface under her feet shifted to a vast area rug. Carpet so thick and reassuring, it could have sprouted like grass at home.

The hotel staff's floral garb kept pace, as speedy as Jackie was slow. Arms to gather the bags, arms to guide them into the vaulted, expansive space, arms to hand them pineapple juice and a warm wet towel.

What to do with the towel? Jackie looked around the lobby for a clue, but only staff fluttered about in multiple versions of the Hawaiian print she'd grown used to as Carl's uniform. All teeth, gleaming white against bronze skin, smiling. More smiles than TV toothpaste ads and talk shows.

This hospitality rivaled Disneyland, though staff there offered nothing free except directions to the restrooms. It bettered Vegas, where staff operated discreetly to not distract tourists from the tables, drinks replenished without bidding.

But never better hospitableness than their Michigan community. Back home Jackie'd longed to escape banality and rust. Now she battled overwhelm, all her secret fears of not fitting in coming to the fore. Bonnie abandoned her welcome drink, shoving into Jackie's hand before she ran to the bathroom to check her look, no permission sought. Was this the way to treat a sidekick? Dump her with luggage and drinks? When the sidekick also needed to pee?

Jackie searched the lobby for Carl and Steve. Untethered

wasn't a good feeling, no matter that they still stood on American soil.

There. The guys nursed glasses of juice, their heads bent to kibbitz. What? Though his single earring glistened in the sunshine that infused the hotel lobby, Carl wasn't wearing one of his trademark shirts?

Jackie downed both cocktails and rapidly swished the glasses with the damp napkins. Instantly glasses and napkins disappeared in the hand of one of the servants. Could she get used to this?

There, their bags sallied forth, piled high on brass luggage racks, which resembled a queen's chariot. It was a blessing that Steve and Carl hadn't worn Hawaiian shirts—she might not be able to distinguish them among the porters.

And, all hail the queen bee, Bonnie returned from wherever she'd vanished to.

The travelers drifted to the elevator. They neither made nor heard a sound as it rose to the top floor.

The room's opulence stopped Jackie and Steve at the door. The ceiling vaulted so high, it reinforced Bonnie's constant proclamation "The sky's the limit!" for this vacation.

Jackie walked on the cloud-like carpet and sank onto the bed. Steve plopped beside her, cupped her face in his hands, and kissed her deep and long. The knock on their door came sooner than either wanted. Their luggage had arrived, unwanted in the moment, but here it was. All needs met except one.

After a quick nap and quicker rifle of her bag for a change of clothes and fluff of her hair, Jackie allowed herself to be escorted to the huge hula show on the hotel's vast lawn, set to begin prior to sundown. She exchanged glances with Steve about the lawn's size—as big as the pasture beside their barn. "Wouldn't the cows love to graze here?" he said.

The show's stage was within site of the ocean but, though the thin line of water constantly undulated in waves, there was no sound to compete or overlay the ukuleles and the murmurs of the guest assemblage. The stage was filled with players in various sizes of stacked, curvy, and plump, but no singing had begun. Jackie turned to Steve. "Wonder how the choir's doing without me back home?"

"Just fine, Baby, just fine." *Baby?* He hadn't called her that since high school!

The breeze ruffled her hair. All was gentle, all was colorful and carnival-like. Many of the hundreds of feast-and-show-attending women wore sarongs, muumuus, and cuddled to their husbands in matching shirts. Steve wore a Hawaiian shirt loaned by Carl and, Jackie noted, it looked freshly-creased but inside out. Bonnie had on a colorful dress, though not matchie-matchie to Carl's shirt, thank goodness. Jackie felt like the plain peacock in contrast with her flamboyant mate. Had she missed a memo?

She missed Fran's direction. *I need a dose of her shoulders-back, head-up, guts in, nothing-can-touch-us aplomb.* Breathe.

She waved off the grass skirt Steve tried to buy from the vendor, a longhaired girl whose hips swayed as she leaned near to hawk her wares. Her breasts glistened—with coconut oil?—and the men leered. Jackie jabbed Steve in his side. Bonnie did the same to Carl.

They claimed four folding chairs at a lengthy white-papered table, reminding Jackie of how the church ladies set up the annual bazaar. Not so fancy, not so different from home.

What? The meal was served cafeteria style. Holy crap! She'd retired and traveled far for *this?* At least she stood on the other side of the serving station, and she sipped a Mai Tai. She wouldn't be required to clear the table, wash the dishes, or even replace the chair under the table when she departed the feast.

Or make the bed the next morning. She clutched that as something to look forward to—after she and Steve massively messed up the sheets in the honeymoon suite. Hallelujah for Hawaii and romance regeneration. If Jackie wore glasses like Fran, she knew they'd be steamed by her thoughts.

Clearly, Bonnie and Carl were having the time of their lives. As was Steve while he and Carl conducted their avowed Mai Tai research. More and more boisterous, keyed up like after one of Brandon's winning games.

She felt as if she were on the other side of a two-way mirror. She should be joining the crowd, but it took more and more effort to breathe. She tried to enjoy poi and rice and pineappled ham. Chew swiftly, swallow, and swig. The meat was super salty. Was it the Spam she'd heard of, from the blue metal cans stacked in an airport display? The long-awaited Hawaiian vacation was letting her down.

Like the sun that set moments ago, leaving them in the dark before tiki torches flared.

The music first came alive with drums. Steve bumped her arm when he clambered onstage, his opaline-and-black hair decidedly askew. Holy crap, what happened to his aching knees and back? He was dancing and prancing, making an ass of himself! Jackie hung her head, staring at her almost-clear plate.

She wished she hadn't left the weed-stuffed cane in the room. She could use it now to hook Steve's neck to return him to his seat!

Bonnie nudged her. "Look up, girl! Your husband is a star of the show." She felt Carl behind her chair, pulling it out. "Do you want him to hula with you or that skimpily-clad Hawaiian girl?"

Suddenly a grass skirt was tied around Jackie's waist. She allowed herself to be led to the stage steps, embarrassed beyond words when she saw Bonnie and Carl clasping iPhones and cameras. The debacle would appear on Facebook, Fran's retirement social life. She'd go viral, and there was no cure.

Jackie fixed her mind on future adventures, glad the travel plans were open-ended. Attention spans were nanosecond. This news would be overlaid with local escapades within days. No worries, said the Aussies. No worries, shake your head, and jiggle your curls. No worries, no worries, bend your knees and let your hips sway.

No worries – what? Her knees already creaked. Alternate knee bends to swivel and wiggle and jiggle booty and breasts more? She wasn't a jellyfish. Jackie tucked behind a dancer. The woman's tick-tocking butt reminded her of their grandfather clock pendulum at home. The analogy calmed her. Lift your arms, cup your fingers, and emulate the lady's movements. *We're telling a story all right...of my eternal embarrassment.*

Jackie looked at Steve, who beamed while he displayed new, obviously Mai Tai-fueled moves. Quite the showman, not at all like his perpetually stoic self.

Well, if he could be an exhibitionist, she could, too. Her

hips moved, her arms waved, she gyrated. She became a ukulele, eager for Steve to pluck her strings.

Hold on! An image flashed in her mind. The weed-stuffed cane had not been among the bags brought to their room. No wonder the porter smiled bigger than huge. That jerk confiscated it, smoked some of the contents, and likely sold the rest. That was a lot of wacky tobacky. He probably owned the hotel bar by now.

Jackie's shoulders sagged. Sigh. The cane contents she'd secured to ease their paths of adventure, so they'd be able to gallivant, prolonged and avidly, without aches and pains. A mini-fortune lost, irreplaceable without a doctor's prescription. She'd purposely purchased a simple maple cane to blend and not attract attention.

Now they were attracting attention. And feeling no pain. Later, they'd both be shoveling Advil. Jackie now embraced Bonnie's fortune. They could continue to buy beaucoup pain relief. Would it be Tequila Sunsets or Screwdrivers for breakfast?

Holy crap! If booze replaced their former reliance on weed as balm, they were headed for AA ranks.

Jackie bowed her head briefly to pray. She didn't close her eyes to avoid stumbling as she swayed. Additionally, she requested forgiveness for hastily blaming the porter. She'd not boarded the plane with the cane. She'd likely left it behind at LAX, stuffed between the banks of uncomfortable airport seats? Bet the DEA's trained dog had gone nuts. She tried to laugh as a vision of their dog's skunking incident came to mind, but the levity wouldn't take hold.

Jackie prayed for more resolve—and, instantly, her spine

straightened to dance. Not gonna happen. Not with music in the air. Who needed weed when Hawaiian music unleashed her inner goddess! Singing gospel tunes as a choir member would never be the same.

Jackie beckoned Bonnie and Carl to the stage. Bonnie's multi-color braids, clipped in among her blonde locks, soon wound into the stratosphere.

And, the crowd went wild.

Nineteen | *Fran*

THE IMAGES SHOCKED FRAN. On a torch lit stage, Jackie and Steve swiveled their fannies and hips more than cheerleaders, their smiles spread almost as wide as their upheld arms.

Steve stepped on his grass skirt, stumbled, and almost fell off the stage. Jackie didn't flinch when a barely clad female dancer broke his fall with a full-bosomed hug. In fact, she appeared glassy-eyed as she feigned a stripper rather than follow the other performers' ebbs-and-flows. A coconut bra, similar to the ones worn by the lithe Hawaiian women on the stage, topped Jackie's outlandishly-colored clothes.

While Carl's wardrobe of shirts had been an anomaly in their town, the stage looked saturated in florals. The sensory overload of color, music, and movement made her nauseous. She looked down at her robe, frowned, and shut down email.

Fran knew she couldn't share this travel adventure with Paul. For heaven's sake, and for his own. Hell, she wished she could unsee it herself. Thankfully the video ended after sixty seconds, Bonnie and Carl beckoned to the stage to join the suggestively-sexy dance. Fran's mind went blank, like the screen.

Stunned, Fran didn't respond as Paul kissed her cheek. "Don't forget the Tim Horton donuts," he said before he swept out the door. This time she didn't grunt in disgust at his unnecessary reminder. Perhaps that's how she'd niggled her friends. Perhaps she'd built in the neediness that sometimes chafed, by not allowing others to problem-solve. She vowed to explore this notion. Soon.

Fran clicked off her computer and saluted her reflection. Let her friends enjoy their drunken freedom. Their antics occurred in a different time zone. History. Fran was the ballast in the community. Someone to keep a lid on values and truth. Her simple reply to Jackie's email would suffice. "Thanks for sharing. Glad you are having a good time."

Fran leaned forward to grab her tea. Elbows planted as she sipped, she resolved to *adult* and behave more prudently than ever to compensate. Allow her friends, a workaholic farmer and wife, to vacation. Allow Bonnie and Carl to bond and achieve a relationship blessed by heaven. Fran would tutor a new student today—Paul's new church secretary.

Fran selected her outfit with care, wishing she'd not hastily donated her suit armada to Goodwill. While she applied make-up, she practiced her fierce face, her empathetic pastor's wife face, and her adoring wife face, trying to memorize the muscles for each. She vowed to repeat this cycle daily now that she'd been released from temp duty.

She also vowed to devote time to pluck her increasing strands of gray.

When she arrived at the church, Fran didn't see Paul's car in his assigned space. He visited hospital patients and shut-ins on Monday mornings, preferring to offer Holy Communion himself. The beige Toyota, rust gnawing its quarter panels, likely belonged to Marge, the new hire secretary. *Ha, Marge's Barge.*

Comic relief lightened Fran's mood. *Welcome, Marge, just*

barge on in. At least she wouldn't be facing the Widow's daily visit on her own; she'd be behind Marge.

"Hi, Marge." Fran plunked the donut box on the desk to shake hands. "Pleased to meet you. I'm the pastor's wife." She paused, watching for recognition on Marge's face. When none came, she continued, "Fran Blackstone, the high school principal for decades."

Still no whoops or cheers, so Fran crooked a finger and bustled down the hall. She tossed verbal directions over her shoulder. "Come with me, and I'll show you your second duty of the morning."

Marge trilled, "What's the first?"

Fran paused halfway down the hall. "Get the usual at Tim Horton's Coffee Shop."

"Oh," Marge blinked. "But I prefer Dunkin' Donuts."

Fran ignored the inappropriate remark. She waved Marge over to the multi-cup coffee maker, waited until the woman was ready to observe, and made the first tank with an extra scoop of Tim Horton's Dark Roast. And a dash of salt.

She punched ON, commanded Marge to record the recipe, and then reviewed the note card in order to assure proper annotation of all ingredients. Fran mentally munched both Maple Dip donuts in the box, the Widow's favorite feast.

Well, hell's bells. The woman was already stationed in front of Marge's future desk, arms crossed over Mary Kay pink. A glistening diamond brooch served as a nametag, yet Fran felt compelled to introduce them.

"Mrs. Braghorn, this is Marge Baylin, the church's new secretary." Smiling like an ingenue, Fran turned to the new secretary, who seemed skittish, perhaps wary that this woman was another foil, as Fran had affirmed that *she* was.

"Marge, this is Mrs. Braghorn, one of our dearest donors, er, church members." Fran felt her face heat, likely matching her garb, as she realized she'd forgotten the Widow's first name. She hadn't planned on Alzheimer's Disease joining her retirement. She had to prove to herself that she was on top of her game.

Fran edged behind the desk and snuggled the pink box atop the papers stacked on the desk to clutch them under it. She desperately hoped the letter to be signed and sent to the Bishop wouldn't be marred by maple frosting. Paul needed his approval of the church's expansion plans.

Paul stepped into the office, put his hand on the Widow's forearm, and stepped around the desk to give Fran a chaste peck. "Good morning to my two favorite women, corralled by God into the same place, the easier for me to appreciate." His eyes widened in surprise as he lifted his head to take in the full room.

Fran realized he'd forgotten his new secretary's start date, so she stepped in. *Must have been a wretched morning.* "Paul, you remember your new secretary, Marge Baylin." Turning to Marge, she winked. "Your name is perfect, my dear, because you'll be bailing out the pastor like I just did."

The Widow lifted her chin and glided into Paul's office. Fran gaped, but Paul didn't react. "Make yourself comfortable while I get us some donuts and coffee," he crooned and eyeballed Fran. His rapid remarks were a decibel below stage whisper. "Remind me to speak with the janitor to assure my office door is closed at the end of the day. This can't happen again. The architect's plans are spread out on my desk."

"For gracious sakes," Fran managed before Paul sped to the kitchen. She sped after him with the donuts, leaving Marge to stare at her hands. Thank God, she hadn't said her first thought, "Hell's bells."

Fran placed the box on the staff room counter, fumbled in her purse, and wrote the new secretary's name on the top. She sneaked the Maple Dip duo out of the box, napkined them, and stashed them in her purse. Fran scooted out of the room before Paul opened the box. Yes, it had been a tough morning for him, judging by the length of his bio break.

Not the best day to devour the Widow's favorite donuts, but Fran was damned if she cared. She was already doomed for adopting 'hell' as a favorite phrase, so pile on the taint of tastes. Ha! This was her last day of work. She'd hurry through secretary training protocols, perhaps forgetting to mention the imperious fool's preference to Marge.

What did she care? Let the Widow Braghorn eat cake. Let the pastor handle his messes. She'd be home in an hour with this snack for her Bran-cam dairy barn review. Her hair appointment was at 10:00.

Brandon Breeden's behavior could not be worse than his parents'.

Mmnm. Maple Dip donuts supplemented green tea very well.

What the hell? The same slender kid is doing the chores. The dog overseer is nowhere in sight. There is definitely something to get to the bottom of here. Something more to cogitate over than hair colors. Gotta go! Who cares if maple frosting dapples my face.

Fran entered Maybelline's beauty shop to no notice, no greeting of welcome. What? It's only Marge's first day. I may no longer be the church's secretary, the switchboard operator of church gossip, but I remain its pastor's wife. Have I lost my community status already? I realize some of my prowess vanished when I retired as the high school principal, but, hell, I'm nearly six feet tall.

Four heads in various stages of hair cut-and-color bent over an iPad, the 70's hair dryer bent back but whirring away. The sound matched the obvious buzz among the group. Maybelline held a pair of scissors in her hand, open-jawed as if poised to stab the screen.

"May, sheath your weapon," Fran commanded. No one lifted their heads. So Fran elbowed in to look for herself—just as the group exploded in applause.

Suddenly the air sucked from the room and all eyes fastened on her. "So, why aren't you doing the hula in Hawaii?" The question bored into Fran's heart. She licked the corners of her mouth, desperately seeking donut glaze to soften her shock.

Fran felt her chin collide with her Adam's apple. Dumbstruck, she blinked before words floated into her brain. "Jackie asked me and Paul to watch over Brandon and the Breeden Dairy."

"You're joking, right?" asked Polly. "Brandon's a thirty-one-year-old man."

"Yeah," said Jennie. "Didn't he successfully captain two football teams? For an aggregate of seven years, high school and college? Wasn't he headed to the pros?"

Fran didn't know where to look, what to say, what to

think? She faced multiple no-wins. Chest-bumped questions to add to her own.

Did Bonnie hand her phone to someone before she and Carl joined the dance onstage? Whatever compelled her to post the foursome's spicy hula performance? Jackie had only attached photos of her and Steve in her email account. Further, the post already had 300 "Likes", which meant it had gone viral in this town. Would the nation be next?

An impossible thought. But first things first. How am I going to manage the fallout from Bonnie's impetuous Facebook post? Worse, Bonnie upstaged my plan to develop a travelogue as a fundraising ploy.

Wait, I've forgotten that Bonnie's massive pledge already preempted church fundraising. But I'm not to tell. Paul and I must mask it some how. Must. Keep. Thoughts. To. Self.

"How do I feel? I feel like going blonde. Whaddayathink, Maybelline?" Fran blurted.

Maybelline beamed. Polly put down the iPad to applaud. "I think blonde highlights would be a great way to go. Do you have the time?"

"I've got nothing but time," replied Fran. "The church hired a secretary to replace Bonnie. Name's Marge Baylin."

"Oh, I think she's a cousin of my husband," said Polly.

And all the hens in the room nodded and clucked.

To regain everyone's attention, Fran announced, "Give me honey blonde highlights and whatever the hell other blonde tints you've got, May. I'm wearing my mink coat to church, and I want my hair to match."

While Fran could sense that the covey wanted to ask where and how she'd gotten a mink, the sole comment emerged from

Maybelline's mouth, "What a way to celebrate the Fourth of July, Fran." She escorted Fran to the chair and placed the tint selections into her hands,

The hens returned to the dryer row and immersed themselves in magazines. Quiet. For a few moments. Then, cluck-cluck-cluck.

Twenty | *Bonnie and Carl*

"DON'T TAKE OFF A grin."

"Say what?" said Carl, "It's after midnight and I wanna ravage your body. Take off your clothes!" He lunged toward Bonnie, but his movements were as slurred as his words. He staggered back, his fingers hopelessly entangled in her plastic grass skirt. "Are you still hulaing, woman?"

To counterbalance Carl's yank, Bonnie's right hip ricocheted. Or maybe her hip hulaed on its own. Giggles erupted like, well like, gasp, the volcano in front of the Mirage Hotel on the Vegas strip.

Strip. That's right. Carl wants me to strip.

But how, when she had hula hips? And hiccups? She couldn't maneuver or think.

Bonnie laughed so much, she doubled over, hiccups intermittent. She stumbled into the easy chair, snuggled in, floundered and flopped a moment, then bounced up like an errant spring. *What was that kids' rhyme Jackie often quoted? Something about an old woman who swallowed a bunch of critters, who wiggled and jiggled and giggled inside her.*

"Raise your arms," Carl said, "so I can slip the damn thing off."

"I am raising my arms," Bonnie murmured as she slumped to the floor. She lifted an eyelid to peer at Carl, grabbed his collar to pull him close, and managed, "That's what my momma used to say," before she passed out.

Carl gaped. He wondered why Bonnie's mother said, "I am raising arms." He realized he knew little about Bonnie. He knew she was determined and fell easily in love.

Further, Bonnie cemented his love and loyalty with her intuitive act to re-bond him with his brother. Steve, the first person who'd loved him in a long while. Jackie was a close second, well third, because he sensed that Bonnie experienced love at first sight.

Quite the opposite of himself. He nodded at the affirmation of the old wives tale that opposites attract.

Bonnie had mended fences with his kids and removed alimony from his life. She was a rich asset in more ways than one. He looked forward to the future, roaming the world, but he knew little of her past. Maybe she'd find her roots in Australia, too.

Carl set their travel alarm, as well as telephoning the hotel operator for wake-up at 9:45. The Quantas flight to Sydney departed at noon. He supposed the bellboy could pack their bags if Bonnie flashed some cash at him. Carl smiled. He didn't mind being a kept man.

"Don't take off a grin," cycled through his dreams.

Twenty-one | *Jackie and Steve*

A FEW BAGS DOTTED the flight's baggage carousel, plucked from the bowels of the Quantas plane and hoisted by unseen hands. Jackie reached into her purse, pulled out her compact, and opened it to check her makeup. She fluffed her curls, hoping her cowlick wasn't splayed flat. It had been a long flight and, though she'd slept, her face looked as haggard as every particle of her being felt.

She longed to yoga-stretch here by the carousel, but travelers, also fatigued beyond reason, milled about. Open space ebbed and flowed, and tempers might flare. She didn't desire to replace vacation with hospitalization-by-baggage-cart, kamikazied by a ten-year-old with a toddler atop five bags. Such a vehicle had nearly battered her moments ago. Not a good welcome to the land of Oz, as the flight attendants had called Australia.

Jackie scanned the crowd. She took a deep breath and relaxed. After her third airplane ride, she felt like a seasoned traveler, one now able to master the gist of snagging bags and remaining calm during the hurry-up-and-wait aspect of air travel. Sort of like the Army, Steve and Carl had agreed. Sort of like being in charge of a church, Bonnie chimed in.

Sort of like being a wife and mother, Jackie knew but didn't say. Let everyone else have the last word. She was on vacation, resolved not to care about egos and turf.

"Take a look at the weather through the sliding glass doors," Bonnie said. "Winter looks grim. Let's dig out the minks."

Despite their men's winces, each woman dove for her garment bag and unleashed her fur. Who needed lipstick and fresh makeup when a mink coat caressed? Who cared about limp hair made limper by foul weather? "Get us to the Intercontinental Hotel." A cab arrived at the curb pronto, and they all scrambled in.

Holy crap. Bonnie was bossy. Worse than Fran and Paul and Steve and Carl—and Brandon, who, in his own way, expected allegiance to his whims and requests. *You'd like frog legs for supper? Sure, I'll have the dog chase 'em out of the pond and fry them in no time. It's no bother, no bother at all.*

Jackie wondered if there was room on the continent for her agenda. Perhaps she should put one forth. Try it on for size, like she had done with the mink into which she now wriggled. It didn't feel so bad. In fact, it felt divine.

By the time the taxi van wheeled into traffic to transport them to their hotel, Jackie was snoring.

The hard roll aside of the van door jolted her awake. She looked at her watch and then at Steve. By the looks of his hair, he'd also snoozed.

"What time is it?" Jackie twisted curls while Steve rifled his hair, dug in his pockets for his folded ball cap, and settled it in place. Thank goodness he never fiddled with his mustache. Wouldn't want to look like Snidely Whiplash on their first vacation foray.

"It's 5:00 somewhere," said Carl, shaking his head like the

dog after a scratch. He nudged Bonnie, then stage-whispered, "Don't take off your grin, honey. We're here."

Bonnie snuggled into the curve of Carl's neck a moment, and then slid her mink off her and Carl's laps. She draped it over her arm and exited first. As the funder-in-chief she apparently felt compelled to lead the entourage. Jackie looked at Steve who just shrugged and hitched his caboose on the train.

The lobby of the Intercontinental was narrow and underwhelmingly beige. As unassuming as the outer space for taxis, cars, limos, and walk-in guests was grand. Bonnie walked almost as quickly as the bell captain who'd waved them forward to the wide swath of check-in desk with a flourish of a circus ringmaster.

Bonnie plunked her Capitol One credit card on the counter and demanded an upgrade to the two best suites. Soon they'd unwind their plane-torqued bodies in luxurious accommodations, rewind their watches, and then begin their adventures together.

Within a couple of minutes all of the luggage was stacked into three brass carts with three uniformed porters ready to earn a big tip. However, as soon as Bonnie signaled the group toward the elevator, Carl spoke after nodding to Steve. "You ladies go up to the rooms and settle in. Steve and I got something we gotta do first."

Jackie cast a worried look of surprise at Steve. He shrugged, nodded reassurance to Jackie, and gave her a hug. "Go along and take an extended nap, hon. I don't know exactly what Carl has in mind, but he's my brother, and I gotta go."

Jackie kissed Steve as warm as could be and released him into his brother's hands. *What could go wrong?* echoed in her head in cadence with her step-run to catch up to Bonnie.

Bonnie lifted a bitchy-arched eyebrow as soon as her long-nailed finger left the door hold button of the hotel elevator. "What took you so long, Jackie? I'm in need of a nap." Her mink hid her plane-wrinkled clothing, but it didn't cover her anger-creased face. Jackie sensed Bonnie was beyond reason—miffed at being left behind by her beloved?—so she smiled and remained mum. No other people occupied the elevator. Thirty-seven more floors to the top.

"If you're wondering where our luggage is, it's in our suites. I took care of the porters long ago. I tipped them twenty dollars each, so you owe me thirty bucks."

Jackie rummaged in her bag and came out with two twenties. "Do they have the same currency as us?"

"Well, the porters accepted my tip," Bonnie stashed the money in her mink and said no more for several seconds. "I hope I won't be seeing that damn Spartan green with khaki pants uniform. That's stupid Midwestern clothing, Jackie."

Jackie gazed woozily at her shoes. "I can't think right now, but I believe I followed your suggestion."

"We'll all get along best if we remember whose cash we're spending."

Holy crap. I didn't even receive change from my $40. Fran's personality has transmigrated. Jackie began to sing to herself, inhaling strongly to suppress quips best not unleashed in a stale-aired small space. Jet lag had curdled their moods. Jackie needed water to revive her spirits, as well as swallow toxic comments. Maybe even drown Bonnie's truculent ass.

Jackie could hear Bonnie rustling the bills in her mink pocket. Jackie shrank deep inside of hers, wishing she'd followed through on the idea to stash some weed in the lining. A toke would take the edge off just about now. Maybe a half-hour ago.

When a bell signaled arrival at their floor, Jackie glanced at herself reflected in the mirrored panels of the elevator. Her smile wavered. Relief, sorrow, and hope chased each other over her face.

She rolled her eyes, blocking Bonnie's view with her purse. Buckle your seatbelt. Bonnie has assumed the position: acerbic, demanding, and bossy rich bitch, as childish as a two-year-old. Lord, give me peace. Because if you give me strength, I'm going to need bail money to go with it.

Carl ensconced himself in one of the concierge's silk damask chairs and motioned Steve into the other. Abandoning the habitual Midwestern ritual of small talk, largely about weather, Carl immediately delineated his requests to a smartly suited man whose posture was more precise than any person Steve had ever met. Even when he visited the VFW Hall, where every stripe of military service strolled cocksure, no one aligned perpetually ramrod straight. This man sat more erect than a staff sergeant could've screamed into a man.

It was as if the staffer was fused to a pole. His waxy blond hair loped over his forehead to emulate the curved handle of a cane—or a staff. If Brandon were here, would he have blurted out, "Queer bait?" like he so often did at guys in TV commercials.

Steve brought his fist to his quivering lips while Carl conducted serious conversation with the gent. Contact with his mustache stayed him. Must. Not. Laugh. Steve didn't glance at the man's brass nameplate and badge. The Staff would be his perpetual name.

The Staff swiveled to a computer and tapped keys without looking at his hands. It was likely that he couldn't bend his neck.

Steve folded his hands and smiled throughout the interchange—he couldn't understand a word the Australian said. Perhaps he mumbled more than most, perhaps not. But Carl seemed pleased, now leaning across the man's mahogany desk to peer at the screen. Mr. Erect shooed Carl away and wrote on card stock that seemed to have been imported from the last century. Steve cringed when he thought of his lined yellow pads at home.

After Carl handed Steve the card, he stood. "Ready to go?"

Steve frowned and stared at the note, idly flicking his thumbnail on its corner. The sound reminded him of the dog's tail beating the barn door when he wanted out. The words looked so wonky, Steve worried his reading skills had been left on the plane.

He looked up at Carl, quizzical in the extreme. "Where? To the University of Wool-on-a-gong? Ha! Higher learning about sheep on a bell?"

Carl grabbed the note back and stuffed it into his pocket. "Sorry, I must have shown you the wrong side. No, Brother, we are headed to the Fortune of War. It's Sydney's oldest pub. It's in The Rocks neighborhood, just steps from our hotel. We need to sample Aussie beer."

He was already walking away when Steve grabbed him by the arm. "Shouldn't we shower, change clothes? Tell Bonnie and Jackie where we're headed and why?"

"You mean get our spending money? I've got credit cards on our shared accounts." Carl patted his wallet. "The girls are napping, so now's the perfect time."

Steve wavered. He'd been married longer than Carl, so he was more schooled in the proper way for a husband to behave. To assure his supper was always salted the way he preferred, as well as served on time.

"The longer you stall, the longer it'll be before we return." Carl smirked. "Come on. I got something to tell you, and it's cool." He grabbed Steve's arm and jerked. "Are you up for adventure or not?"

The Fortune of War Bar was, indeed, steps from the Intercontinental Hotel. Many, many steps, all of them down. Steps they'd have to climb back to their hotel, *if* they could find it in this vast unknown. Mind-numbed by jet lag and this concern, Steve absorbed himself in Carl's chatter and the Sydney harbor view. No way out except forward, so he went.

"Sydney Harbor, or Sydney Cove, was a march away from Captain James Cook's initial landfall at Botany Bay."

Steve had already lost track of their route. While he was beyond fatigue, Carl seemed buoyed by his ability to info dump.

"No British citizen saw the place before thousands of hapless debtors, often Irish and Welsh, were shipped to the island. The journey was a one-way ticket to a unique penal experiment, distant from the gallows back home."

Steve considered Carl's drone a cruel sentence, too.

"Cook reported to England in 1776, around the same time

we unruly Americans cracked the Liberty Bell. Captain Cook extolled the distant land's botanical glories to King George, a monarch who needed good news." Carl paused to turn and look Steve in his bleary eyes, though the former seemed not to notice. "It turned out that Cook lied."

While Carl paused for emphasis, Steve took several deep breaths, so pleased with the reprieve that he didn't process the import. He could see that a response was expected, so he used his fallback, "Not copacetic, I take it," adding several shakes of his weary head.

"Definitely not cool, but what did the King care? He was rid of a vexing problem. The prison population was thinned so that more beggars and petty thieves could be incarcerated and off his capital's streets." Carl turned to walk.

Steve took another breath, another glimpse of the magnificent Opera House, and tucked behind Carl, who'd already resumed his monologue.

"Though it was summer in January, 1788 when the First Fleet arrived, the flora and fauna were instantly recognized as dissimilar to home—and not at all abundant. Sydney Cove was lusher with its own fresh water source, but Cook hadn't explored for that. He and his botanist extracted plant samples and left, sated and eager for fame."

"There's no greenery here now," Steve chanced an interruption. "Sydney seems pure concrete and stones, with a shining Opera House and harbor for glamour."

"Well, that's now. Let me return to back then." Carl was in full tourist guide mode, so Steve could only be unctuous. On top of being tired to the bone. "The commandants, soldiers, and crew of the First Fleet understood their plight. The eleven ships departed with the tacit expectation their venture would become a cannibal kingdom."

"You're not serious, are you?" Steve cringed at the thought—and at his present circumstance. He was not an athlete, not anymore. He could have been, but Vietnam stole his prowess from him. His lungs heaved, his legs cramped. Each sighting of Sydney Harbor's water reinforced his thirst.

Steve fixated on thirst over exhaustion, though both undermined his ability to listen and absorb. He was certain his ears had blisters as well as his feet. Even his mustache seemed to bristle—with sensory overload and chill.

"Ah, The Rocks, the original settlement. We're near beer!" Carl exclaimed.

Steve salivated at the sight.

The Rocks neighborhood was just that, surrounded and built upon rocks as big as Steve's barns. Tourists filled the bar-lined streets, the bar interiors, as well. They bypassed all of the lively establishments until Carl spied their destination.

Its sign proclaimed that the Fortune of War Bar opened in 1828, less than forty years after the first white inhabitants arrived. Now, it was a raucous enclave, filled predominantly with male patrons. The wood-paneled walls reverberated. Steve vaguely wondered if the nails would hold.

Fans of the Australian team, the Kangaroos, congregated on one side, projecting buff. And gruffly intense in their butch haircuts in all shades of Scotch-Irish heritage. The New Zealand rugby fans—dressed in all black, intimidating as a murder of crows—occupied the other half of the cozy bar. Except for the fan wear, the host sported identical hair and musculature and was indistinguishable.

Brandon, the former All-American football player, shriveled in Carl and Steve's memories. These men, with bodies as big and solid as goal posts, smelled of abundant sweat and spilled beer. All hundred eyes focused on the new entries. Carl and Steve exchanged looks. Carl decided. "It's taken generations of Australian history to get us here. Let's go in and have a hella good time."

The cheers, divvied between corners of the bar, were rollicking. "Aussie, Aussie, Aussie." Returned by, "Oy, Oy, Oy." The All Blacks brandished tongues, shaking fists, and rude glares. Silent menace was their brand. Steve and Carl managed to thread among the throng to order via point-and-mime. "I'll have what they're having."

Carl and Steve knuckle-bumped when two beers scooted in front of them. Each drained their mug, signaled for another, and helicopter-watched multiple big screens to keep themselves awake. The din rivaled any football game experienced in the US. Between the brothers, they'd been faithful fans of several teams. Neither planned to wimp out by stuffing bits of bar napkins in their ears.

An hour later, their ears ringing, Carl edged Steve outside and along the harbor-side walk. Steve didn't protest. He just walked. They could catch a cab later. He needed to sober a bit before he returned to the hotel. Flat sidewalk seemed a good choice.

Suddenly, the sidewalk shifted pitch. Had the earth heaved? Steve deep-breathed to suppress a puke. Despite taking in significant amounts of night air, he felt bushed. Though he worked briskly in the barn every day, his calves burned with every step and his sides ached. Oh, to find a sidewalk escalator.

Suddenly Steve spied to a familiar-looking word ahead: Wooloomooloo Hotel and Bar. Were all Aussie words alike? He elbowed Carl and pointed. "Let's sit. Have a drink. I'm famished. I'm beat."

Carl clumped to a table with a harbor view, Steve plodding behind him. The Sydney Opera House lorded over the harbor again, an improbable jumble of conquistador helmets which seemed unrelated to music.

A waitress materialized and Carl ordered, "Two Fosters, please."

The woman, tatted shoulder-to-wrist, didn't bother to equably flirt. Carl's credit card was on the table. Instead she squinted, scrunched her nose, and pursed her lips as if in mid-sneeze. "Suit yourselves, Mates. But that's piss beer, if you'd ask me. You might as well crack a tinnie at home, 'cause I'm not likely to bring you two of those."

"What would you suggest?" Steve asked.

"Victoria Bitter or Toohey's New."

Steve eyed Carl and then turned to the waitress. "Bring us one of each."

The waitress scooped up the credit card. "Run a tab for you, Yanks?" She wiggled away before Carl agreed.

"Lively," Steve said.

"Women get straight to the point when you're mildly drunk." Carl winked.

Steve leaned toward Carl. "When are you getting to the bit about our ancestry? Do we have Aussie roots or not?"

"Oh, that. Yes. While you were correct that Breeden was

Welsh heritage, no one of that name had his death sentence commuted to seven years service in a penal colony thousands of miles away. Your dad's line of relatives weren't crooks." Carl eyebrow-boogied, and Steve returned the gesture. As a means of urging Carl on, because his brain power was collapsing. And because his brother had adopted his signature look. Copacetic and cool.

"But..." Carl inhaled deep, savoring his dramatic build-up, looking about as if clandestine info was about to leave his lips. "A man named William Edwards, age 29, convicted of stealing a heifer in Monmouth, Wales in 1785 was aboard. Over three hundred years ago our mother's forebear herded a cow, only it belonged to someone else."

"Is the intel solid? After all, you got it from a hotel staffer whose looks as well as accent confused us." Steve stared at Carl, perhaps too long, because his eyes almost went to sleep.

"You could chip a tooth on it," Carl replied.

Steve shook his head. "A herder murder." He chortled, inciting the entire bar.

Startled, Steve looked around. Did all Aussie bars convulse with noise? Ah, another rugby game.

When the beers arrived, Steve studied Carl over the rim of his glass. His Reagan resemblance oozed masculinity. He was the personification of Mayhem, the State Farm ad character. In the moment, Steve didn't know if that thrilled him or scared him. He winced, hoping it was imperceptible to Carl, his only anchor in the room.

The brothers hoisted their glasses to salute their heritage, its infamy and sin. They high-fived. They drank. They listed in their seats.

Just then the rugby crowd swept into this bar, too. Were he and Carl being stalked? "Would you look at that, Mates?" a voice boomed. "The bogans have come to the Big Smoke!"

Carl wheeled to reply, "Isn't Paul Hogan a bit yesterday, Aussies?" He signaled the waitress for another round. "Did you come here to see my big knife?"

"Blimey, a knife ain't a fair go, Mate."

"Harry, he's only spit the dummy, not got a knife at all. Leave the bloke be."

There were more remarks, more shouts, more men edging near, bustling and bumping, beery. The room had to be tilting on its axis, because that's what Steve's head registered.

Suddenly, Carl's head was soaked, along with his shirt. The one he'd been wearing for a day. Or was it two? Steve was grateful that his mustache served as an Air Wick to block some of the body odor and beer reek, but still his head arched reflexively away.

The fight started soon after. It wasn't the Hokey Pokey Senior Citizen type. It was Maori Haka-fueled brawl, all nasty faced-menace and fists. Like the All Blacks pre-game ritual Carl and Steve had watched in horror, but the TV screen didn't show the spit.

Apparently fans of both teams, 'Roos and All Blacks, took umbrage with Yanks. Discrimination. Something neither the Californian nor Michigan native had expected. Or experienced. Was this a usual welcome to the country? Not like Midwestern hospitality at all.

The burly host pummeled their rube targets. For a few seconds. Then, their breath coming hard, they took on each other, equality among blocky-bodied hooligans shown, just as in the televised rugby game. If there had been women in the bar, they'd either run out or joined the brawl. The scene bore zero resemblance to Happy Hour back home.

Officers appeared *after* the mirror behind the bar became the target. No one desired seven years of bad luck. Or incarceration in Sydney's police centres, though it looked like that's where the lot was headed.

Carl grinned. Now, he and Steve knew, they truly and bruisingly knew, who were the champions of the world. Aussie, Aussie, Aussie. Oy, oy, oy.

Twenty-two | *Fran*

SUNDAY MORNINGS SUSTAINED A lonely pattern. Soon after he rose, Paul drove to his church office to rehearse, highlight, and annotate his sermon. No more pancakes or waffle spreads with whipped cream, berries from Jackie's bramble patches, and mounds of crispy bacon. Just coffee and a fistful of cereal in a plastic cup carried her husband out the door.

Fran learned to brush past the resultant hours of home hush, leisurely readying for church. She avoided the Bran Cam on this, the ordained day of rest. Thank God for *CBS Sunday Morning's* hour-and-a-half.

No closet finagling to fill time. A principal's garb had required thought. Firm, staunch, yet approachable was the look. While these elements carried forward for a loyal pastor's wife, she covered all with a choir robe. She'd once toyed with the notion of wearing her fur to niggle the Widow Braghon, but Paul voiced an emphatic, "No." A pastor's wife should wear a cloth coat. He didn't want his salary to plummet, he said. Because she'd negotiated staff salaries, Fran understood.

Besides, it was summer. Michigan in the midst of its roasty humid climate.

Church attendance had risen so two services were necessary to accommodate the crowds. The buzz generated by the stained glass window installation, refreshed carpet, pews, and interior paint attracted them like watermelon remnants attracted raccoons. The seats and coffers were full, and Paul was ebullient as he bested the Catholics across the street.

Fran's sole boon was to sing worship songs twice. Though she missed Jackie's alto, the new robes attracted several additional tenor and bass voices to the choir. The new members enhanced the harmony of the entire congregation.

Her husband was swamped on the patio in the half-hour between Sunday services. The furor over Bonnie's Facebook video spurred much gnashing of teeth around the donut table, along with the usual gossip and sports scores. Soon, the donuts disappeared. Marge, not Fran, was tasked to retrieve the cash donation cup and replenish the trough.

Christ on a bicycle. Marge purchased five dozen from Dunkin' Donuts, not Tim's. Fran's impromptu-and-persistent battle with the Widow over the Maple Dips was done in.

Fran self-soothed with the Maple Dip she'd secreted in her voluminous sleeve, now that she knew Marge would shirk her Tim Horton donut run. The better comfort was that Marge would be the one to field the complaint calls—which Fran admitted to sparking—and the Suggestion Box notes, some of which Fran stuffed. The woman would recompense with the correct donuts soon.

Hell had no fury like a thwarted ex-administrator accustomed to running the show.

Fran regretted not having Bonnie and Jackie to crow to—or join her co-fixing.

Fran dearly missed the trek to the bank to deposit the cash, after tallying and posting the collection plate haul. A chat with the bank manager, Harold Prince, used to enliven and inform her day. He behaved in a more ritualistically self-possessed manner now that his bank was stuffed with church cash and Bonnie's lottery LLC accounts. He no longer worked to charm Fran's socks off. She'd liked the man better when he was unctuous. Who else could she trade polysyllabic verbiage with in this town?

Sally, the Koffee Kup waitress, was no longer sycophantic when she and Paul attended Taco Tuesday, sans the former entourage. Fran's status as a regular ceased with day and nighttime pals gone. Paul always received a slice of pie on the house, as if that would assure Sally's entry to heaven. Fran gritted her teeth.

Each Monday rolled out with no agenda, purpose, or plans. Nothing calendared for a has-been, a realization to which Fran settled into several months ago. The first day after her last day in the school system had been joyous, but the shine was off the apple, so to speak. Mondays flattened more because Sunday afternoons no longer afforded coveted time with her husband. Paul was absorbed with architectural plans.

Tuesday portended worse. Another bad morning loomed, like a classroom of bored summer school students. She could feel depression, thick and heavy as fog, enveloping her brain. She toyed with the notion of revisiting Facebook to see the extended reactions to Bonnie's video, but decided not to reward her friends' sin by adding to the views.

Then she recalled her Bran Cam duties. She'd been delinquent for two days. She had a mystery to solve; perhaps a lengthy email report to Jackie and Steve would be required.

She microwaved her Darjeeling and settled in for a lengthy observation session, swathed in her favorite robe. An aromatic candle nuanced the scene. She felt less alone in her vigil.

The familiar interior barn appeared, reminding her suddenly of the single camera TV sitcoms that predated "I Love Lucy." Desi Arnaz may have been a philanderer, but Lucile Ball laughed all the way to being a star. Fran chuckled at the thought while she watched the black-and-white images on her monitor.

Fran actually empathized with Brandon, though a miniscule amount. He'd been a shoulder injury away from being a pro football player, failed at marriage, and missed two trips out of town. In neither instance had his parents given him a choice, though they coddled him in every other way. He was a has-been, too.

Still, Fran wondered. Since Brandon was engaged to sweet Julie, studying pharmacy at Purdue, he was scarce around town. Her recent witness of a possible laborer replacement intrigued her, though, truth be told, the ritual of watching nearly fully-automated milking numbed. Fran felt assured she could handle the milking herself if Brandon's surrogate, the high school quarterback, was injured and unable to fill in.

What? The young man's frame loomed larger than she'd grown accustomed to in her vigils. The limbs moved with more beefy confidence, less kinetic charge. Then, he turned to face the hidden camera.

The milkman was Brandon, not Seth Thomas. Was she that prescient? Had her thoughts made it so? Was the power of the Lord upon her? Hell's bells. Brandon handled the chores for which he received handsome compensation. Fran gave the teabag an extra swirl and ran to fetch a hard-boiled egg. She required fortification for what might be an interesting sit.

She'd been in place mere seconds when a scene rolled that shocked her more than the travel foursome's dance video. A massive brown wad sailed smack into Brandon's face. One of the dairy cows apparently pooped, mooed, and coughed simultaneously, and a cowpie in the face resulted.

Fran nearly gagged, but then she laughed and snorted, splashing tea on her favorite robe. She longed for a rewind option on the Bran Cam. She longed for sound—though Brandon's body language shouted his shock and anger for him. Ha, it served the kid right for neglecting his duties. Ha-ha-ha-ha-ha.

Fran wavered between applauding Brandon's initiative for hiring a replacement and scolding him, but realized she couldn't tip her hand by letting him know she'd witnessed the cowpie incident. It was her and God's secret, and she could not have imagined a better *come to Jesus* moment if she tried.

Fran composed an email to Jackie, but she didn't hit SEND. She fist-pumped, danced around the room, and then ran to the laundry to dab the tea stain. She hustled upstairs to dress for yoga, where her serene, self-satisfied smile would not seem out of place.

She vowed to not check the Bran Cam for a few days. She wanted to savor the final image. When the shit finally hit Brandon in the face. Ha-ha-ha-ha-ha.

Tuesday afternoon she happily read more of Jan Karon's recent book, her tutorial for being a pastor's wife. Peace was served with the pot roast and potatoes for supper, but no report. Fran craved conversation, but Paul's preoccupation with the church plans made for a silent meal. He didn't seem to have room in his mind for a funky Bran Cam secret, so Fran

ran and re-ran the scene in her mind, assured that she was having a better time.

Wednesday, hump day of the camel commercial's fame, began merrily. A little grocery shopping, not daily like the European custom she and Jackie learned while studying Portuguese. She considered anything daily to be a drudge. Routine didn't appeal to one of high intellect. She wished Paul would expand Marge's job description to include supper prep.

She slung the *Hiawassee Highlights* newspaper into her heaped cart. *Holy crap,* she could almost hear Jackie say. The picture and headline were as salacious and strident as the *National Enquirer,* racked beside it at the checkout stand. Waylon must have lifted a picture from the online video, Jackie's breasts covered in coconut shells and Steve's ass in the air. Bonnie and Carl in the background, though blurred.

Lord save us all, this story would not go away. Yet again, Fran felt dismayed. She hated missing the free-spirited fun. Could she have stopped the zany antics, or would she have joined in? She felt chained, rather than released in her retirement. Maybe she'd cycle back through the store to purchase Hawaiian chips. Maybe the liquor store carried Mai Tai components. She could practice her chicken dance, mind and body well-oiled.

No, her career as a pastor's wife would falter with the consequences. She wished for a local bookshop like the one in Jan Karon's fictional village.

When she returned home, Fran read through the afternoon, put leftovers in the microwave with instructions for Paul on how many minutes to zap his meal. Then, she went to choir practice, where she intended to hide behind the sheet music or in her choir robe sleeve to avoid potentially embarrassing conversations.

Thursday morning began with Fran nibbling her thumbnail while she schemed about opening a bookshop as a place to shelve her trove of *National Geographics.* She'd tried to engineer a bequest of her Nat Geos to the school library. The Board spurned her offer, stating Google Earth had long surpassed the need for forty years of monthly mags. The high school library also lacked shelf space, but would she like to make a donation for new computers?

She logged into her email account, but didn't linger overlong. Her inbox was filled with requests for political donations, offers of penile implants, and charity requests. Not a single invitation that would fill in one of the Monday-Saturday squares in her calendar's empty month. Had she contracted leprosy of the social life? She only received calls from folks curious for more details of the uncharacteristic antics of her friends or praise for Fran's good judgment for not joining them on the trip. Marge, the new church secretary, was useless. Rather than squelching loaded whispers, she embellished them and/or referred callers to Fran and Paul's home.

To avoid calls, Fran trundled around her Craftsman cottage, leaving her cell in her robe pocket in the parsonage. She dusted and vacuumed, washed windows. She lit a cinnamon-scented candle while she mused, but her memoir failed to find. Her home might smell like a cookie, but she couldn't flash that fiction to save her life, which she took to be the purpose of memoir.

There were twenty messages on her voice mail when Fran returned to the parsonage. She listened to one, then deleted them all. Gossip wasn't the lively life she sought. Meatloaf and mashed potatoes for dinner. Microwaved. Zap. Paul noticed nothing, not even her. Hell's bells. She began to feel peeved.

Fran slept until noon the next day and dressed for her Friday pick-up-the-mail task. Although Steve put the mail on hold, the local postmaster complained about having no room for a mound. Though Steve pre-paid all potential bills, she received circulars and junk mail from the post office.

Fran placed the rubber-banded stack of mail on the kitchen table. Ah-h, a letter fell loose. She teased it out, but the return address fuzzed. She'd neglected to clean her glasses again.

Postmarked California, an envelope with a considerable heft, fine linen weave stationary with an address embossed. A lawyer? Dare she open it or should she email Jackie first? Forgiveness rather than permission? It was difficult to choose with a pastor in the house.

Had to think. Had to nourish one's body. Fran whirled around the kitchen, seeking something that didn't require cleaning her glasses for a thorough pantry search. Ah, bread. White—what a perfect metaphor for her humble small town life.

Hells bells! Fran burned the last slice of bread, a heel, when she attempted toast. Of course, this set off the smoke alarm. She clamped her hands over her ears, unable to think of how to put this genie back in the bottle. She hoped she looked like Jeannie on the late sixties TV show as she danced to the pantry and to the garage, desperately seeking a cease-and-desist button.

Even without stalwart Steve, the volunteer fire brigade arrived so quickly, she greeted them in her frumpy house frau garb. She rued the phone call from her pastor. Perhaps he'd paddle her when he got home. Wouldn't that be naughty and nice!

By 2:00, she relented to the suspense, the clanging bell in her mind, perhaps a reverberation of the fire brigade. The letter opener in her hand seemed to move of its own accord, and soon she stared at what seemed to be a summons.

A woman named Stephanie Edwards was the complainant. Or was it Carl? Fran had never seen this type of document before. Ms. Edwards asserted that Carl had snaked her out of alimony. In addition to feeling cheated, the woman had mounted a claim on the lottery win.

Hell, publicity from the Hawaiian incident yielded more than Warhol's remark about fifteen minutes of fame. In the shared lottery win euphoria, Carl flippantly neglected a duty that yielded far-reaching consequences—into Bonnie's deep pockets.

Fran ran to the Internet, looking for YouTube...hell, five hundred thousand hits? The count ticked up while she watched the short segment. Her husband would kill for that amount of interest in his church.

Fran dithered. What to do? She checked the clock. What time was it in Australia? Should she call Jackie or her brother, Judge Blackstone? Fran would not interface directly with Bonnie, the increasingly bitchy millionaire, certain that she'd knock Bonnie's block off over the phone.

Fran refocused on preparing something especially tasty for supper, something to overcome the smoke smell that swarmed their home. She needed to pull Paul into this dilemma.

Hell's bells! When and how did she become subservient to a stomach? A keeper of secrets and divisive details?

Then, Fran chuckled. *I'm relevant again!*

Twenty-three | *Bonnie and Carl*

"BONNIE, DON'T PAY THE ransom. I'm—"

"What ransom, shithead? Where've you been? I sat in the Jacuzzi tub until all of the jasmine-scented bubbles collapsed and my toes wrinkled, the water long-chilled. The view from our Bay-facing bathroom window was serene. I got my rocks off, if you know what I mean."

Carl couldn't help himself, despite his dire need for Bonnie's assistance. Her peevish tone begged for rebuff. His tongue-in-cheek doubled down. He couldn't resist. It was how he'd handled controversy throughout his life. His brain cycled through replies like a Wurlitzer on steroids. The boozy fight high dissipated. In its place, electrically recharged word choices surged.

But he chose to ignore the rocks.

"Did the people on the cruise ships wave when you saluted them with your sweet bare ass?"

"I'm hanging up on this content. I'll leave the mooning to you, when and if you return. Make it quick before my libido fades. Bye, Buster. I need to slather my backside with lotion. Gonna be awkward because you're not here to help. Should I call the bell captain or concierge?"

"Wait, wait. Don't—"

"Why? I bought a slutty red lipstick in the hotel spa and had my nails polished to match." Bonnie switched the phone from one ear to the other so she could loft each hand in turn and watch her fingers dance in the reflected Bay lights. Now, she saw her nails as weapons rather than sex toys.

Carl decided to alter his tone to abject begging. He wasn't about to bear this setback stoically alone. Besides, he had Steve to consider. "I'm in a paddy wagon on my way to jail."

"Who is this?" Bonnie held the phone at arm's length, re-admired her polish, and willed the caller to not be Carl.

"Bonnie, honey. I'm captured, about to be incarcerated, in the calaboose. Steve and I had a hella time. Got into a gnarly fight with giant Sequoia guys."

"What's a Sequoia?"

"Bonnie, please don't digress. The cell battery is lower than low."

"Answer my question. Inquiring minds want to know." Bonnie's mind conjured several irrational revenge fantasies. To prevent tears. Tears of anger, frustration, and fear. She'd seen many couples traipse in-out of the pastor's counseling session, and she knew weeping did no good.

"It's a ginormous tree. Often thousands of feet tall. Not many left due to climate change. Now, can we resume our discussion of a release plan from jail?"

"So, you found your Australian convict roots in the present.

Did you find them in the past? Is that why you celebrated with bar hopping? Let me guess, did you make it to three?"

"Bonnie, I'll let that slide because I need a quick fix to a situation. A situation compounded by hunger pangs. My last supper was an airline snack."

"Well, buy yourself something. You have my credit cards in your wallet!"

"—about that, too, Bonnie. I'm afraid my wallet got thrown in the Bay during the fight—"

Suddenly the voice in Bonnie's ear changed. "Sir, how may I describe you?" Bonnie heard Carl's voice in the background.

"G'day, mate. Name's Jake. I'm a freakin' badass, a member of the All Black Rugby team. World champs, New Zealand. Second string. My neck sports a dog collar 'cause I can't afford tats. Your bloke's a fine man, though he busted my lip. Not sure I want to share a cell with him since the police centre's overcrowded due to our overhauled bail statutes."

Bonnie blinked. She blinked and blinked and blinked, but the tears still spilled over the edge of her eyelids, like the slim stream of Bridal Veil Falls. She knew what a Sequoia was. She'd seen them in the California state park named for the trees.

"What? No words now. Check the web and come get 'im released. I dislike Yanks. Mind if I use his phone to call my solicitor? I'm tired of taking one for the team. Jail guards are dicks." The phone went dead.

Golly-gol-darnit-dang. This wasn't what Bonnie's mapped for the trip. You'd think when his wife won the Boffo Lotto—not a banal amount like a hundred bucks won in yokel poker—Carl would be obedient and tame. Because of her lovely presence, her presents, her gift of funds for life. In Carl's case, the money seemed to have robbed him of all good sense. She married a strong, smart, and bold person, who now seemed as inept as an ape. Should she get him out of jail or should she let him cool his heals in a climate-controlled cell for a couple of nights?

Bonnie envisioned a straightjacket and muzzle to amplify the lessons Carl needed to learn. A better plan than wringing Carl's neck.

Bonnie shook her head to clear the images, and then clutched the receiver to her chest. She reached back to rub her neck, regretting she'd not sprung for a massage. She caught sight of herself in the mirror. No wonder she felt chilled. She was naked.

Naked and...afraid. And alone, except for Jackie who was as out of her element as she was. Maybe more flustered. They'd only been in Australia a day. Outlandish wealth had helped her escape, but she'd left her brain at home, and now her heart was going to jail.

Who could she call? Not her former boss, Pastor Rankin. Should she, could she call on his boss, the Lord above, on her own? Fran, who would lord her assistance over her? Forever.

Then Bonnie recalled. And nearly melted at the thought. Carl had Superman skills. She tossed the phone, scrambled out of the tub, donned the thick hotel robe. No time to lose. She accessed the hotel Wi-Fi.

Twenty-four | *Jackie and Steve*

"YOU DON'T SAY." IT was dark, so Jackie didn't spy a clock when her eyes swept the room. She couldn't see herself in the mirror, which was likely a good thing. She avoided a glance at the trash. She knew she'd shredded an entire box of tissues during her hours of fret.

"But I do, dear. Life is not exactly copacetic. Carl and I are headed to the Sydney Police Centre in Surry Hills."

"How far is that from here?"

"How should I know? We walked uphill, downhill, and over many blocks. Without coats. I've got blisters on both feet. No food, though plenty of fluids were imbibed." Steve paused, and Jackie could almost see him riffling his hair. "I think I left my brains in the barn."

"So, you went walkabout like an Aborigine, like in that movie I watched on the plane? While I've been holed up in a hotel with a revoltingly wealthy witch as my only companion. You've reverted to Brandon at age sixteen."

"Jackie, let's not meander off-message. I'm. In. Jail. Not a jaunty nightclub or a café. This is my one call, same prison policy as the U.S. I'm on a phone in front of a long line of squirmishers, rugby fans built bulky, not slight. In the interest of good foreign relations, the warden let me call first."

"You're not joking? Sorry, Steve. You know I'm a little ragged when awakened from deep sleep." Jackie heaved a sigh, repentant to the core. She was supposed to focus on Steve, not herself. "Take some yoga breaths and then tell me the particulars. All of it. This is going to make a great story later, and you need to practice."

"Jackie, I need a lawyer, not a damn Lamaze class!"

"Fine. If you won't deep breathe, I will." Jackie patted around her scalp, unable to locate a lone curl to fidget. Her hair was twisted as tight as her stomach felt. "Steve, while we are not wealthy, we are the invited guests of someone who is. Bonnie has enough money to fill the hotel swimming pool, cavort in it, and then lounge in the spa. She could buy the hotel chain, probably the town. Find Carl and suggest he phone his beloved to induce her to post bail or bond or whatever-the-hell amount of cash is required to free you, for cripes' sakes."

She heard Steve's long, long sigh. She'd gone into lecture mode, as if he was Brandon. Again.

"Sorry, honey. I truly want to hear the details, if you don't mind reliving the events—" Better to keep Steve talking than for him to inquire about her and Bonnie's status. That would go nowhere, but Steve still had Carl's tail to tweak. Bonnie was at least as in love with Carl as she was with her cash.

Incentivized, as Fran used to say about her students and staff.

"You know Carl had a mission to explore our convict roots." Steve groaned when he heard himself utter those words, and he hurried on before Jackie caught its pertinence. "The hotel concierge accessed a central data base in seconds. We didn't even have to search out a government archives building. We left with full disclosure in hand."

"Honey, you can relate that another time. I wanna hear

about my hero in his bar fight. Wait a minute while I get the door. I ordered a shrimp cocktail for room service delivery at 5:00. You know I listen better when I'm not starved."

Steve shrugged his shoulders at the scowling men in line behind him. He began to sweat through his over-ripe, worn-on-the-plane clothes. He didn't know where Carl was, but he did recall that both their wallets got lofted into the Bay. A longing to be in his milk barn almost incapacitated Steve. Oh to be safe, secure, and in Jackie's arms. In Michigan, where he belonged.

The nearby guard stood, back to the wall, eyes not moving, but seeing all. The guy's fohawk helped him clear six feet. Though trim physiqued, the guy's biceps bulged his shirt, telegraphing a bully-prone nature. Would he stay the angry men in line for the phone or push Steve out of place soon?

Steve angled his head away from the guard and alternated moving his lips as if in deep conversation or, the better half of that, listening. After numerous years of marriage, he had the act down pat. No Amateur Hour for this inmate.

Now to frame the fight while he waited for Jackie's return to the phone.

He'd punched his way out of a couple of bars in Michigan. In Jackie's presence, when they were young, her eyes bright with tears as she kissed his pummeled face afterward. But none of the bars in Michigan were populated by rugby fans, a breed of Paul Bunyan stature, legs like tree trunks, jaws firm, arms spring-loaded to bust chops.

The truth would be hard to tell. Steve's innards churned

with chaos times ten, major organs rearranged by multiple blows. He exerted tremendous will to cope with Jackie's dining on damn shrimp.

Ohh-h. It was a relief to consider that his abdominal pain was hunger, not damage unleashed by Aussie fists.

When Jackie returned to the call, he stood taller. He'd recalled a famous Rocky Balboa fight scene and referenced it to his loving wife, with her inevitable cringe immediate. "You know I hate blood. Don't tell me any more!"

Steve tried not to hear Jackie's chewing and was glad when she hung up with a pledge to call Fran pronto to enlist Pastor Rankin and Judge. And to bang on Bonnie's door after the ducks were in a row. Bonnie's duty was to quack cash.

The pep in Steve's step stopped at the cell door. The door slammed hope in its face. The austere accouterments contrasted strongly with the comforts of his home. True fright settled in. He attempted to appease himself with comparison of the hosed-down simplicity of the concrete cell similarity to his milk operation.

He heave-hoed himself onto the thin, rough-blanketed mattress, envisioning his body as the bales of hay he'd easily hefted to the wagon when he farmed with his dad. To circumvent thought of the disappointment his dad would project if here, Steve recycled memories of Brandon's football games, skirting the perimeter of his son's unheroic job efforts. Visions of Sparty, his building of the dairy business. Then Jackie, his true home.

Steve knew he hadn't spilled details of the actual bar brawl, specifics returning as his hangover cleared. Fine points punctuated by pain. Would Carl be complicit? The *Rocky* version wouldn't hold for long.

Steve began to rehearse his spiel with little or no fabrication, none that he'd readily confess to at any rate. It felt important to reshape a repugnant scene. He appeared to have plenty of time.

It was the second bar they shouldn't have entered. He and Carl should have slept off jet lag with their wives rather than derail a dream trip. Steve blamed it on the intoxication of ancestral roots discovered in the country their group intended to explore. He blamed fate. But he didn't blame Carl.

Despite the lack of sleep, Steve recalled feeling superhuman, able to handle the significant swill in his belly, as virile as in Vietnam. He recalled the odd odor of linoleum wax, the product Jackie applied ritualistically each spring. It rid the house of winter's closed, stale air and returned the kitchen floor's spiff as well as removing boot heel scuffs. It smelled like renewal, and Steve's mind and body longed to be rendered anew, too.

He smiled. He knew Jackie would appreciate the analogy. So, he repeated it, again and again, to establish his sense memory.

But the barroom recollections cut in, demanding attention like the Aussie fans had. Filled with over-tall men with hair punked to add to their height, cast-iron tonnage jerseyed in fan wear, all blitzed. The bartender was wiping down the expansive bar top with a white cloth, extending his arm as he mimicked the steady, even strokes of a windshield wiper. Steve felt like he'd walked into a bowl game after-party, something he and

Jackie had missed when they attended the Alamo Bowl in 2008. Or was it 2009?

Damn! His eyes darted between the TV screens that lined the remembered bar, the volume of each obviously at max. Vertigo surged, even bunked in the cell. Steve reached for the cold concrete wall, then recoiled.

He had relished the partisan roar, answered by the opponents at regular intervals. As Steve recalled, during Brandon's winning high school and collegiate careers, the other side had little opportunity to cheer.

The noise discouraged conversation, and Steve thought they'd ordered by mime. Remarkably, they seated themselves at rough-topped table unsplashed by beer. Not remarkable, really, because all other bar occupants stood.

He remembered the skinny waitress talked them out of ordering Foster's, the only Aussie beer known in the States. Her hair could have been any color, but her bar apron, at their eye level, was black, pockets stuffed with cash. Steve was reminded of a kangaroo.

Yeah, Jackie would like the apron detail, though her pockets were lined with love, delivered with each hug and peck on his cheek. He'd omitted the kangaroo comparison and their ill-fated interaction.

Steve remembered the casual bump that caused the waitress to douse Carl with beer. "Bogan!" she'd cried. "You've wet me cash. The bills will bond to become a lump sum. And, not in a proper way. I've got a car payment due."

Then a big dude stepped in. "Yeah, Bogan." Though it was another word unknown to the Michiganders, his tone of voice signatured its slur.

His mind's eye watched Carl reeling back to appraise the tormenter, and then tap the gargantuan guy's shoulder as he marched toward the restroom, an act of capricious reflex on a generously splashed playing field. He remembered trying to snag Carl's arm. He wanted to affirm the golden rule of spectator sports to Carl, a guy with less-than-professional experience: one cannot take on sports fans on their home turf.

The guy swung around, bringing a roundhouse punch with him. At the sight of his brother's chin hitting the table edge. Steve launched himself into authentic jungle fury, a remnant of Vietnam he thought he'd forgotten. He imagined Jackie cheering him on like when she sat beside him in the bleachers. It kept his fight alive.

He punched. He grabbed shirttails. He dodged. He turned. His fists flew. He smashed and trashed and received it all in kind. He forgot the old guys' rule: one could not pretend the prestige of a Marine's ripped muscles presided over a body of middle-age flab.

Soon their table was surrounded. Then over-turned. Steve thought briefly to hunker, as he'd done in Vietnam. He longed for the bartender's white cloth to claim surrender now.

He was certain he never screamed in agony, but he feared the open palm smack to his cheek might leave a permanent mark. Then, somebody struck a blow that made his teeth freeze. Fade to black.

As a headache emerged, Steve regretted bypassing the offer of medical attention. Things might never be fully copacetic again. But, the fight story would grow with gossip, a small town talent Steve now appreciated. He and Carl would become legends.

Twenty-five | *Fran*

FRAN CONTEMPLATED A SHOWER, to wash a week's worth of non-grit, when her cell phone rang. "Amazing Grace". Yes! Just what she needed, a dose of Jackie's charm.

"How sweet the sound—" Fran began, as she glanced at the clock. 2:00 Friday. *Better get crackin', Betty Crocker. You don't want to eat crow when your husband gets home.* "What time is it there, Jackie?"

"It's 5:00 a.m., Saturday morning."

"Why are you keeping farmer hours on vacation? Haven't you let that habit go?" Fran felt the return of command-and-control: advice to whip via phone.

Only sobs sounded in the receiver. Sobs so symptomatic, Fran could almost see Jackie's blotchy face, almost feel tears drench her soiled robe. She bit her tongue to suppress snappish remarks. It was clear Jackie was a mess, likely causing a puddle on an expensive hotel carpet. Fran watched the second hand sweep round the clock face three times.

"Fran, it's all going to shit. Bonnie's an uppity bitch and Carl and Steve are in jail."

Fran held her phone away from her ear and quizzically looked at it. Did that compound sentence contain any truth about her longtime friends? Had Jackie lost her mind? Cusswords littered Brandon's views, but not the Christian farmwife's. Was she channeling her son because she missed him?

"I'm not sure of our connection, Jackie. Would you please repeat what you said?"

"I don't know how it happened or why—"

Fran interrupted. "Let me get a pad and paper while you get ahold of yourself. I'm going to need the 5W facts. Remember the five fingers on your hand? Take deep breaths and think clearly. I'll be right back."

Fran sailed a fervent thank you prayer to the Lord. Just when she felt thoroughly extraneous, He placed a problem in her lap.

For the next twenty minutes, Fran listened, scribbled, and doodled. While she tried to maintain an orderly, logical list, Jackie rambled. She fretted about Steve, but almost unintelligibly. A tirade about Bonnie sounded more strongly worded and comprehensible. Apparently Bonnie's arrogance had swelled beyond her wealth, and her sharp tongue harassed Jackie's ears. Fran's notepad resembled the wandering of a lunatic chicken, pecking to find some facts.

Carl and Steve were currently incarcerated in the Surry Hills Police Station in Sydney. *Hell,* Fran thought, *that sounded like a tony Detroit suburb.* In holding cells, not together, hardly fed. Steve hurt and afforded no medical care. There was something about bail and remand. Not a mere wrist slap and off-you-go for Yank tourists who made a teensy mistake. Worse, Aussie TV swirled with rumor-laced news.

Since there seemed no pause in Jackie's sobbing, Fran grabbed the remote, clicked on the TV, searched, and found the BBC. Hell's bells. The priggish manager of a hotel with an impossible Woo-woo-woo name stared fixedly at the world audience rather than a reporter phalanx. *Hmm, already coached and lawyered-up.*

It was then that Fran recalled the lawsuit letter. "Jackie, stay in your room by the phone. Let's not waste more cell minutes, okay, honey? I'll do some research."

While Jackie deep-breathed to calm herself to say "okay"—Fran wouldn't hang up until she heard the affirmation—Fran sized up the hotel manager and nicknamed him, a lifelong technique that helped her mentally whip an opponent.

Starchie Archie didn't look beleaguered. Smiling broadly, he didn't look stressed. He looked composed, rehearsed, and expectant of compensation for his bar's pain and suffering. Something about the charges amped beyond public drunkenness and into the stratosphere of alcohol-related violence in a public place, an order he was empowered by law to issue at the time of the incident.

Steve and Carl could be barred for up to a month from re-entering his bar. But it would take many, many months and many, many dollars to rebuild. He knew his regular patrons ached for the recently refurbished Woo-woo-woo-hula-balloo Bar.

Yes, yes, there were security tapes, but he wasn't prepared to share them. After Starchie Archie cited the outrageous sum of his lawsuit, he altered his manner to harried and bereft as he stepped away from the microphones on the arm of his fierce-looking lawyer.

Smug bastard. Fran wished she could reach into the TV screen and wring his neck.

She looked aloft. Lord, I know bastard to be a Biblical word. Do not convict me, your loyal servant and Jackie, Steve, Bonnie, and Carl's ally.

Fran decided it was time to call Bonnie. First a shower, perhaps dress in a suit, and replace post-lunch tea with a nip. Fran knew the best means to align was to listen to Bonnie's queenly temper tantrum. When Bonnie was spent, Fran must insert the now additional lawsuit. Booze would bolster her resolve.

Fran never considered calling Carl, with whom she had little rapport. He'd caused too much uproar too quickly when he'd brought his California antics and attitudes to their small town. She might never truly trust a man who'd always be an outsider and a scamp.

Fran looked at the clock and did the math. 5:45 in Australia. Surely the pea under the princess' mattress—the incarceration of her husband—had the new bride awake. And ripe for new conundrum, followed by Fran's advice.

The hotel bar manager was the focus of Bonnie's wrath. Yesterday it was a probably a hangnail, Fran thought. Bonnie shrilled about his overblown expectation for cash, without a word about Carl.

But then, Carl's name did come up, but not as expected. It seemed that Carl landed the punch that broke the star player's jaw, and he would be out for the season. The 'Roos were suing, and Bonnie felt sunk. Though she had millions, the funds were encumbered in LLC accounts for which she had no access. Not only had Judge set it up that way at her request, Bonnie also lacked his phone number. Could Fran interface?

A paraphrase of one of the Beatitudes flashed Fran's mind. While Bonnie may not have inherited the earth when she was enriched, the formerly meek miss certainly felt she owned the world. Then Fran said, "Yes, I'm on it." How could she refuse her friends? How could she pile on the gnarly ex-wife's lawsuit via pit bull LA attorney? Now Fran applauded herself for resisting the meltdown-inducing jab.

There was much too much to attend to, but Fran was the woman for it all. She had a team to assemble. Stat.

Fran glanced at the clock. It was 3:30. Judge was known to have already drunk two fingers of Scotch, one from each bottle of single malt that he stored in the bottom drawers of his desk, both left and right sides.

She needed time to conjure a plan, but she also needed to calm Jackie's nerves. And her own. Let Bonnie flounder and squirm a bit.

Then, it came to her. A nickname for Bonnie. One Jackie might enjoy because her traveling friends' relationship had unraveled.

Jackie answered at the first ring, desperate for good news, but settled quickly into Fran's distraction. Fran sang, to the tune of 'Happy Birthday' to evoke Jackie's spontaneous harmony, *Naughty Bonnie, you're screwed Haughty Bonnie, you're screwed.* Jackie hiccupped several times and joined in.

When Jackie finally wound down, Fran ended the call and raced to the kitchen to search her recipe files, compelled to prepare Johnny Marzetti, Paul's favorite church lady casserole. She needed comfort food—and for the oven to do all the work.

Fran recited the *Serenity Prayer*, learned when she attended an AA meeting with Judge, to get him to go. She needed to override the Haughty, Naughty Bonnie refrain before Paul arrived home. He'd note the tone and might embed in his building plans to ignore her.

As supporters of friends-in-dire-need, she and Paul had

much to discuss, and he frowned on nicknames and snark. It wasn't his idea of wit. He'd prayed for her on the spot when she first reported Bonnie's wealth with the snotty aside, "It must be nice to have millions to bank. How's Christmas going to go this year? Here's our tree. Here's our luxury car. Here's our mountain of cash."

Fran smiled wryly. Paul had moved beyond her quip and plied his superb skills, honed for the Lord. Fran knew a righteous portion of Bonnie's stash was marinating with interest in the Building Fund account. He'd be mighty invested in helping his investor-in-chief. Ha and hell's bells.

Paul smiled beyond ear-to-ear when he sailed in the door, nose lifted like a bloodhound on scent of a quail. "Johnny Marzetti, one of my favorite men!" He removed his coat and sailed his wool cap to the coat rack. He hugged his wife before he removed its matching striped scarf.

"Ew-w. That coat scratches like three-day stubble."

Paul's smile didn't waver and he winked. "Please share how my former school administrator wife knows about an emerging forest on a chin."

"Don't josh with me, Paul. You recall when the menfolk of this town grew mustaches in solidarity with Handy when he endured testicular cancer last November. Did you know the nonprofit movement started in Australia in 2003? *Movember* raised $21 million in 2013."

Paul's face blanched as he recalled. "Yeah, you kissed all the gentlemen in town—and a few strangers, too. Unseemly for a public school administrator. I was embarrassed for you!"

Eager to seat him for supper, Fran ignored his remark. "Aus-tra-li-a." She extended each syllable, trilled the 'r'. "Where your friends are?" Paul continued to look clueless, so Fran doubled back to 'staches.

"Don't you remember the scruffy upper lip *thing* you attempted. I had to apply copious amounts of chapstick nose-to-chin. Julie told me her dad made a minor windfall as the product, coupled with mustache wax, flew off his drugstore shelves. Ralph Watson donated all profits to testicular cancer research.

"But enough about cancer." Fran turned toward the kitchen. "Hang up your scratch-ass scarf, wash your hands, and let's eat. I'm eager to share news of our friends' travel." She turned to look directly at Paul while she sheathed both hands with oven mitts. "You might want to contemplate the best prayer of your life while you're washing your hands."

When Paul returned to the table, twin tapers sided the casserole, flickering to settle the mood. Paul lowered himself into his chair without a word and reached for both of Fran's hands. "You mentioned Australia earlier. Have you gotten over not being invited on the trip, my dear? I've felt badly. I know my responsibilities prevented us from adventuring with your longtime friends."

But not badly for practically making me a widow while engrossed in your building plans? Fran smiled to override her attitude and mime a good wife. There was much to accomplish while she and Paul broke bread. Mindful intervention definitely needed—as well as saving grace.

"Honey, we mutually agreed to remain here, to attend to Brandon's work ethic on his parents' behalf. Tonight I have news to share. You'll need to hear it without food in your mouth. We've already clasped hands, so commence with a comprehensive prayer."

Paul complied, earnest and sincere. Fran relaxed fully for the first time all day. Finally, she felt in the safekeeping of the Lord and His servant, her husband, Pastor Paul.

When Paul lifted his head, he didn't let go of Fran's hand. His face appeared to be set on neutral, ready to go either way. "Please serve my meal before news. I worked through lunch and there weren't even stale donuts left for the ride home. The sweet tomato tang of this fancy spaghetti is tantalizing. I'll listen better when I'm not famished."

Fran scooped a generous portion of the casserole onto Paul's plate. He promptly snuck his forefinger around the perimeter and dumped the dollop on his tongue. He almost knocked the salad bowl from Fran's hands as he fanned his tongue and grabbed his water glass. His sheepish look caused her to double his portion of salad.

Fran hurried through portioning her own plate, because she sensed Paul couldn't be polite for long. He practically hyperventilated with hunger.

"Paul, I have complicated news from Australia. I was going to give you options among the layers. However, in the interest of good digestion, I'll provide the local news first."

Fran commenced. She didn't mince, got straight to the cosmic joke. She provided simple imagery for what didn't require embellishment to discern. After all, they were eating, but if she didn't get to it, she felt she'd explode. God had exacted vengeance for Brandon's unseemly shirk of dairy farm duties from a cow's ass.

"The shit hit the Bran!" Paul laughed so hard, Fran feared he'd choke, but it was all good. It was good to get Paul schmoozed before he began shoveling his food at an amazing pace. Didn't want spaghetti sauce soiling the parsonage walls.

"It's God's vindication for our need to remain here. I can show the event to you because it's on tape." Paul's gasp reminded her she hadn't told him about the Bran Cam. Fran's words came fast, speed-dialed to save her skin. "It was necessary, Paul. I needed an inside witness. The cows weren't going to tell."

Paul backed off, acquiesced to the sense of that, and returned to beam ear-to-ear. Fran hung her head and near-whispered. "This funny episode stays at this table, not to be bandied around town, Agreed? Like we quashed the news of Bonnie's Boffo Lotto win." *Like we're going to keep the next news under wraps. Except for Judge, whose help we need as much as our Father's.*

Paul nodded. He winked. "Show me after dinner." He began to shovel his food at an amazing pace. He ate in silence, alternating between salad and casserole, and then scooped another helping of the casserole onto his plate. "We won't alert his folks, either. Don't want to intrude on their fun."

"Speaking of fun." Fran paused, but not overlong. She'd wordsmithed and rehearsed the one-two-three-four punches, but she needed to get to the point. Bonnie and Jackie's frantic texts and emails reproduced like rabbits every time she left her desk to circle the house to walk off emotion before she replied. She'd finally given up and walked to the kitchen to have another nip. Searched for some candles, lit them, and awaited

Paul. God knew how many messages there were, and she didn't want her phone or computer to implode.

"Apparently the first words out of Carl's mouth were 'We're screwed.'" Then, she dispensed the bad news. Paul's eyes widened, on red alert. Fran shot her arms out to steady his hand and prevent him from falling backward with his chair as each punch landed.

But, Paul didn't fall backward. He pulled his cellphone from his pocket, studied the screen and, looking shot through the heart, pulled back his chair. He donned his coat and ran out the door, leaving the scarf like a comma in her story.

Call that a false start. Her expository skills were going to hell with her retirement. Fran hummed *Amazing Grace* as she finished their meal alone.

Twenty-six | *Bonnie*

WOOSH. ALL THE AIR left Bonnie's lungs. Not until then did she realize she'd been holding her breath. She felt like a day-old birthday balloon, helium spent, tumbled to the floor.

Moments ago the lobby scene with Jackie was bad—well, she admitted it had been a fight. Not like the grasping-and-clawing, utterly gross mudwrestling Bonnie had glimpsed during an online search for one of Pastor Rankin's sermons, but it couldn't have been described as a discussion, either. Jackie had pointed an unChristian finger at her and shouted her inadequacies to the world.

Bonnie felt shaken, verbally mauled, and maybe, just maybe, deservedly so. As Jackie recounted some of her slights, using all of the fingers of each hand twice, Bonnie admitted it sounded like soap opera dialogue. As if having their husbands jailed wasn't enough.

Then, Jackie stormed off, despite their shared quest to feast rather than text Fran again. Anxiety fueled hunger in both, neither wanted to nibble on their manicures while they waited for Judge's plan. Crullers and Maple Creams and Bear Claws while they awaited reply. Oh. My.

Bonnie looked at her watch, but the glimpse didn't help. She didn't know if it was morning or afternoon or yesterday, today, or tomorrow. All she knew was she stood alone in the Intercontinental Hotel in Sydney, Australia, clutching her arms to her midsection to prevent herself from retching out of control.

Bonnie quickly lowered her arms. Though affronted, she still had her dignity. And she wasn't alone. Inside a French handbag she knew to be worth more than Jackie's van, her wallet showcased a rainbow of credit cards as well as lipsticks, lotions, and tissues. While she dabbed moisture from the corners of her eyes, Bonnie collected her thoughts.

When she crumpled the tissue, a polished nail grazed a substantial diamond stud. Bonnie tossed the tissue in her purse, just to touch her wallet, to remind her ego that she had access to cash in uncommon denominations without the LLC account numbers. And Australia had to have ATMs.

Ah, the heady power of plastic, buttressed by beaucoup bucks in beaucoup banks. Who needed a fleshy sidekick when another could be bought?

Bonnie flicked her hair and flaunted her walk, wrapped in new leopard print pants. She popped over to the concierge's desk, got a proper suggestion for nearby eatery as well as an ATM, and swooshed through the hotel's brass-trimmed revolving door, bidding its self-propelled swirl to revive her.

Carl would soon be by her side, when she posted his bail. How high could the amount be? Bonnie assumed he and Steve would help to mend fences with Jackie. Fran and Judge would subvert the lawsuit trifecta, and the foursome would be free to travel on. Bonnie felt self-confident, brimming with resolve.

Her tenuous mood suddenly collapsed. A dozen big-lensed cameras lofted on the shoulders of squint-eyed and swarthy men, bulked further by hooded parkas, swiveled as one to her. Instantly, a dozen microphones, wrapped against potential whistling winds, jabbed at her like drawn swords. She backpedaled to call Jackie, but her former best friend hurried down a wide, chandeliered hall of the hotel, reduced to Lilliputian size, not within earshot.

Bonnie burrowed into her mink coat. She fumbled in her purse in a vain search for some irresistible words or her cell, neither there. A pair of little white gloves, like those she'd worn on Easter Sunday as a child, would be useful as well: to accessorize her salute when she flipped off the gaggle of reporters.

Bravado shriveled. She could only manage a single syllable, a mixture of a plea and a sob, "Carl." She needed more than a handbag plan. She needed her man, but he was *unavoidably detained.* Bonnie deep-breathed and strode back outside.

She scanned the reporters. All male. She searched for one not crowding, shouting, or stabbing a microphone at her chest, one she could maneuver past to escape. She shook her loose-curled hair into a curtain to shield her face from the spit of their rapidfire questions. She glanced over her mink-covered shoulder, hoping for hotel staff reinforcement, someone to call a cab to haul her Cinderella-like to the ball. Better yet, to possess Superman's ability to fly and airlift her to safety, since Carl was jailed and couldn't unfurl his cape.

Carl. Bonnie forced a smile. She'd get to him somehow, but now she craved a human sidekick, preferably someone in law enforcement. She craved a whistle to call the hounds off.

With Carl and Steve incarcerated and the hotel staff apparently on break, Bonnie's boots might be her only tool. They were the costly boots of a prosperous cowgirl, but still... She wished she hadn't been so snarky to Jackie in the past twenty-four hours. Well, for several weeks. A minute ago, her best friend snapped, "Haughty, Naughty Bonnie, your comeuppance is here," and left.

Bonnie Voss Edwards abandoned to the jackals? She'd expected money to bring cache and respect. Was this how that "Born This Way" Lady GaGa star felt?

Well, she hadn't been born this way. Nor did she have staff to inoculate her from this throng of pushy ill-will wishers. She wished she hadn't grabbed her mink to wear to the police station, but good Lord it was winter. She hadn't yet unpacked her several suitcases.

Haughty and naughty. Was that how she came across? She clawed at her loose curls to untangle them. Their shower curtain effect hadn't worked, and she must look a sight. Tomorrow, she'd see herself in every newspaper in town. In the world. Back home, Maybelline would shriek at the mess Bonnie'd made of her handiwork.

Bonnie kept churning thoughts to keep her mouth sealed, a grim smile glued in place as the cameras clicked and tape rolled. She tried not to capsize from fear and grief and the unknown. *Darnit! I brought my merry band with me, but a series of badass acts banished them from sight.*

Everyone at home knew Jackie was the kind of person who helped anyone with the door when hands were full... *But, when my hands are full, Jackie's scarce.*

Wacky Jackie, come back! Bonnie wished she'd recalled that nickname as retort when Jackie had hurled *Haughty, Naughty* at her. *Tit for tat, imagine that!* An old jump rope rhyme.

Crapola, I wish I had not thought of rope. Bad imagery for the situation, for the jailed men and for me.

Bonnie bolstered herself with the fact that Judge Blackstone was involved. That man could be docile as a doe or snarly as a rabid dog, but he was always wise. While Fran was far away, too, she would involve her new husband and Bonnie's former boss, Pastor Rankin, who should entice the Lord to intervene.

Bonnie unobtrusively patted herself on the back, while cameras flashed and video whirled. She prided herself that she'd handled every word and deed available to sinners, er, church members in her capacity as the secretary, with the preacher in the next room and the Lord above to back her. She expected returned favors now. She needed support, dang it.

Bonnie ran her palm down the lengthy front of her mink. Cameras click-click-clicked. The men apparently thought she was imitating Marilyn Monroe, though, in truth, the languid movement was her effort to stop herself from stomping a boot. A tantrum would not do, but a sexy photo would suffice. If the jackasses wanted coverage, she'd give it to them. They needed pictures to match the judgments already made: an American vixen, a millionaire whose husband had blown up the country's chances to win the World Cup by decking the star player, would pay and pay and pay. Mix in an ex-wife's lawsuit, and the money is gone, gone, gone.

All her life Bonnie'd craved attention, to be at the head of the line, the class, the role call. Now she had it, but the pedestal wasn't so cool. Vertigo caused nausea to rise in her throat. Public puking would not do, especially in coveted boots and mink coat. She couldn't clean it up with these lovely nails.

Contrarily, Bonnie began to rock. Back-and-forth. It was difficult to emulate an heiress in these conditions. She could feel her pulse popping her neck. She also had to pee.

Bonnie made a choice. *Judge, I need you more than the Lord right now,* she half-whimpered, half-shouted into her coat sleeve. I can't face the tasks of posting bail, visiting the jail, and finding a suitable barrister on my own. I wish I hadn't become so brash and controlling that Jackie backed out of sight. I can't handle abandonment now.

Just then, Jackie appeared with two tall paper cups of coffee. Bonnie could almost smell the fresh roast from her cornered animal spot, fifty feet away. She watched Jackie maneuver up the middle of the reporters, parting them like the Red Sea. Her elbows hoisted to the men's eye level, her mink buffering her moves.

Bonnie heard, "Back off, Buster!" emerge from Jackie's clenched jaw several times. Her demeanor suggested that Jackie could happily muster blithe atrocities, anything required to free her friend from this hoard.

When Jackie arrived at Bonnie's side, she turned and held one of the cups aloft. "Everyone back off, or I'm going to take the lid off these Flat Whites and fling the contents." Using her lunch lady bellow, Jackie boosted the second cup. Bonnie watched her dare a dozen reporters with her lunch lady stare. One by one, the men became teenaged boys and obeyed.

Bonnie proudly witnessed jackals being intimidated by a Midwestern farmwife. Her sunbeam smile returned when Jackie hurled a final remark over her shoulder as they bolted from the hotel entrance. "Tell that greedy bar manager he can't soak an American citizen without expecting someone to get soaked in return!"

Bonnie laughed so hard, she almost fell and ripped her

mink as the women charged away. It was difficult to run in her stiletto-heeled boots. Mid-run Jackie ripped the lids from the coffee cups and overturned them. When Bonnie saw no liquid splash out, her knees almost buckled. Empty cups! Wacky Jackie was back!

Jackie pulled Bonnie down the street, as both laughed like hyenas. They ducked into the coffee shop, where they requested American coffee, Super Bold. Their order evoked a quizzical look from the barista, similar to the reporters they'd left slack-jawed in their wake. Perhaps it was the mid-morning wearing of minks.

"Bonnie, Fran telephoned Judge. A plan's in action, but guess what day it was in Michigan?" Jackie grinned like the Cheshire Cat in Alice's Wonderland.

Bonnie looked blank.

Jackie plowed on. "Yesterday afternoon."

The barista shouted their names just as Jackie's face broadened into a grin.

Bonnie rose to claim their coffee orders. By the time she returned to the table, she still hadn't fully processed the time zone differences, Jackie filled in, "Like it was the time yesterday when our men went off to celebrate something unknown."

Bonnie just sipped. It was as if all of the bossy and bitchy and haughty and naughty had drained like her cup, and her energy was spiraling to nil. *What good was money if you didn't have your man, your friends?* Bonnie felt like a four-year-old in time out, glum and forsaken, a disconsolate child.

Jackie's voice intruded. "Don't you wish it was still yesterday, and we had a do-over?"

The liquid she swigged was so strong, it made Bonnie's eyes

water. She stalled by clearing her throat, then tipped her cup to show Jackie. Its contents were almost gone. "I need a refill. Be right back."

When she returned to the table, she replied to Jackie. "I can't help thinking that, if we'd gone with the guys, we'd all be in jail." She squirmed and turned to face Jackie. "I regret my arrogant attitude. May we have a friendship do-over?"

Twenty-seven | *Jackie*

JACKIE DEMURRED. SHE FELT depleted, squirmy at the prospect of being used. Her bold, swash-buckling display to free Bonnie from the reporters tapped out her reserves, already frail due to Steve's jailing.

Rather than return Bonnie's imploring gaze, Jackie stared at her Hawaiian pedicure. The right big toe polish was already chipped, a metaphor for the start of their round-the-world trip. Their husbands had devolved into toddlers who abandoned thought to fists. Was Aussie beer that potent?

Her gut constricted. She relied on Steve's level head, his constancy, his desire for all elements to be *copacetic.* Carl had been a wild card since she'd met him, but she'd hoped that Bonnie, a former guardian of the faith, would domesticate him. How could she and Steve have trusted a Californian?

She returned Bonnie's gaze, willing her to be the vibrant one, to lead, to decide. *Just tread a little lighter this time.*

After a few more sips of coffee, Jackie found her voice. "Bonnie, perhaps we need to establish some boundaries, like Pastor Paul coached all of us in the church several years ago. You probably typed all his sermons. Do you recall any of his phrases or the precise steps of his advice?"

Bonnie nodded. Slightly. Coy. Maybe she'd apologized from rote courtesy rather than true remorse. Not ready for real change because she held all the cash. "Well, if you need me to think that much, we ought to eat. Let's return to the hotel and order room service. We've got some powerful strategizing to do. We know Judge will pull through, but doing it will be better than quivering with anxiety." Then, she leaned her head into Jackie's to sotto voice, "I sure wish we had some weed."

Jackie threw back her head to laugh at the memory. Not that long ago, she'd craved the same escape. But her stash was long gone, fueling someone else, likely an airport janitor. Oh, well. She met Bonnie's eyes and tapped her cup to Bonnie's. "We enjoyed Hawaii so much, we didn't need it, but it'd lift our moods now, wouldn't it?"

The euphoria evaporated fast. She gulped more coffee and swirled it with realization. "If we did manage to get it aboard the planes, who knows, though. We might be the ones jailed, and on vastly more damaging and more permanent charges than Carl and Steve."

"My knees suddenly feel weak. Bonnie, please get us a cab."

The cab ride was quiet. Jackie caught the driver peering too frequently at them in the rear view mirror, which partially obscured his badge. She didn't want to meet his eyes, didn't crane her neck to learn his name and say, "Hi." Shove Midwestern manners in a pocket. What if he insisted on asking theirs? Had their photos hit the news already?

So, she signaled Bonnie to zip her lip and Google-searched news entries on her phone. Thank the Lord she'd gotten a Sim card at the airport. Best $20 investment she'd ever made.

As the women hit the pavement, Jackie noticed Bonnie tucked close behind her, allowing her, a middle class farmwife, to run interference and be the primary blocker in their sweep through the hotel lobby, looking neither left nor right. *Lordy, it felt good to use an American football term.*

Yes, Lord. It feels good to lead the charge.

The elevator seemed swifter than previously, yet the hall to their rooms was longer than long, the green carpet extending like a sideline the full length of a football field. Thank goodness Bonnie had sprung for a cab to return strength to their legs.

When Jackie was safely inside her suite, she quickly undressed and showered. She wished she could wash away their troubles as easily as the neck grime and armpit sweat. Rub, scrub, rub. When Jackie exited the shower, her first act was to scoop up her sweat-sopped tee shirt and toss it in the trash. She searched for stains on her mink.

Jackie toweled her hair and put on heather gray sweats, leaving the Michigan State shirts tucked in the suitcase. She didn't bother to unpack. She picked up the bedside phone and dialed Bonnie's room. "Let's dine in. That way, we won't miss Fran's texts or calls. My room or yours?" In the pause before Bonnie invited her over, Jackie bit her lip. She'd just said "my room" rather than "our room." She felt like she'd betrayed her longtime union with Steve.

She'd never been one of the farmwives who thought of their home as *hers* and *the* barn as *his.* Historical accuracy demanded she refer to their homestead as his, because it was his family heritage, but Steve had never overpowered her with this fact. They shared everything, fifty-fifty, "Even Steven" his community-wide nickname.

Jackie winced. Mama Bree had admonished her at their wedding reception. "A good wife stands beside her husband, ready to step in front, to be his flak jacket at any time." Good gravy! Steve was in jail, and all she'd done was blubber to Fran, bicker with Bonnie, and nap. She hadn't felt this guilty since Steve's tour in Vietnam. She prayed the Lord's Prayer and recited every Bible verse she knew as she traipsed to Bonnie's suite.

Bonnie hugged her at the threshold of the suite, in the first privacy the wives-of-suspects had. Jackie hugged her back and walked into the room. Bonnie had already raided the mini bar to prepare two Scotch and water cocktails.

Jackie placed her iPad on the desk and looked quizzically at the drink. "I don't even like Scotch."

"Try this one. It's expensive," Bonnie shoved the glass into Jackie's hand. She lifted her glass to prod Jackie to toast. "I'm rich."

"Uh, is this the way to begin our planning to free our men?" She stood and glared at Bonnie. "I'm rich, too. I'm the daughter of a King, our good Lord, and a much-loved wife and mother." Jackie brought her fists to her hips. She hadn't forgotten intimidation skills honed by her high school cafeteria duties. That boundaries talk hadn't quite taken hold of Bonnie and her frivolous rich bitch attitude.

"Take off your mink, you dolt. You need to be a wife first, a friend next, and leave the heiress in the closet. Put your attitude in a pocket before you put the mink in the garment bag."

Bonnie took a step back and did as she was told.

Jackie beamed. First battle, er, boundary won. She'd been married longer than Bonnie, and her skills were better honed. She took a sip of the Scotch to toast herself.

Jackie pursed her lips and slid her tongue across the roof of her mouth. She scanned every surface in the room, desperately seeking a napkin to further scrub. She would not allow herself to spit the drink into the sink.

Jackie swished to summon more saliva to dilute the drink and then swallowed. "If I'm gonna down Scotch, I need a picnic spread to offset this battery acid. I don't want to scar the tonsils and adenoids I still have."

Bonnie laughed. "You still have those? It was kind of a fad, a means to build an ENT's medical practice, when I was a kid. Snip, snip, easy money." She rifled a large basket resting atop the room's refrigerator. "How about macadamia nuts and cashews and almonds. Cheese spread and cocktail crackers. I'll take the Milky Way and you can have the Snickers, okay?"

Jackie pulled the decorative fabric swath, draped near the foot of the gigantic bed, and spread it on the floor. She settled in with her Scotch and ate all of the Oreos. Life became more sublime all the time. Sorting out life with snacks and Scotch worked. She tried to envision Steve being fed to subrogate guilt.

"Good golly, I like Oreos."

"I know," said Bonnie. "Bogarted the entire package. Didn't even give me eye contact during your personal feast."

"Don't scowl, Bonnie. You'll wrinkle your famous lottery winner, wife-of-an-incarcerate face." Jackie extended her glass. "Speaking of Bogart. May I Bacall you for more Scotch."

"Fine," said Bonnie. "But you have to fetch the

water yourself."

"I will, but for cripe's sake, you didn't even notice my pun." Jackie got the water first, then dribbled some Scotch on top. She swirled and swallowed and then remarked, "I've never tasted water from a gold-handled tap. Didn't notice a difference. Did you?"

Bonnie turned to speak, rich-woman assertive again. "We need to shed our uncultivated skins. Like the *Silly Hats & Caps Society*. In Michigan, it was all good fun, but now we need to co-think with Fran and Judge to bring our men home." When Jackie bored a hole in her, she softened her manner. "Besides, I haven't unpacked."

Home. The word resounded in Jackie's head. Bonnie's suggestion marked their local hotel as *home,* a slip that Jackie'd caught herself in earlier.

If *home was where the heart is,* had Australian adventures replaced their farm routines? Truly, Jackie fretted about Steve but, Holy Mother of God, she hadn't thought of Brandon in nearly two weeks. Further, she'd referenced the mother of Catholicism. *I've only missed two Sunday services and my faith has swerved?*

Worse, I missed two weeks without a thought of my beloved son? Have I gone senile or narcissistic, to abandon my reason to be on Earth? Has some sadist stolen my motherhood gene?

Jackie hoisted herself up from the floor. "Bonnie, would you please excuse me? I'm too woozy to problem-solve just now. I think I'll go have a soak, sober up a little. Can we revisit this topic in an hour? Take good notes when Fran and Judge call. Or voice mail me."

Bonnie didn't answer as Jackie scooped her iPad into the crook of her arm and backed out of the room. She was too busy rummaging for more food.

Several attempts were required to open the suite door. Jackie fumbled, missing Steve more with each fail, willing herself not to cry. She needed to see to gain the safe haven of her room, undress, and climb into the tub. She needed to recline in warm water, to rebirth her motherhood instinct. Weariness and wariness, first with Bonnie and now of herself, were not a good combination.

Besides, in the tub her tears would blend with the bath water.

Blubberingly, Jackie fixated on the world's most famous mother for support. Hail Mary, your support for your son never flagged, did it? The Bible tells us so. I've betrayed my kind. I need your help. Get me back on track. Release Steve from jail and help me figure out why I've relinquished Brandon guardianship.

P.S. Do I want to resume guilt, the core of motherhood? This is a question for you specifically, Mother Mary, and not for God.

She remained in the tub until her fingers and toes puckered. She climbed out, toweled off, and dressed. Two home-based realities came to the fore in the process 1) Her curly locks remained damp from the shower, so she'd now bathed twice in one day, something she hadn't done since she helped with farm chores, and 2) I'm so uncomfortable in my own skin, that my new clothes won't fit. My soul has shrunk.

Likely her Michigan State garb, which jammed her closet at home, wouldn't fit either. Home, where style crapped out to comfort. Aprons hid a myriad of stains. Gloriously grubby ruled, to better display motherhood's toils.

Home, maybe soon, since Australia was proving too hot for them to handle. A return trip portended as many transitions as she'd slid through since departing. Would the travel home be safer?

Home, where she'd mired her self in wifely and motherly roles. Had she abandoned *smotherhood? Did she even want to return?*

Twenty-eight | *Fran*

FRAN LIKED THAT IT was tomorrow in Australia, though she didn't like that it was a weekend in the Midwest. Judge habitually sustained a three-day drunk, from midday Friday through Monday brunch. Husband Paul repeatedly tried to church the sinner, but he left the matter in the Lord's hands via steadfast, earnest prayer.

Paul justified his acceptance of Judge's $50,000-year donation as penance for them both. That Paul could achieve this balance tempered Fran's guilt for not having pulled him into the fold regarding the lawsuits. Sinners needed prayers, and Fran knew her friends hadn't wronged. Lawsuit and incarcerations could be healed by cash. Judge, the keeper of the LLC, was needed. Stat.

Fran made the obligatory round of calls. Judge's office, his legal secretary's home, Judge's home, his housekeeper's cell, Milton's liquor store, and the local hospital. All knew to be discreet. The point was not to harass Judge—nor to merely harness his talents to rescue Jackie and Steve and Bonnie and Carl—but to rescue her brother.

That's what Fran told herself as she turned the lock of his office suite. His office gal was on restroom break, so she could be bold rather than be seated, as directed by the sign. The longer she was retired, the more she relished breaking rules.

Fran sank deeply into the wall-to-wall carpet, ankles quivering with unease. All sound squelched except her galloping heartbeat. She'd never brazenly interloped before.

Oops, there was the time she'd sneaked into the jock locker room to filch a football helmet for a church fundraiser. She'd also broken-and-entered the Principal's office to fast track Jackie's resignation. She giggled as she recalled how she'd twirled and then spat on the new guy's office chair. She'd become a leprechaun in her old age. She'd not only had fun, but she'd come out clean. The ends did justify the means.

Fran traversed the room. Surfaces were stacked with plump manila envelopes, legal-looking briefs, memos on letterhead, and Post-it noted reports. Thick rubber bands of various hues secured the piles. Chaos was thwarted. Fran felt at home, because this had been how her office had looked. Hoarding must be in her and her brother's genes. She slowly turned the knob of his inner sanctum and peeked around the door.

No motion. She noticed Judge's swivel chair wasn't scooted into the kneehole of his expansive desk. She inched forward, glad she'd worn sturdy shoes. She flicked the marble-inlaid globe beside the desk. As it spun, her nerves steadied. Fran took a deep breath and looked down.

Yup, her brother snoozed on the floor, still dressed in his black robe. Ugh, the black robe opened for a peek of red skivvies and a fairly hairy gut. Another secret to add to her pack of facts. Locked in her computer-like brain.

The big gut rhythmically lumbered. Fran decided not to dial 911. She knew the location of the built-in fridge—so she could slide a couple of ice cubes into the red skivvies. She also could perform CPR.

Fran savored the power intellect gave her over others, but she felt saddened by her brother's fall from grace. She'd idolized her older brother, who had beat up recess bullies for her. She figured it was high time to return the favor, so she slid his desktop computer around in order to sit on the other side of Judge's desk.

A single key tap brought his computer to life. Fran began to guess-type potential passwords. She fervently hoped Judge didn't snore. She'd be unable to concentrate, just like when she was street-address-scanning while driving and she couldn't allow the radio to blare.

Tap, tap, tap. Think, think, think. Nothing worked so far. Her brother didn't awaken to assist. A good thing. She wouldn't need to explain herself, nor would he. She paced the room, rifled his bookshelves, and opened file drawers. Hell's bells, those were locked.

Ah, but the desk drawers weren't. Fran knew his password instantly when she spied the near-empty bottle of Bombay Sapphire nestled between the Macallan and Maker's Mark. Sapphire had been the name of her horse. The one he'd helped her to groom and then taught to jump, to earn ribbons the color of the horse's name. This bond allowed them hours of retreat from their mother's and father's wars.

The computer sprang to life, churning out websites, databases, and all things lawyerly in Australia. Google was great, but some of the resources led her down blind alleys. Aussie Bail Bonds, for example, resulted in a male escort site of dubious repute.

A half-hour passed, forty minutes, and more. Judge remained inert, tacit permission to continue her search. Fran scanned names and copy-pasted promisingly credentialed firms into a file and emailed it to herself. She'd compose an email to send to Jackie later, at home. She'd do better when relaxed and away from the aroma of booze. The situation warranted a couple of sips, but she had a public reputation to maintain. While the small town community accepted her brother's *eccentricities,* Fran's pride precluded a fall from grace.

Then, she remembered her brother passed out on the floor. Perhaps she should check him into rehab. She couldn't lift him, so 911 would be the only way. She lifted the receiver, listened to the dial tone, and then paused to pray. *Please, Lord, give me Your best solution.*

The answer came pronto. Judge sat up, shuffled his robe, and then shambled to his chair. "Lord bless us, you're all right! Want some aspirin, you old buzzard?" Fran paused. Her feelings fluctuated between exasperation and relief.

She knew her brother would refuse a hug.

He might also feel somewhat embarrassed. Even angry that she'd trespassed, though he didn't know how far. To cover her anxiety, Fran filled the air with words.

"Want to join me for dinner or should I set up a church lady brigade to deliver meals to your home?"

Judge threw back his head and laughed his characteristic belly laugh. "No, I'll pass again, Sis. You know I think the ladies will poison me as much as your husband's words of righteous religion."

Fran stood, slowly turned the computer monitor around, and gave him a peck on the cheek. Then she lifted her head as if she wore one of her hats, turned and glided out of the room, good deeds done. Mum's the word to allow her brother to sober by himself.

Fran silently thanked the Lord for not offering His answer until she'd completed her Google search. She thanked him for pulling her brother midway through the weekend and prayed for hours of sobriety.

She also thanked her brother for not saying, "Don't let the door hit you in the ass." That phrase would have absolutely broken the spell.

Fran slowly drove home, contemplating all things. She admired her frosty, in-control demeanor, but she didn't admire the distance that judgment required. How was she able to accept her brother's behavior and not that of her friends? Was it because he was her personal hero or because he was blood? Was it because he'd fallen so low so many times that she'd been forced to accept him or go crazy? Did she dare take this up with her pastor husband, if and when he became available to anything other than his grandiose plans?

Many people sinned, some as outlandishly named as their pranks, some blessed. Wackie Jackie, Even Steven, Haughty Bonnie, Cut-up Carl. Fran felt disinclined to muster nicknames for her husband and brother. Let them handle their own collision course with conscience; she was done with names for the day.

Besides, Fran knew she should include her *hell's bells* habit in the tribe. She had to get a handle on that, rein it in, access her robust vocabulary. Substitute an Italian term.

When she arrived home, Fran went directly to her computer, not even bothering to call out for Paul. She accessed her email, printed the list, and admired the heft. She gave herself a pat on the back for her efforts. She contemplated a few moments. The email letter to Jackie practically composed itself.

Dear Jackie, I hope you are well. Bonnie, too. Hope she hasn't gone silly rather than secretary on you. The latter skill set would be more helpful. The former would undermine.

I trust Carl and Steve are in comfortable cells, not in the common drunk tank. Who knows what unhealthy infestations lurk on the floors?

I also hope they are behaving themselves. I've done some research and discovered that the courts in Australia offer a legal aid 'duty solicitor', who can give advice and may be able to apply for bail on the guys' behalf.

But, of course, with Bonnie's millions, you can afford top-rated counsel. I've determined that a solicitor, not a barrister, is your first step through the legal system. A highly-rated firm, Watson & Watson, is near your hotel on George St.

The news of their arrest has not hit the local paper, like the Hawaiian dance did, but the Detroit Press picked up an AP article about it as well as the hotelier's furor and intention to sue, so the news of Bonnie's Boffo Lotto win may seep into the local gossip mill.

I have not yet told Pastor, but, with your permission, I will. Engaging the congregation in prayer will be particularly prudent if the gossip starts to fly. Paul can even enlist the Catholics across the street. For heaven's sakes, with Bonnie's millions, the priest may be able to beseech the Pope.

Steadfastly your friend, Fran

Fran read and re-read the email before she hit send. She knew a call would be more expedient, but Paul would kill her over the amount of the phone bill. Hell, she'd kill herself.

Speaking of Paul. Could she squirm into his dinner meeting with the Widow at the country club? Could she wrest him away from the church expansion plans, now including the neon sign on the Interstate and the ginormous education building bearing the Rankin name? At least he'd been able to dissuade the Widow from placing Braghorn in huge letters on the façade.

Without his friend, Deacon Steve's help. Now, to get that noble man and Cut-up Carl out of the drunk tank. Curtail the lawsuits and mend fences between her gal pals.

Her phone rang before her computer shut down. She watched screen icons vanish, replaced by black as she reached for the receiver.

"Hi, honey." Paul's voice sounded so exuberant, he was almost shouting. Fran instantly pulled the receiver away from her ear. When she turned toward the window, she watched several wilted magnolia blossoms sail to the ground. Hell's bells. Fall loomed. Fran shoved the prospect from her mind. Her friends' troubles must be tended to first.

"Something came up in the Widow's schedule, and she'll be unable to dine. Rather than cancel the reservation, she suggested I invite my wife. Can you freshen up and drive to meet me at the club by 5:00?"

"I was born ready for someone else to cook." Fran laughed. "I just have a bit of work to do on my memoir, dear. I've been multi-tasking all day. You'll be so proud when I share."

"Of course, I will, dear. Thanks again for helping me find Marge. She whips up such a storm, I can multi-task, too. I can waste time, be unproductive, and procrastinate all at the same time."

Fran laughed again. She knew her husband to be single-minded—and what he meant. He allowed Marge the Barge to handle all everyday tactics while he devoted himself fully to the church expansion plans. If he knew what went on behind his back, he might faint—or fire Marge. Oh well, Fran was out of that mess—and fully engrossed in another.

Fran turned on the computer, glanced at its clock, and set the volume high. She prayed for the bell that signaled an emailed reply, permission from Jackie to share the sad, bad news. She prayed she'd hear the 'bing' throughout the house, because she needed to hustle-bustle to get ready for the club. Hey, how could Paul sneak away early from the church? And, why?

Fran buried her questions. She bounded upstairs to bathe in bubbles, hoping each would capsulize polite, yet to-the-point phrases to set the proper praying machinations in motion. And pop all of the troubles away. God bless it.

After she toweled dry, Fran selected Chanel #5 scent to dab behind her knees. She rifled her clothing, hung in colored coded sections, all hangers turned the proper direction. She settled on a V-neck shirt with bell sleeves in a deep ruby color, slim black skirt, and pumps. Her pearl necklace, with matching button earrings, rooted for her success. As Fran arranged her hair, she wondered, yet again, if Paul would notice her new blonde highlights.

As Fran walked resolutely downstairs, she clutched her

black purse handle like a lifeline. This would be as vital a conversation as any in which she'd been involved, including the sexual harassment case of the assistant football coach and the cheerleader who accused him.

Fran wished for the hundredth time that Jackie's easy warmth was contagious, able to beam across the Pacific Ocean and thousands of miles of U.S. soil.

Twenty-nine | Bonnie

BEWILDERMENT OVERPOWERED BONNIE. SHE needed to settle, to unpack. But she couldn't consider any action or task without Carl. Waiting for the Michigan input was awful. Shoulders slumped, she sank her bedraggled butt onto the bed, rocking and clutching her sides to stop dry heaves. She flopped back and attempted angels-in-the-snow atop the bedspread, but the movement fell short of a massage.

Carl was absolutely a Larrikin, or a Lar, which seemed to be the Aussie term for leprechaun. *I liked him better when he was a lech.* That thought kinked Bonnie's body with electricity. Carl gave sensuous massages.

As abruptly as the sexual response surged, Bonnie's body dropped it and she returned to sulk mode. No one in her experience had been in a drunk tank. No man, woman, or teen. That circumstance wasn't part of a small town pastor's purview, let alone that of a long-single church secretary. The only fights she was aware of were marital, limited to broken china and drawn forks. Not brawl-scale rowdy bouts with broken limbs or damaged pride. Australia had rendered different escapades than she could have imagined. Even at his wildest, Bonnie hadn't figured fisticuffs as part of Carl's repertoire.

Any more than my win of millions would become mine. Reportedly behind every lottery winner, the payout board rolled collective eyes: *Another one's going to tailspin.* She longed to prove the mystique wrong. But how with so many cash demands hanging over her head?

Wish Jackie would hurry with her sobering up. I need her to march to the ATM with me. I've forgotten my PIN. Two heads were better than one, Bonnie felt certain she would experience recall. In the interim, better to ponder something else.

Bonnie didn't feel certain Carl and Steve would be released, nor did she know if her companions would resume exploration of the city, the country, the world. She didn't even know if the men would be acquitted of the charges, whatever the charges, or if any funds would be left if an outlandish lawsuit was filed. In addition to the other lawsuit. Much was in Judge's competent hands.

Bonnie stared out the picture window, saddened by an unfamiliar vista.

Remote! The word exploded in her mind. Bonnie clicked on the TV, flipping past soap operas to news. Blah-blah-blah-blah-blah, blessedly inane for a while. She hoped the news wasn't as inaccurate as the soaps' dramas. More comprehensible, too. These people slurred their words in a strange way, and the product commercials were quaint. Cookies called Tim Tams and biscuits called Anzacs?

She turned up the volume and leaned in to squint. That might improve discernment. Crapola! Blah-blah-Carl-blah-Bonnie-Boffo-blah-blah-Steve.

There was much speculation about her and about Steve and Carl. She yelled "Jackie's here, too!" but quickly clamped a hand over her mouth. Suddenly Bonnie felt highly responsible for fate. She took out her frustration on the remote. Bam! Bang! Broken!

Not that long ago she'd felt like the sky was the limit, practically levitating with glee when she'd received the initial news in a truck cab. All of life lighter than air for a near-month. But the euphoria of the Boffo Lotto winnings had subsided. Now she knew there was a bottom to hell.

Was this a rational outcome for a woman who only wanted to live a little and do good after years spent in a secretary's less-than-padded chair? The chair singularly unequal to the pastor's, which had a high back and padded arms. Single, in a small town with few eligible men. She'd finally met her mate, but dang. I don't *deserve* this bad karma. I was a God-and-pastor obeying secretary for umpteen jillion years.

Bonnie whimpered and sniffled for several minutes. Then she washed her hair and blew it dry, an abbreviated process now that the dang extensions were gone. This activity cleared her sinuses, always bloated after a cry, but it didn't clear her mind.

She recalled Carl's blithe "ransom" comment. Also his lost wallet. He couldn't bail himself out. It was all on her.

Feeling overwhelmed, Bonnie almost succumbed to full wail. She wanted to run away and join the Barnum & Bailey Circus she recalled from her youth, rather than remain in this one. *Not my circus here, but definitely my monkeys.*

Bonnie shook her shoulders, waggled her head, and then swept up her locks in a Scrunchie, trying to get a hold. If she felt traumatized, Carl and Steve might be, too, although she doubted they'd be contrite. Probably, when Steve and Carl were released, they'd want to cocoon. Michigan was the best place on earth to achieve that state. They'd revel in the rumpled ease of multi-washed jeans and sweatshirts, ball-capped and self-aware, the steady rhythm of routine. They'd likely kiss the cows and the grass, maybe even the barns, upon their return. Maybe even the hapless dog, who seemed incapable of earning a name.

Bonnie might want to kiss the ass of a cow, too. She certainly was willing to kiss anyone's, including a solicitor, barrister, and the police, if the charges and lawsuits were dropped. She didn't know anything besides the fact that she needed to sleep. Fortunately, she'd tucked her negligee on top of one her Disney suitcases. Unfortunately, her lover wasn't present.

Yesterday she'd thought Australia and the world, emboldened with bottomless bucks, would be the perfect place to reinvent herself. Today Bonnie felt trampled.

She sprinted to unleash her mink from the pile in the tub and toss it over her shoulders. Ooh, better.

Tomorrow, or sooner, she and Jackie would empty their purses to hold the ATM cash, the PIN perfectly recalled with their mind meld. Together, they'd spring their men from the Surry Hills Police Station. Bonnie schemed that she and Carl would go hand-in-hand to follow-up on Judge's suggestion to hire the Watson & Watson solicitor, allowing Jackie and Steve a free day.

Gosh, she missed Carl, his love and ability to reassure her. His agency to keep her worst impulses contained. It took too much energy to achieve without him.

Especially when screwing up was her best achievement, as it now seemed to be Carl's. Maybe they were well matched in all departments. Crapola. Agency, which Carl claimed being a California gave him, was lame. Time to change the topic.

Bonnie wanted to weep. She also needed to shield herself

from her image in the suite's multiple mirrors. Her saucer-sized Jackie O sunglasses, a stupendously overpriced purchase while in Vegas, still sat parked in their case. Winter hadn't warranted their wearing, but the TV coverage did. Better keep the glasses close.

Bonnie opened her over-sized purse and rummaged around for the glasses' case. Funny, the purse interior felt roomier than usual. She dumped everything out on the bedspread and poked around. Lots of lipsticks, lotions, and blush. A partial tissue pack and a special hairbrush. Yeah! Bonnie seized the glitzy oversized sunglasses case.

But no wallet. Crapola! She opened her purse and rifled again, her fingers scrounging its inner nooks. She now regretted her refusal to purchase dime store readers—*add it to the list!*

Bonnie scratched her scalp, but only dandruff fluttered into the air. When and how—and why oh why—did that happen? She quickly dug in her pocket.

Yes, her Capitol One was there. Better not cancel the card despite Carl's swimming with the fishes in the Bay. Bonnie snatched up her glasses and donned them, the better to hide from all the problems.

The lawsuit publicity train was coming. Bonnie felt creeped out. Everyone in Australia probably knew her face. The populace of the world, including their hometown, aware of her fortune and misfortunes. Threatened by forces in California, too. There would be no going back.

Besides, it was spare-no-costs to get her one-week husband out of jail. Fond memory now eclipsed methodical thoughts, single-minding her purpose. She had to spring the only man who could do anything about her desires and cure her despair.

So be it if the solicitor was avaricious.

Bonnie felt drowsy and Jackie was taking overlong. Her last waking thought was they should make an appointment with the Lord before any others. On their knees.

When Bonnie awakened, she looked at the clock. She'd slept two hours. She felt drugged. She also felt lonesome.

Within two minutes, Bonnie'd donned a velvety sweat suit, raided the fridge for the final champagne, and snuggled her personal pillow under her arm. She used the bottle to rap Jackie's door.

Jackie's ringlet-prone hair appeared more vigorously coiled than ever, but Bonnie refrained from fluffing it. She also refrained from unkind comments about the dang fan wear. She'd promised to maintain Jackie's boundaries forever more.

She set the champagne on the desk and unleashed its cork. As she watched it bounce off the vast harbor view of the floor-to-ceiling window, Bonnie thought what a backwards-and-forwards metaphor a sailing cork could be. But, at least the window hadn't cracked. The sky was still the limit, and she was behind a glass shield. Time to evoke God's.

"Jackie, doesn't this panorama evoke prayer? Certainly our painful situation does. I haven't given this matter to the Lord yet, have you?" One look at Jackie's face, blanched with embarrassment, sufficed. "On your knees, friend. Pretend Pastor Paul is in the room." Jackie obeyed before either of them realized Bonnie had already transgressed their agreement to not order Jackie about. Each bowed their heads. Silent prayers said, Bonnie lifted her head as Jackie lifted hers. "Let's call that

Watson & Watson." The words leapt from her mouth.

"It's the weekend. We shouldn't bother them," Jackie protested before she accepted the overflowing flute.

"Bail is what solicitors live for, Jackie." Bonnie took a swig. "Besides, with a name like Watson & Watson, there are at least two of them, and one should be on duty. If you won't call them, I'll get the concierge to do it."

Bonnie didn't want to take charge. She just wanted to swill champagne. But one look at Jackie suggested that she was as tired as Bonnie was not. Besides, Bonnie was a veteran of placing calls hither, thither, and yon on the Pastor's behalf. Now she had *staff.*

Bonnie paced the room while the concierge contacted the firm. She'd requested that an attorney from Watson & Watson call within the hour. She opened the refrigerator to the bottle of champagne chilled inside and refilled their glasses. She handed the Room Service menu to Jackie. "Select three things that we'd both like and three things you've never heard of before."

Jackie blinked, but she did it. They were not going to war hungry. They drank and drank and nibbled, gobbled, and snacked. Neither worried about weight watching, nor did they worry about DUI. They weren't driving anything except release of their men from jail.

Bonnie fondled her Capitol One Card, nestled deep in her jeans pocket. It was her rosary, her amulet, her power. Funded to the tune of $500,000 float, this was her sole plan. Unless the champagne—or God's whispered answer—rebooted remembrance of her ATM PIN.

She'd shake her man loose, no matter what the feat required. All of Bonnie's freshly-washed tresses slipped from her Scrunchy. Dang, she couldn't even manage her own hair.

Thirty | *Jackie*

BONNIE HAD JUST CALLED for prayer, but Jackie was too jumpy to focus on the Lord. She felt like a voyeur in life, like a shadow self without her better half in the room. What could Steve be thinking now? Surely, he couldn't cause more ruckus beyond what the "roots" discovery had unearthed. Surely he would trust his wife to rescue him in due course. Surely, he'd be eating well in an Australian jail, as well as she and Bonnie sipped room service champagne.

Bonnie's head had popped up from prayer with the best idea of the day. Watson & Watson could come to their room and release their men on bail. That way, she wouldn't have to face the publicity hounds.

While they awaited the arrival, both agreed to ditch the champagne. Jackie slyly stepped into the suite's bathroom, nearly as large as her kitchen at home, and fumbled around in her luggage to find the Tylenol. She swallowed a couple, glanced at her reflection in the mirror, and then grabbed her brush. She raked it through her hair, scratching her scalp as if exacting penance for allowing Steve to languish in jail. Now she prayed: *Lord, help Steve forgive me for this lapse. Mama Bree, forgive me for breaking my promise to stand by my man.*

A knock sounded on the suite door. Man, that was prompt. Watson arrived before the Tylenol kicked in.

Jackie went to the peephole. A tuxedoed gentleman stood a

full stride back from the door, holding a bulky leather briefcase with brass-tipped edges. It appeared to weigh a ton. Holy crap! Was it a means of ramming his way into the room?

After she surveyed the room and her and Bonnie's attire, Jackie opened the door. She was about to welcome the gentleman when Bonnie darted in front of her and stuck out her hand. "Mr. Watson, I presume."

Behind her, Jackie rolled her eyes. *Really?* Then she blinked. Watson was Brandon's fiancée's last name, she of Watson's Drug Store in their hometown. A God-incidence, as Pastor Rankin often remarked.

The man lizard-eyed the ladies. His sliver of red licorice mustache didn't move, though his orangutan red hair was fully askew. An odd juxtaposition, as if he was half-liberal, half-conservative, half-unhinged, with the other half enslaved by the law. His arms didn't gesture in greeting any more than his lips. He merely glided into the room, and handed each woman a thatched linen card the size of their palms and embossed with the solicitor firm's name, number, and address.

Jackie couldn't shake the image of gekkoes she'd seen in the Southwestern U.S. Did his greased hair, slick from his forehead to the nape, or Botox keep his eyelids in place? Jackie had seen people in Vegas whose foreheads didn't crease when they suffered a huge loss. She and Bonnie had whispered about Botox' known effects, info gleaned from the pages of *People* magazine in Maybelline's shop. Perhaps this was how Australian solicitors appealed to an international clientele.

Jackie bit her tongue. Dear God, this man was here to help them. It wasn't the time or the place to deploy snarky observations, like the women she knew back home, but her first impressions had most always been right...

"Charmed to meet you, madam and madam. Welcome to our country. How may I assist you?"

"Please sit, Mr. Watson," Bonnie said. "Anywhere." She wheeled the ruby red leather chair from under the desk and ensconced.

Jackie's eyes surveyed the suite. There were only three seating selections and one of them was the room's king-sized bed, covered in shimmery taupe silk damask. Quilted and heavy, the bedspread weighed a ton. Good grief, a firm, double-armed tug was required to scoot it to the end of the bed last night.

Hours ago, she'd climbed into that bed—and experienced insomnia on Egyptian cotton sheets. 700 count. She knew because she had read the label. Silkier than any fabric she'd ever sewn in 4-H. Pillow cases ironed by a laundry service and smoothed by a maid's hand. She wondered if the maid changed the bed linens since Steve hadn't slept on the other side? Sigh.

Jackie further scrutinized the room to thwart tears. There, shadowed by the matching drapes, was an ottoman of the same muted hue as the spread. She couldn't risk throwing her back out to lug it over to be conversational. Its matching club chair reminded of her chair nestled in her family room, beside the empty space where Steve's matching chair formerly presided. Chagrin and sigh again.

Jackie hoped she hadn't whimpered aloud. Steve, in whose arms she'd not nestled last night. Ah, to be safe, snuggling under the granny square afghan her mother had made for Brandon. A memory revived her spirits: how Steve would aim a fart and cover her head with the afghan when she'd fallen asleep in her chair while he completed the night milking chores. Something to sweeten your dreams, he'd explained.

Something to revel in if she spent another night without Steve: clean air. No rush for the air freshener. A suite to self. Time, precious time, to do anything I please. Silence with no moos in the background, no barks. God forgive my sliver of selfishness—and help Steve forgive me, too.

Jackie sidled over to the bed. She almost collapsed, not from exhaustion or concern, but from renewed grief. Over Sparty who used to cavort in the bedcovers when she tried to refresh the sheets. Every Monday, a ritual she missed. She scurried back to the ottoman and sank to its depth.

Sparty, the late favorite pet, not replaced in their hearts by the new Dalmation. Not because the dog had allowed himself to be skunked, almost derailing their trip and resulting in the trashing of Steve's beloved chair, but because the dog was dumb. *Note to self, don't be dumb as the dog. You know this is displaced grief. Keep your focus on Steve.*

Mr. Watson didn't sit. Didn't blink. Didn't react to her sad musings, likely written in all caps on her face. Relief. Despite the Australian Watson's oddly opposite hair and mustache, Jackie felt like she did in the presence of the mid-Michigan Mr. Watson, who also stood. Behind his pharmacy counter. Both men were professionals. Their posture fostered trust. Jackie had faith that all would be copacetic soon. She could almost feel Steve's hug.

Solicitor Watson set his bag down near the desk and sat on its glass-topped edge, closer to Bonnie. It was if he knew the millionaire by sight, though Jackie had to admit her lower status might be signaled by the height of her seat.

Jackie frowned because the solicitor didn't click open the hefty briefcase. She noted Bonnie's nod when Mr. Watson pulled out his phone.

"Ah-h, you are using the 'Notes' function," she said. "What a champion idea!"

Champion? Who was Bonnie channeling, the Queen of England?

"My husband, Mr. Carl Edwards, of Michigan—"

Jackie turned away. Bonnie made it sound as if Carl owned the entire state.

"And, my friend, Jackie Breeden, by the way, and I'm Mrs. Carl Edwards." There was an unspoken undertone of 'You may kiss my ring.' Holy crap!

The man refrained from shaking their extended hands. He also refrained from comment on Bonnie's manner. One hand remained in his tuxedo pants pocket and his other cupped the cell. He'd apparently be taking notes with his thumb on the keyboard, as dexterous-fingered as his facial muscles were restrained.

"Our husbands were wrongfully incarcerated in the Surry Hills Police Station within the last twenty-some hours. My friend's husband, Steve, has a serious medical condition and may require hospitalization if he isn't released forthwith."

Jackie's brow creased as much as the solicitor's didn't. Where in the heck did that lie come from? From the same source as the pomposity? Watson's thumb flew for thirty seconds. He requested their cell numbers, input them, and re-pocketed the phone.

Jackie raised her hand. "Uh, Mr. Watson." She waggled her arm like an urgent kindergartener who'd burst if she wasn't called on. When the solicitor swiveled to observe her in her corner, she asked the terms of the arrest and potential length of jail time.

"Well, I can tell you, Madam, it was more than two Yanks having a bluey with rugby blokes. It's serious, so we are glad that you called." Now Watson mustered the crack of a smile under his red licorice 'stashe. He edged off the desk, clicked open his bag, and retrieved a single sheet of crisp paper. Jackie longed desperately to flick it out of his hand, to hear the snap of the fine linen, to set a match to the truth.

"It appears that the charges levied are more serious than merely 'drunk in a public place'. I've delineated in this document, but have elected not to read the full text aloud. You'd be gob-smacked and likely faint."

Jackie did feel faint, but she bridled at hearing it from a man she'd never before met. Watson didn't know her. Her reception of him and the situation fluctuated between assurance and extreme dislike.

But Bonnie had summoned him and his call was on her dime, so Jackie sealed her tongue in the roof of her mouth and imagined peanut butter and jam. Jackie winced. Bad imagery. *Make that my homemade jam, not the one Steve and Carl are in.*

Solicitor Watson flicked a piece of invisible lint from a shoulder, as if to signal that he was shouldering the problem and it was a cinch. Jackie's puns were helping her accept the situation and she silently applauded her aplomb. "The officials have moved beyond 'drunk and disorderly', which is quite usual in the Kings Cross bar area."

Watson paused to place one hand on a hip. "I assume you're aware of this locale."

Bonnie didn't reply, so Jackie didn't either. They felt the heat of the other's embarrassment fill the room. They had no idea. They hadn't even known their men had gone bar-hopping.

"I can show you a map if you'd like." Bonnie waved him off, but he added a killer blow. Of course. "Kings Cross is populated by rowdy rugby players and fans who are more than a cheeky lot." Now the man paused, flicked the other shoulder's invisible lint, and intoned, "I'm afraid prostitutes are drawn to the area."

That. Did. It. What was he insinuating about *Deacon* Steve? Jackie glared at Bonnie, who decidedly avoided eye contact. Everyone at home knew Carl to be the cheeky character. He'd obviously drawn Steve into this. Holy crap!

As if to affirm he recognized that fact as well, Watson placed the letterhead into Bonnie's hand. While Bonnie's face remained impassive, she flicked one paper corner with a luridly polished fingernail. Tick-tick-tick.

"As I stated previously, it wasn't deemed a simple incident of blokes having a bluey. Your husbands have been branded as troublemakers, who can and will be banned from the Woolloomooloo Ovolo, if the manager has his way. And there may be an impending civil lawsuit."

The solicitor peered over the paper from which he'd been reading and swung his eyes back and forth between the two women. Tick-tock-tick. If Bonnie didn't say a word, Jackie wouldn't either. She couldn't, because she was holding her breath. Listening to Watson's recitation left her fully depressed.

"I'm afraid your lads didn't merely get on-the-spot fines and then carted off to a four-hour pokey. I've taken the liberty of securing a bail bond for your husbands, Mrs. Breeden and

Edwards. We have an in-house bondsman, as this is a frequent reason for our services. Australians can be a bit foolhardy when it comes to drink and sports."

"So, it's free," squeaked Jackie, happy to get a word in edgewise.

The lizard-eyed head swiveled four degrees. "Bail has been set at $10,000 for each man, so release is gained by ten percent, which our firm fronted as a courtesy. A retainer for future court appearances and lawsuit representation is $500,000 US."

Jackie looked at Bonnie and Bonnie returned her gaze, mirroring each other's blanche. Jackie led their mutual exhale, choreographed as if in the church choir back home. Bonnie was the best sidekick a Midwestern tourist could have. Never mind her manners, she had access to the necessary cash.

Bonnie shook her head, imperceptible to some, but a signal to a friend's keen eye. "May I charge to my room?

"I'm afraid not, madam. That would be most irregular."

Bonnie's hand reached into her leisure suit pocket. Jackie watched in wonder. What magic would Bonnie pull out? Ah, her Capitol One card. "Kindly put the full amount on this."

Solicitor Watson stooped to unlatch his case. He retrieved a small plastic Square and attached it to an electronic tablet. He slid Bonnie's card through a slot, invisible to Jackie's eye.

Then, Watson blinked. Twice. He handed the card back and then moved a step forward to position the tablet for Bonnie's signature.

"Aren't there documents to sign? I'd like a receipt." Bonnie blustered.

Jackie, the hopeful voyeur, remained mum.

Mr. Watson retrieved a small printer from the briefcase and

clicked a few times. While the tiny implement spit out a document, he retrieved another tablet from the briefcase. He tap-tapped and handed it to Bonnie. "Sign here."

After Bonnie completed her assignment, he handed the tablet to Jackie with the same terse direction. His well-tailored tux creased no more with these movements than had his face throughout his time in the room. Jackie complied, too stupefied to speak.

A moment after the signatures, the tiny printer spat out a single double-signed document. Jackie wanted desperately to snatch off his red licorice 'stashe. She dared not look at Bonnie, because she knew her friend wished the same.

"Thank you. Your husbands will be released within the hour. Should I retain a limousine for you?"

Thirty-one | *Fran*

FRAN RELISHED HER RED Mini Cooper's scoot, another personal possession she'd declined to abandon when she married Paul last spring. Her spirits and resolve bolstered with each m.p.h. increase the vehicle achieved. She loved having a clock-like needle as well as a numerical display to track acceleration. Zippety-do-dah was the car's name.

She also loved that the smaller wheel-based vehicle cornered well at high speed. She loved that it easily squeezed into miniscule parking spaces. The country club self-park lot was full, and she'd be damned if she would valet. Too often the young lopers were young men she'd too-recently disciplined at the high school, individuals she feared might opportunistically key the exterior, or worse, fowl the interior.

Fran quickly checked the clock and did some mental math. While it was supper time in Michigan, it was already tomorrow in Australia. The men's release from jail had assuredly been secured and her friends were...let's see...eating breakfast at some delicious Aussie restaurant, perhaps one where shrimp was roasted on a barbie. Fran winked at her reflection as she checked her makeup and hair in both the rear and side view mirrors and the collected her purse. Ready. Set. Emerge. Do-dah.

Mildly hobbled by her skirt, Fran planted both feet and cantilevered from the car. Pausing to smooth her skirt and right her skewed pearls, she strode into the grand lobby and up to the maître d's stand. Thankfully the gentleman was older and not one of her former students.

She smiled broadly, lips cupped over her teeth, in case she'd landed a smudge of lipstick on her slightly-snaggled front tooth. She'd always counted on Jackie to tissue her teeth when the duo sang in the choir. It was in these simple instances that Fran felt most bereft. Email correspondence didn't suffice despite the recent uplifting news. It was as if her friends' wanderlust unraveled the fabric of Fran's daily life.

"I'm here—"

"Let me lead you to your husband's table." When Fran placed her arm within the crook of the maître d's elbow, she recognized cashmere. His dark, casual jacket wasn't casual at all.

No one lifted his head as he squired her across the room. Again, it seemed like her lease had expired when she resigned from the schools. Marriage to the prized local pastor had not renewed it. She felt invisible.

Until Paul spied her and flashed his smile. Fran felt her face color as he popped from his chair and sailed across the room to remove her from the man's escort. She nearly puddled when he planted a swarthy kiss on her cheek, then her mouth, and hugged her full on. She hoped his desire didn't diminish with the news she'd been entrusted to share.

Perhaps his tongue kiss was intended to clear lipstick from her tooth. Yum.

Fran plopped weak-kneed into the plumply upholstered chair, and she relished the scoot forward as Paul pushed her closer to the table. Seldom did she receive a free ride.

Not until she was seated did Fran notice the champagne

nestled in a silver tureen. No, that wasn't the correct term. She shook her head, certain now about the loss of her vocabulary prowess.

Well, it didn't matter in the moment. Carl Edwards was the only man who'd ever ordered champagne in her presence, and he was in jail. Coincidence, this could not be. What a set up! Fran convinced herself that this was her entry to the jail dilemma, to hark back to that peak moment of friendship for life. Ready, begin.

Fran beamed as she lifted. "I'm proud of you, dear. I've never seen you pour champagne before. You didn't spill a drop, despite the rush of bubbles. How might you know how to do that?"

Paul flushed his confession.

Hell's bells! What a scoundrel! Paul's expansion planning meetings with the Widow had been fueled by champagne. Fran fumed as she recalled that this last-minute meal had been at the woman's behest. She almost kicked Paul under the table, but her mission to be pleasant stopped her foot. She worked to not squint-eye her beloved.

Fran understood her husband's schmoozer tendencies, the Widow long his prime mark. She felt her eyes narrow, despite her wish, and lifted the flute high to cover. *No sense getting your panties in a bunch, not with a flute of champagne at your lips.*

She gulped, and then cleared her throat. "Paul, you and I have spoken many times about a fact of life that perpetually puzzles us both." She paused to look in his eyes, willed him to place his glass on the table, and ask her, "What?" Paul complied. She metaphorically patted herself on the back. She just might excel at this wife stuff.

Fran mirrored his move, as she had during many a difficult parent conference. The body language caused people to align involuntarily, rapport established without a word.

She reached her hands across the table, clenched his more fervently than intended, and began. "Why are some people devoted to chaos and determined to live in turmoil?"

Paul eased his hands out of her over-zealous grip and shook them a few moments before he re-clasped them in his pastoral listening posture. "Who now?"

"Let's finish our champagne—" *Too soon, too soon.* She didn't want to ruin her future inexpensive, expensive meal. She planned to order escargot, prime rib, filet mignon, oysters. Surf and turf, lobster, whatever was the highest price main course, since all would be on the Widow's tab.

That woman owed her big time. Fran had practically felt like a widow herself in the past month, with Paul's endless absence due to regular church business and his extensive consults. The imperious witch was no longer the primary source of funds, though Paul couldn't tell. Both of them were sworn to secrecy on Bonnie's behalf.

"You know I don't like suspense. Is there more to that Bran Cam business? You know I can't approve its insertion. It's an invasion of privacy that I can't condone."

Fran again mirrored Paul's lean-in, the move he made for emphasis. She parried his glare with a broad smile. "Let me convince you of its worth, by the change it has wrought in young Brandon's behavior. You'll be pleased to know we won't have to confront him for being a slacker and not working on his parents' behalf."

"And his own." Paul just had to grumble. He just did. He

probably looked forward to the lecture, witnessing Brandon's discomfort at their awareness of his renege on his promise to work hard. Paul would relish allowing Brandon to believe God and His Holy Spirit had seen all and whispered directly into his pastoral ear. It was a means of churching many a dupe, er congregant. God as witness, as planner of the planet, was real, and Paul was well wired.

Fran withdrew her hands, folded them primly, and then rested them on the table. She needed more liquid courage to divulge the full drama. "Pick up your champagne for a toast, my love."

"Uh-oh. When you revert to 'my love', I know someone's in trouble." Paul picked up his flute and smiled. "Forget the drumroll, Fran. Get on with it, because I know the story's gonna be as ginormous as your grin."

Fran could no longer suppress a chuckle. She gingerly nestled her flute so as not to spill. She required both hands to shape the story. Gestures would be called for now. "I witnessed a different confrontation than we'd planned. Better, I fervently believe."

"Better?" Paul wiggled his eyebrows, in imitation of Deacon Steve. Though it was an attempt at humor, Fran's demeanor almost capsized with the burden of the bad half of her news.

But she yoga-breathed and continued, resolute. "That young high school quarterback I'd seen, the one likely employed at minimum wage to complete Brandon's milking responsibilities, came to work, but Brandon chest-bumped him at the door." Fran enjoyed Paul's sudden clutch to his throat, one that signaled disbelief and a glug down the wrong pipe. She paused to assure his status, and then continued, determined to dispense this tidbit and then get to the downside of the conversation. And enlist Paul's aid.

"I've watched the scene several times to memorize what Brandon said to his teenaged fill-in. Here goes...'Dude, you're dead meat. I saw you surfing porn on your phone while you hosed the stalls yesterday. You wasted lots of water.'"

Paul smiled at that line. He'd likely listened to Steve complain about Brandon's wastefulness, just as Fran listened to Jackie's rant about Brandon's overlong showers.

Paul winked and flashed his patented smile. "You imitate a male voice well. Perhaps you could call some of our members who are delinquent with their tithe."

Paul quickly withdrew his hands to his lap to avoid Fran's smack. "Let Barge do it. She can give them half a mind because that's what she's got."

"Tsk, tsk. Is that dissatisfaction about your replacement?" Paul chuckled briefly, squelched by the slam of Fran's fist.

"Don't make me digress. You know I hate that." Fran swept her hands across the table to signal Paul was out of line. He stopped, replacing his grin with his placid pastoral counseling face. Satisfied, Fran spoke. "I always dislike your smirk, too. If you smile when things go wrong, you have someone in mind to badger or blame. And believe me, there's plenty wrong. May I continue, please?"

Fran didn't wait for Paul's reply. She stuck a finger in his face. "Then, Brandon widened his stance and put his hands on his hips to emulate Coach Uhrig on the sidelines. A posture that a principal and a pastor would never use, but coaches rely on, especially when their gifted athletes towered over them." Fran smiled as Paul nodded to affirm. "Brandon glowered and then shouted, 'You're supposed to focus on chores. This is my livelihood.'

"The kid replied, 'Well, it ain't lively enough if you ask me. I quit.' He rousted himself to full stature, dramatically sweeping invisible wisps of straw from his shoulders, chest, and legs. He cock-walked to the barn door and scraped his work boots against the opening, almost toppling his athletically agile body with the unnecessary jab. A few moments later, I heard Brandon mutter, 'First Julie dumped me, now the kid. And, what the hey, the damn cows are pregnant again.'" Fran sat back. The first half of her news landed. Kerthump.

Paul shifted in his chair, his active listening posture melding into counselor mode. Grace was his role. Fran could see his eagerness to empathize, call Brandon into his office for counseling. Maybe wrangle weekly attendance and a monthly tithe in exchange.

But into the moment of his mulling, Fran interjected an opinion, one she'd never imagined she'd say. The words spewed like bullets.

"Let Brandon mind his own camera, as well as his young man, his chores, his pregnant cows, his love life, too. Micromanaging Brandon's micro dairy management seems neither gratifying nor necessary. Most of the time it's tediously dull. You have a church to run, and I have a memoir to write."

Paul frowned. Fran knew he couldn't let the balloons fly away that easily. "But, cow gestation is nine months, and who knows where Jackie and Steve will be at that point? What will Brandon do? What would Steve want?"

Fran righted herself, stiffened her spine and her upper lip. "Well, now that you mention it, Steve needs all the help he can get." She paused, not for effect this time, but to gather her resolve. She almost cried as she dipped her head. She couldn't, she just couldn't look in her husband's eyes. She almost whispered her next words. "Steve's in jail."

"What?" Paul gasped. "Where? In Australia?"

Feebled beyond her capacity for words, Fran gratefully nodded in reply to Paul's next words. "Carl, too?"

Paul came alive, his role defined. "Sons of Baptist preachers!" Paul exclaimed. "I hope and believe that Jackie and Bonnie aren't incarcerated, as well." His eyebrows shot up, incredulous rather than to tease.

Fran refolded her hands, squeezing them to hold herself together, close to her chest. "Jackie and Bonnie are in a premium hotel. I've enlisted Judge, at their request, to suggest an Australian attorney to expedite the men's release. However, matters are complicated by a cash-fueled imperiousness Bonnie has adopted. Primed to be pissy is how Jackie described her behavior. And apparently Bonnie is self-righteously angry at Carl, while poor Jackie is befuddled by everything."

Paul extended one hand across the table. Fran fiercely grabbed it. Her lifeline. "This calls for prayer. Let's get the congregation involved."

Now Fran fell apart, something she'd never done in life. Her champagne flipped to douse her new blouse as she swept her hands to the side of her head, tears falling on her mother's pearls. "Welcome aboard, one and all. I'm so relieved to not be alone with this multi-threaded mess."

Thirty-two | *Bonnie*

BONNIE AWAKENED TO A strange sound, one that emulated the scraping and scratching of a mouse. She lifted one corner of the sleep mask she'd permanently borrowed from the plane, spying her watch, laid out like a corpse in front of the hotel clock. The clock's red digital display shrieked, "Jet lag's a bitch!" At least, that was the sound Bonnie heard in her head. Her watch face declared 3:30 p.m.

In Michigan. What time was it here? 6:30 a.m.! Why wasn't Carl released?

The sound from the edge of the room shifted from a scratch to a scoot. Bonnie scrambled to remove the sleep mask and turn on the bedside lamp, painfully yanking her hair in the process. Long hair was more of a challenge than she'd expected. She could almost hear Maybelline's "I told you so."

Her eyes darted around the room and then attached themselves to bold, thick capital letters she could read from here. YANKS JAILED! FANS CHEER AS BAR MANAGER SUES. The morning paper's rustling slide under the door may have awakened her, but its headlines, blanketing the entire front page along with fight photos, bolted her upright. Carl's incarceration and a lawsuit! The bar manager *had* filed.

Bonnie flung the eyeshade at the corner lamp, which wobbled with the force of the weapon's strike. Beyond conceivability, beyond challenge, beyond her capability, even when blessed by cash. Gosh, darnit, dang!

As abruptly as everything else this morning/afternoon/night, the phone rang. Was God calling via an Aussie landline?

"There's been somewhat of a glitch with your card, I fear, Mrs. Edwards."

"Watson, is that you? How's the mustache hanging?"

"There's no need to be glib, Mrs. Edwards. Especially under the circumstances." Watson cleared his throat to ensure the clarity of the next news. "Your card has been refused. We couldn't conceive of it here at Watson & Watson, I dare say, so we took the liberty of inquiring via channels. It seems your Capital One account is overdrawn by ten cents. Yank banks have been quite fierce since they dumped your country into recession."

Bonnie hiccupped. "Is that why my husband isn't released?"

"Quite so, Madame. The other Mr. Watson suspected a scam. We're unable to assist until you can secure the funds."

Bonnie slammed down the receiver. She felt like she'd swallowed the newspaper whole and concentrated on not throwing up. She longed to expel the semi-digested contents of the mini bar on the hotel's superfine sheets. The feeling was quadrupled by guilt, because she'd not visited Carl, expectant that Watson handled all.

In fact, the thought of visiting the police station and its cells repelled her. Coffee, lots of it, was called for. She had oodles to contemplate and then do. Crapola. She lounged in a luxury hotel—without a purse with its coins and bills and cadre of credit cards—while she had millions locked up at her request in LLCs.

Bail is like the ransom Carl jokingly alluded to in his lone call. But neither ransom nor bail can I pay now. Money seems to not be enhancing my life. Bonnie suddenly wished all the troubles would evaporate—and take the dang cash with them. Well, maybe not the cash. Money could buy temporary happiness. Self, let's start with me, and let Carl rot.

Rather than succumb to handwringing that might have damaged her expensive mani-pedi, Bonnie booked massages for Jackie and herself after calling room service. She scheduled arrival of a full array of breakfast selections at the civilized hour of 8:00 a.m. There were kinks to work out of their bodies from the lengthy plane ride, Carl and Steve's improvident behavior, their incarceration, and their non-release. Bonnie knew she planned better when it was her skin and not her brain, that was well oiled.

Jackie was used to getting up with the roosters, so Bonnie rang her room. Her disheveled friend, garbed in the hotel's complimentary plush white robe and slippers, rapped twice on Bonnie's door four minutes later.

Bonnie pulled Jackie into the room and held her gaze. Then she picked up Jackie's hands and rubbed them between hers. "Our men remain in jail..."

Jackie began to hyperventilate and nearly collapsed to the floor. Rather than urge Jackie up, Bonnie nestled beside her to whisper, "There are as many kinks in our bodies as there are in the situation, so first things first. You've got to learn that, before you can take care of others, you have to take care of yourself. Okay, Jackie?"

Jackie nodded lightly and then dropped her head to her hands.

"Good idea," said Bonnie. "Let's pray."

The Lord's Prayer echoed into the hall.

"Now, let's go," Bonnie replied. "Let the masseurs ease the pains they can, and we can apply our imaginations to solve the others. Anxiety is a brain hindrance one can not surmount," Bonnie paused to wiggle her tush, "without the support of a few unincarcerated men, our masseurs."

Eighty minutes later, the loose-limbed lasses floated back to Bonnie's luxury suite, headquarters for the duties that lay ahead. Bonnie allowed Jackie to explore her suitcase stuffed with carefully folded leisure sets, a rainbow of velour. That kept Jackie occupied, so she didn't fret.

"Jackie, I took the liberty of ordering in rather than venture out. We need to avoid reporters all the more."

"Amen to that." Jackie slid her fingers down the length of each sleeve. Bonnie knew, by the look on Jackie's face, she craved Steve's arms around her—after taking care of the problem, of course. That Steve was the problem, not Brandon, was not customary in the Breeden household. Jackie's eyes glistened with tears.

"Besides, Carl and Steve will be home soon. Our plan to hock our minks is good. All good, to bail our men out." Jackie smiled wanly and didn't taint that expectation with truth. They needed to muster their courage. Stat.

Bonnie knew to distract Jackie fast. "Items we'd not sampled remained on the room service menu, their print yearning to be touched, but I decided on scrambled eggs, wheat toast, an assortment of jams and juices. American coffee and lots of it. Food and an action plan. Let's do this!"

Jackie nodded, consigned. The two women settled into locating a pawn shop, one rifling the phone book and the other accessing the Internet. How hard could hocking a gently-used fur coat be in Sydney, Australia? After all, they'd strolled through the famous place in Vegas where *Pawn Stars,* one of Carl's favorite TV shows, was filmed, while they awaited their turn to be married by Elvis.

Several businesses' phone numbers, addresses, and opening times were soon scribbled on the hotel stationary. Jackie chanced a call to Steve, but the Surrey Hills staffer would only take a message, with a promise to deliver it with the breakfast tray.

To not cry, Jackie squeezed her eyes. Bonnie just rolled hers. "Guess I won't bother trying to phone. Carl might refuse my call, and I dare not risk the collapse that would follow."

Jackie nodded. Time to read the paper until room service arrived.

Jackie perused the Aussie cartoons, and then shucked them to the floor. "Aussie humor's different. Lots of weird characters and words." As she headed to the desk to fetch a pen for the crossword, Bonnie handed the first section to Jackie, eyes fixed on her face.

Jackie gasped as she read the 'Sydney Morning Herald' headline. Her knees buckled, and she plopped hard into the over-stuffed chair. *Holy God-fearing crap!*

"Room service!" accompanied a knock. Muffled, discreet, an imperative to calm tourists' nerves. Before Bonnie could reply, a black-and-white uniform swished in behind a linen-laden cart.

"Holy Catholic Communion!" Jackie whispered at the

sight of the multiple silver domes. Also on the cart were creamy china plates with burgundy and gold rims, perhaps plundered by the proletariat from Russian palaces. "One platter probably costs as much as my entire set of Fiesta Ware. Do you suppose the scrambled eggs will taste better or the same?"

"Get a load of the jam choices in the silver compote," Bonnie regaled as the uniformed maid whisked off one dome after the other. She then lofted the coffee pot above her head, daring the waterfall of coffee to spill a drop, willing the women to notice as the china cups filled. They didn't.

Bonnie spread butter on a wheat toast point, but that was as far as she got before the veiled-eyed woman repositioned herself, nearer than was polite, shoved the bill at Bonnie to sign, and then backed away. The door neither slammed nor hit the silent maid in the ass, but the friends' heard her distinct cackle, "American rubes! You just signed for a nasty surprise, served on a platter."

The women looked at each other. More Aussie slang they couldn't ascertain.

"The pawn shops don't open until 10:00. We'll get the cash, and then we'll head straight to the police, right, Bonnie?"

"Jackie, we've gone over this ten times. Maybe your brain is not fully-caffeinated." Bonnie shook her curls to consider. "Nope, mine either. Not ready to take on the day."

"I think I have an additional fortification." Jackie scooped up the discarded newspaper. "See here in the lower right corner of the back page, with a sumptuous sailboat? It's an ad for Bundy Rum. We might want to re-open the mini bar. Black Tea, I think as the Aussie's call their rum and Coke drink."

"Oh, my favorite form of caffeine!"

Bonnie prepared Black Tea, half rum and half Coke in each glass. The drink's look reminded her of summer tea back home. She knuckled the bottle of Kahlua to augment their black coffees, too. "Two-fisted drinkers we'll be, a new path to female bail bonding."

Bonnie handed Jackie the filled-to-the-brim Black Tea. "Let's get well-oiled so we can well-and-truly laugh."

Jackie hoisted her double, not minding the splash. "I didn't have cleaning duty in a hotel, so I'll toast that, too."

Bonnie tapped her glass to Jackie's. "Down the hatch." The longtime friends could face-read their solidarity. No more verbal mauling. They'd go forth and create copacetic.

Before Jackie swigged, Bonnie spat out her gulp of Black Tea, plucked both glasses from the table, and sped to the bathroom sink. She dumped the drinks, rifled her toiletries for Scope, and gargled for a full minute. "Blech-k! We *paid* for that crapola," Bonnie sputtered as she returned to the room. Bonnie sat, heavily, in the chair. "If I'd ever tasted gasoline, I'm sure it would be better than Aussie Black Tea. I'll stick to Kahlua-spiked coffee, if you please."

"I'm anxious again, after that boozy near miss," Jackie replied, her voice husky with concern. To suppress whimpering, which both knew Steve despised, Jackie lifted her coffee cup to toast. "Let's drain our Kahlua coffee, and then get ready to swash buckle release of our men."

Thirty-three | *Jackie*

IMBIBING BREAKFAST CONTINUED AT a boozy, leisurely pace. As was her custom, Jackie read snippets of the front-page article between bites. Within seconds she emitted a blood-curdling shriek, so shrill it might persuade God to change His mind if used in an appropriate situation. "Holy crap!"

"What's up?" Bonnie asked mildly as the papers fell from Jackie's hands.

Jackie opened her mouth, but no sounds emerged. It was as if the scream had stolen more than its share of the room's air, and there was no power left for words.

"I'm not enjoying the drama, Jackie. Should I grab the paper and read it myself? I can swallow words as well as you, I'm sure."

"Re-load our cups. Your socks are going to rock, and you're not even wearing any." Bonnie lurched to obey while Jackie bent over to stretch, wiggling her arms to release tension. Jackie righted herself and inhaled deep. "I'll speed read and give you the gist."

Though Jackie's voice was light, Bonnie's hands shook while she bartended—as if they'd absorbed all the tension Jackie had released. "Get on with it," she insisted as she slammed down the pot.

"The rugby team owner launched a lawsuit. Seems Carl

landed the punch that took out his star player. For the season. He's suing for damages with expectation that his team won't win the World Cup."

"Bugger all." Bonnie slapped her knees, too overwhelmed to say more.

"But that's not the end of it, Bonnie," Jackie continued. "You may want to sit down for the next news. It seems that a Mrs. Edwards, Carl's California ex-wife, read a newspaper headline—or heard the nightly news—and hired a pit bull attorney to gain her half of the half-of-half-billion." Jackie peered from the corner of her eye, anxious for Bonnie's reaction, but she'd fainted. Fainted dead flat in the red leather chair, ass slipping to the floor. Jackie ran to the bathroom, hoping for ammonia, but returned with perfumed bath salts to thrust beneath Bonnie's nose.

Bonnie sneezed as she came to. She shook her mane. Her lips snarled, and then, "Can you believe the gall of that tweaker and that twit? Wish I could bitch slap both!" Her eyes blazed and her nostrils flared. "My windfall has definitely depressed my attitude toward humanity. What the devil's gotten into everyone?"

Jackie hovered, rocking on her feet, as if she didn't know where and when to alight. Her fingers alternately fanned Bonnie's face, feathered her hair, and lamely patted her hands.

"Relax, Jackie. Guess vehicles for the ex-wife and her kids wasn't the right price for peace. Help me up. I already have plans. Came to my subconscious, which is great, because my conscious mind can't deal with this double scoop of shit."

Jackie bug-eyed. "I've never heard an ex-church secretary swear. Is this a stressed empress trait?" escaped her quip-prone lips.

Bonnie convulsed with laughter. "You mean, you didn't catch the Aussie swear term *bugger?*"

Bonnie collapsed to the uber-thick carpet and grabbed Jackie's hand to join her. They rolled, tickled as pink as their skin had been post-massage. Laughter proved to be the best medicine. It rekindled their sense of ease and redirected their trust to the Lord. Jackie jumped up to fetch the Gideon International's Bible from its bedside berth.

"Did you know that the Wisconsin-based group is working on its second billionth Bible placement in hotels?" she asked-announced.

"Who do you think grabbed that fact off the internet for Pastor Rankin to use in a sermon?" Bonnie replied as she hoisted herself back into the leather chair. "Who do you think solved the congregations' problems, large and small, un-credited, the valiant little woman behind the man?"

Bonnie pounded the desk. "God and Pastor Rankin always got the credit. I'm sick of it! Sick of it all! Let someone else solve-and-serve. It's my turn to be Queen." Turning to Jackie, she said, "My first command is for you to sit, my friend. I have some confessions to make, so keep the Bible handy."

Jackie took her time to seat herself well, her anxiety returning with Bonnie's sober tone.

Bonnie tossed back her hair and thrust out her chin, the better to be forthcoming. "I, uhm, seem to have misplaced my wallet—"

Jackie gasped, but only by half because Bonnie squint-eyed her for the interruption. "It also seems that I've forgotten the PIN to the ATM card I'd kept in a secret pocket of my suitcase—"

Now Jackie escalated to hiccup, leaving no doubt to the genetic source of Brandon's trait, reciting the already known fact, "And, hic, your Cap-, hic, itol One card is maxed. Holy crap! Hic."

Jackie grabbed the Bible and thumbed, seeking appropriate passages. She took a sip of spiked coffee to muster the spit to read the Psalms 23 and verses for many of Paul's preferred, including the re-affirmation of "Love is patient...love is kind, etc." She level-eyed Bonnie as she recited the final verse by heart. "And now these three remain, Faith, Hope, and Love. But the greatest of these is Love."

Bonnie grabbed the Bible from Jackie and re-cradled it in the drawer. There was a legal length envelope in the drawer, too. She nestled under her arm, picked up the phone, and directed the concierge to call a new attorney, barrister or whatever the hell would work. "Just peruse the winningest barrister list. Surely this country has one. Find the closest, the one who'll arrive at my suite within the hour."

Across the room, Jackie rolled her eyes. She knew that Bonnie was too paralyzed by the paparazzi's presence to venture out, but seriously!

Though fully exasperated with her longtime friend, Jackie couldn't throw the babe out with the bath water. She had to rely on Bonnie, the only free citizen she knew in Australia. If what was happening was usual here, no wonder the locals called their country Oz.

"Bonnie, have you forgotten that we won't be here in an hour? By then, we'll have secured enough money, by pawning the minks, to free our men from jail. Remember how you told me to take care of myself first? Well, taking care of my husband *is* taking care of myself."

Bonnie had the grace to blink, but not the grace to call back and change her command. Jackie read her friend's body language. Unclenched her fists and read it again. "You're afraid, aren't you?"

Shamed, Bonnie collapsed, head to chest. A mumble emerged from her lips, "It's my form of denial. If I don't see Carl, maybe this disaster isn't real. It's all a bad dream. This is not my idea of a sweet honeymoon."

"Well, Rapunzel, I'm going." Jackie pointed in the general direction of her suite. "Doesn't it seem unfair that we bask in luxury while our husbands are guests of a foreign country's police?"

The more inert Bonnie remained, the more Jackie's resolve galvanized. "I have a battalion of Band-aids in my luggage. Steve's hurting, on many levels, and he needs a mega-dose of me. I'm going to post bail."

Jackie didn't wait for Bonnie's nod. She didn't need her permission; she had Master Card. She had a conscience.

Jackie ran from the room on shaking legs. Though it took several times to swipe the credit card-like key to elicit the green light for entry, when she did, Jackie burst through with the vigor of Wonder Woman. She freshened her minimal make-up, re-combed her curls, and gathered all the first aid supplies she could find. She scooped the Gideon Bible from the bedside table drawer and stashed it in her purse, exiting the room without bothering to turn off the lights or TV. The door slammed on the news coverage that cycled her personal bad news as if it was the largest calamity ever in the Emerald City, which Sydney apparently was called.

How ironic, her favorite color, the color of her eyes, her team, and the green pastures of home, where she longed to return.

Her breath uneven and jagged, Jackie ran to the limit of her knees' speed. The elevator snailed down, allowing others to enter her space of grief and chagrin, with stops at other floors. This was the local, not the express.

When the doors finally opened in the lobby, she shifted to the left to allow a smiling, white-haired couple with red-leashed golden retriever to pass. Now she burst into unwanted tears. Good grief! Jackie missed the dog.

She stumbled to the concierge, not bothering to perch into the over-plump seat where Steve had plunked not so long ago. She stood at attention, a polite distance from the desk, while the straight-as-a-stick, uniformed man completed his call.

Stepping forward unbidden she tumbled out her request for transportation to the Surry Hills Police Station. Thank goodness, the man's expression remained flat. Thank goodness, he didn't expect details. Thank goodness he had pen and paper on which to write. Jackie knew her addled brain wouldn't retain the facts.

Thank goodness, a tram set out every seven minutes, for a reported thirteen-minute ride. There was a proximate tram stop. Yes, Yank dollars would suffice.

Jackie smiled for the fist time in minutes; Steve would be proud of her frugality. That might mediate his anger over her delay to free him.

Jackie bolted from the hotel, glancing at her upper legs mid-stride. A reflex because she'd often left the house in

Michigan with her apron still around her waist, providing endless local commentary. The velour tracksuit Bonnie loaned her looked as good on the outside as it felt on the inside. It caressed her legs as she hurried, almost like hugs to bless her resolve.

At the tram stop, Jackie used the sun's reflection off the glass shelter to give herself the once over she'd neglected in her haste. While the tracksuit's green enhanced her eyes, shimmering with hope. Soon, all will be as copacetic in Oz as it is had been at home. Amen.

Thirty-four | *Fran*

FRAN SNICKERED AS SHE read Jackie's latest email. The boozy jottings of a tourist had resumed now that she'd released Steve from jail. No mention of Bonnie and Carl. Perhaps Bonnie had not reformed, despite the discussion Fran had coached. An imbalance of cash had capsized abidingly friendly goodwill. Love of money the root of all evil.

What if Bonnie'd denied her husband release—like she'd apparently threatened, according to Jackie—abandoning sanity and every instruction in His good book. With her former church secretary compassion eviscerated and replaced by an unattractive queenly belligerence, Fran hoped Bonnie's hair extensions fell out.

One positive note—Bonnie, so pre-occupied with *whatever,* she no longer posted questionable pictures on Facebook. As surmised, local attention had moved onto another craze. Perhaps Bonnie was hiding out because of the ex-wife's lawsuit to garnish a share of the lottery loot. Were Facebook posts admissible evidence in court?

Midway through the email Jackie confessed she'd seldom thought of Brandon. Fran felt entitled to remotely disable the Bran Cam. Let the young adult wallow in his conundrums, figure stuff out. While it might afford cheap entertainment to watch Brandon muddle, Fran knew she'd feel compelled to help the kid if she witnessed the birthing process.

Fran also wanted to assure that new footage didn't erase the video of the cowpie incident or the surrogate worker's quitting episode. And let's not forget the dog peeing on the impersonator's (poor Seth Thomas) pants. Those would be archived to show Jackie and Steve, if/when they returned.

Fran confessed to her heart of hearts, she unhooked the feed because, despite the profound moments of hilarity, the task wasn't necessary or fun. A retiree should have fun, the women's magazines consistently asserted. During increasing forays to Maybelline's shop, she'd thumbed the pages. And, in spite of herself, she became addicted. *Real Simple* was the most apt.

Now that she'd let go of Brandon's leash, Fran regretted not accompanying her friends. Paul, his head stuck in his church expansion plans, certainly wouldn't miss her. The round-the-world fling, without her leadership knack—and compounded by both men being less than level-headed—had become a brainless operation. And Judge was little better than the other men on an increasing number of days.

Fran began to fret a nail. Should she call Barge to rally the church ladies to enforce low-key alcoholism rehab via continuous casserole brigade? Would that be proper use of her power as the pastor's wife? Would it rend her relationship with her brother, one of her few family members?

Just then the parsonage doorbell rang. Odd, everyone who sought advice or solace from the pastor respected his boundary to bring their affairs to church. Fran had declined Susan Carrigan's offer to deliver Avon to her door, and now that Fuller Brush had filed Chapter 11 bankruptcy, she couldn't imagine who it might be. The paperboy eager to make more money by mowing their lawn?

Fran slid her slippered feet over the wood floors to peer through the peephole. Hell's doorbells. The Widow Braghorn, be-suited, be-pearled, and well-coiffed. She stood erect—and off the welcome mat, as if she didn't accept its message. The Widow clutched her handbag, matched precisely to her leather stilettos, in one hand and a handled casserole carrier in the other.

Fran felt like Armageddon had arrived at her door. She surveyed her robe and swept upstairs, calling "Coming" loudly over her shoulder. She hurried into her closet to don a fresh robe. The pearl necklace she'd worn to the club and not returned to its silken pouch sprawled across the counter between the sinks. Providence. Fran pinched her cheeks and combed her hair for good measure.

Fumbling with the necklace clasp, she raced down the stairs and then slowed, willing her heart beat to match. Pausing to inhale deeply while mouthing the Lord's Prayer. She gathered benevolence to countermand the administrative tone rising in her gullet. Best not to piss off this woman and destroy the peace of her home.

The door nearly swung off its hinges despite Fran's intention to be welcoming yet controlled. "Is this a good time?" the Widow crooned. A phrase that Fran had never considered the woman might know. "I've called Judge's office several times and have been deflected by his receptionist. I was concerned so I prepared mac 'n cheese with chicken breasts, which I know to be among his favorites. Would I be overbold if I delivered it myself, or may I leave it with you for his consumption?"

Ordinarily Fran wasn't in the deferential mode required to

deal with the Widow. But these were, indeed, extraordinary times when the overly endowed-with-entitlement broad behaved in a deferential manner. Shock couldn't describe the depth of Fran's sense of the situation. She held her passive-aggressive sarcasm in check with the Golden Rule overheard when she trolled the teachers' lounge. What one said about others would be said about you. There weren't many women in this town who'd learned that lesson. Certainly not Marge, the barging church secretary.

Tact wasn't Maybelline's knack, either, but Fran so wished she had a salon appointment to run to, to avoid this conversation. "Come in, come in. Set the casserole on the hall table. Do you have a moment for tea?"

The Widow was too cultured to allow full shock to register on her face, but Fran saw the flicker anyway. She'd watched too many lying teens to let emotional *tells* get away. Not for the first time, Fran wished she'd applied herself to poker as her retirement game.

Haltingly, as if she hadn't walked in heels since age one, like the town's wags said, the Widow crossed the threshold of the parsonage.

And, in those moments, Fran crossed a threshold, too. She realized the Widow's influence with Judge could be just the ticket. As a preeminent influencer in the flock, the woman could be enlisted, as needed, to rally the congregation, too. Something was up in Australia, and Fran needed an ally.

"Please sit on the sofa, while I put the kettle on and prepare appetizers to accompany our chat." Fran turned on the stereo, already set on Michigan State's symphonic station to mellow herself and her guest, and scurried out of the room.

"Thank you, thank you, thank you, Lord." Fran said as she rifled her pantry. Ah yes, I spy my Lent-is-over box of chocolates. Though several months old, its remnants could be plundered. Let me try one. Mmn-n good. And, an unopened box of Pepperidge Farm's Milano cookies with the $5.99 price tag untouched. Oh, yes. I sliced the banana bread before placing it in the freezer. The microwave will ready that in no time. Christ on a bicycle, I'm as good as Becky Home Ecky.

As Fran assembled a platter, the tidbits reminded her of Marge. Rather than squelching juicy congregational gossip, Marge embellished and sometimes changed names. Not to protect innocents, but to shift blame. While Fran stayed far from the church office, she listened to her husband—and half the town—and she kept score. Brain-bitching the woman was a secret pleasure, but banishing her would be more beneficial for all. She was a mediocre typist to boot.

Marge's latest affront featured Polly, who lamented loudly that Ron's prized bull escaped their farm lot and meandered the county before being found in a ditch, fried by lightning. The Barge's in-your-face retort: "It was God's will."

No wonder collection plate offerings were going down. The nerve of that woman, undermining her husband's Christian efforts. Paul was near frantic. He had a steeple, roof repairs, an education building, and neon sign to erect, as well as a flock to tend. He hadn't intended to tap Bonnie's LLC so early and so—

Paul had frequently been in the company of the Widow and her wealth. Further, he flopped onto the king-sized mattress, later than late, and sometimes still fully clothed. Fran knew she was beyond the baseness of jealousy, but she begrudged the lost time. This had not been part of her retirement plan.

Hmm. The phrase *strange bedfellows* popped into Fran's mind. She knew she needed an ally to corral her brother's longstanding alcoholism and to fetch her friends home, safe from the jaws of Aussie justice.

Fran reframed her mind, putting on her brightest face, and sauntered into the living room. She placed the delicacies on the coffee table and poured tea. "One lump or two?" she inquired sweetly.

"Three, please. My-oh-my, that platter looks lovely. Yes, I might have a nibble or two."

Ms. Mimsy is simpering. Might she have an agenda, too? I'll just sit and sip and allow the sweet aroma of new information to restore my upper hand.

Music waltzed around the room, lilting, swaying, and circling warmth around the two women's shoulders. Presently, Fran spoke, "I'm quite flattered by this lovely, impromptu visit, Mrs. Braghorn. Did you have a cause? Or merely a casserole? Which, by the way, smells scrumptious."

"Please call me Charlene. We're long past due for that, Mrs. Rankin. May I call you Fran?"

Charlene pointed to the casserole parked back on the entry hall table. "I'll get right to the point. I'm concerned about your brother. He's sustained intermittent weekend benders, when his caseload took a bad turn over the years. These rough patches have become more prevalent." The Widow paused to crease her brow. "I fear for his health."

Fran bit her tongue to not append *and your wealth.* Transferring funds from Big to Little Cayman this time,

Charlene? Hope your make-up doesn't crack with your feigned concern.

Fran double-bit. Because that was precisely the scheme Judge had formulated to shield Bonnie's Boffo Lotto funds. Time to turn this twist to favor all intents.

At the lightning speed of which she was proud, Fran formulated a plan—without Jackie as sounding board. A first. "Let's visit him together," she heard herself say out-of-body-experience-like. "Help yourself to more crumpets while I get dressed. I'll place the casserole in the oven to keep it warm." She swept off the couch to do the deed.

In a flash, she circled back, with a pad and paper, and placed them by the silver platter. "Would you mind preparing a list for a church lady casserole brigade, Charlene?"

Fran flew up the stairs, humming. Chumming with Charlene might be just the thing. And, better yet, she seems to be sweet on my brother, not my husband. Thank you, Lord.

Twenty minutes later, Fran scooped up the final cookie from the platter. "Let's not bother with two cars, Charlene. Would you mind driving to Judge's chambers?"

The formerly at-odds couple embarked to Lodenburg, where Judge's office occupied a full block on the west side of the courthouse, holding pride-of-place on the town square. Fran had to admit the Cadillac's suspension was far cushier than her Mini, kind of like driving on a couch.

The weather was mild, as was the air inside the Cadillac. Charlene listened, uh-huhhed, and beamed while Fran laid out the plan. Filtered, of course, because several details couldn't be entrusted to a twenty-minute ally.

"First, I must thank you for coming forward. As you might suspect, I've been missing my gal pals. Moreover, Jackie and Bonnie are embroiled in a bit of a problem. I need you and Marge to enlist the church ladies to form a meal brigade to help keep Judge sober enough to achieve a large number of billable hours."

"I'm eager to be useful, Fran. You have no idea how quiet a large home can be, with only a stable of deferential servants about. The staleness of the air, without Big's constant cigar smoke and bourbon breath, is suffocating. I'm so lonely I even miss our arguments."

Fran empathized, but did not say so. She also didn't embellish the full basis for her request. She'd counted on the Widow's narcissism to make the situation and its solution all about her. Her gamble had paid off. Charlene came through. No one in the community read international news, so none might ever access the full truth. Carl and Steve languished in a drunk tank Down Under rather than cavorting with their brides, one of whom was richer than rich because of the Boffo Lotto win.

However, the news had reached California. Had to scurry-hurry to cap the gnarly ex-wife's spurious lawsuit.

A ferociously adamant letter from Judge, citing the chronology of the lottery win, would suffice. Perhaps a deal sweetener that only Bonnie could affirm, though prodded by Fran's negotiation skills. The full matter could be mopped up in-house.

Fran was about to applaud when her mind recycled to the close of dinner last night, when Paul had pledged to engage the entire congregation in prayer. Hell's bells. Fran fervently hoped he'd not already prompted Marge to put the jailing in the bulletin.

Thirty-five | *Bonnie*

ONLY AFTER ALL THE suite's pillows and towels were flung, with every article of her massive wardrobe hurled atop them into the Jacuzzi tub, did Bonnie realize she'd made a mistake. What she needed was a good soak. Crapola! She needed to get Housekeeping up here, pronto, to clear the tub and replenish the bubble bath salts. Maybe bring chilled Prosecco and shrimp toast.

She'd just reached for the phone tucked in the discreet toilet stall when it rang.

"Bonnie, where the hell you been?"

"Carl, oh Carl. Is this really you? Are you okay? Are you out?"

"No, and I've been given three minutes for this call, so I've got to get right to the point: What's the plan for bailing me out?" Carl's brusque tone jolted Bonnie back to the reality that her plan to gallivant the world had gone seriously off the tracks. It was tough to be a queen when one's knight was incarcerated.

"And, by the way, did you know that you are not ensconced in the best suites of the Intercontinental Hotel? I wasted a precious minute while the operator traced you to *our* room."

Though her tantrum had ebbed that bald fact ignited Bonnie's torch. "I have half-a-mind to ring the front desk, the concierge, the manager, then corporate headquarters. Maybe get the bar manager, who was suing to contact the

Intercontinental, to vouch for my net worth's need for the premium suite."

"Don't hang up on me, Bonnie. You must get me released. Jackie already bailed out Steve. What about me?"

Carl's imploring tone centered Bonnie's guilt. She'd neglected wifely responsibility again. Jackie's forty years of love was a stronger beacon than a deferred romp. The room may be a mess—and it may not be a suite—but she'd used it to cocoon. She'd abandoned Carl. She had to get a move on to get him released. To be here with her.

"Bonnie, are you there? The desk captain, with whom I traded the call for a couple of future bucks from your stash, is glowering."

Bonnie deep breathed, still incensed. But the feeling was over-arched by lust. She tugged on the phone cord, able to stretch close enough to the heaped Jacuzzi tub to release her mink. She rubbed it between her index finger and thumb, willing herself to calm.

And, as she remembered the pawn-the-mink plan, Bonnie whimpered. Once, just once, because she'd purchase another as soon as she sourced some cash. She wouldn't want to get her precious coat out of hock. The thought of other people pawing her fur gave her the willies.

Speaking of willies, Carl didn't catch her mention of a lawsuit. That was a gigantic oops. She resolved to keep a lid on that unfortunate by-product of wealth, to not waste valuable phone minutes telling Carl all. Her lost wallet and bounced major credit card. Or her failure to recall her PIN. She'd never intended to withhold from Carl—or lie to the Lord—but circumstances called for her to keep it simple. Be strong.

"Carl, honey, it's handled." Bonnie pulled the toilet lid down and plopped. She needed a moment to regroup. "I'll be at the jail within the hour. Get your best smooch ready."

"Bring an aerosol and tuck a change of clothes in your purse. My travel outfit of comfortable clothes became somewhat looser due to a couple of rips. I look and smell like a vagrant. See you soon."

Bonnie re-cradled the phone, after alerting Housekeeping to her needs, and began to paw the clothing pile. She paused to admire the colorful mound of clothing that nearly reached the chandelier suspended over the tub. What did a millionaire wear to spring her man from jail? When the potential of worldwide publicity was disproportionate to the actual cash she, the Boffo Lotto winner, had on hand. *Holy jeopardy!* as Jackie might say.

Bonnie paused in front of the full-length mirror, taking in the ultra lacey lingerie and the body underneath. *Not bad, Babe,* she imagined Carl would say as she straightened her spine. She'd had booze, meals, and a massage to bolster her spirits when Carl's body was as battered as his ego. This was not the time to fold due to blondeness, bitchery, and half-baked Carl disregard. It was time to curb her hedonistic detachment and whip up more sympathy, like a church lady carrying a baked something to the home of the bereaved.

Since her coffers were near empty for the moment, she should find a way to filch a blowtorch to pry Carl from his cell. Maybe hijack a Brinks armored truck that'd limo them back to the hotel. After she offloaded its cash to pay bail.

Bonnie teased out her royal blue leisure suit. She wedged her body gingerly past the water handles to retrieve her silver sneakers. All make-up supplies were within easy reach, so she beautified to become the best jailbird visitor in decades. She'd be legendary, though not in a full-length mink. Sigh.

The mink was easy to pluck from the pile. Jackie O sunglasses completed her look. She enjoyed a few moments of vamp in front of the mirrored closet doors. She smiled, threw kisses, and plunged into the world.

Bonnie almost retched when the cab pulled in front of a weary-fronted store on a dank street several miles from the hotel. She said a small prayer and collected her self-control to alight, telling the driver to wait... Please.

Fifteen minutes later the man remained in the same pose as when she'd entered the pawnshop. He didn't utter a word when she directed him to the Surry Hills Police Station. All business, no inquiries, no smart remarks. No backward looks in the rear view mirror.

Which was good because Bonnie was willing her pulse to relax while her hands belied calm by gripping her handbag like a neck she wanted to wring. The pawnbroker had furtively offered Bonnie $750 for her gently-used mink. But, when her handbag flew over the counter at his head, he'd swiftly padded his offer. Seems PETA had the store under watch, so the owner pulled an extra $375 from his rusted metal cash box, to get her off the premises fast.

Bonnie put the money in her purse and zipped it shut. She fondled the mink one last time and vamoosed. She didn't want to allow the man to recant his offer. She ran.

Outside Bonnie displayed her exuberance by high-fiving

the air. She'd cobbled the cash to pay ten percent of the bail, the amount required to release her man, as well as drinks and cabfare!

The cab stopped and, as the driver reached over his shoulder for his fare, Bonnie shuddered. *Crapola, what a crowd!* Before she'd fully slammed the cab door, the driver sped off.

A fleet of paparazzi had staked out the police station, already converging and hoisting cameras as they spied her, rising to their infamous task. Bonnie gripped a thigh, so her foot didn't stomp. As a secretary she'd been well-schooled to not be a busybody—and had elbowed quite a few out of the pastor's path—so she could fend off this riff-raff.

She needed to project an aura of resilience, of her doing the cameras and the cops a favor, rather than the reverse. Her brief prior bout with the paparazzi, bolstered by Jackie's take-no-prisoners support, had been practice. This was prime time.

Bonnie gave her hair a what-the-hell fling, threw back her shoulders, and wiggled her fingers, readying them to fork over the cash. She might relish laying it on the counter, bill by wrinkled bill.

Amidst the clicks and the flashy din, Bonnie sauntered into the Police Station, ready to brush past the banter and sign-in procedures. Though his posture improved as she neared her goal, she withered the lone officer with a look. Stacking the bills took awhile, but not as long as the dumb jerk's recounting, fumbling for paperwork that he insisted she sign.

Bonnie had to pee, but she wouldn't yield turf until Carl

was in her arms.

Neither of them would wave "Bye" as they left. Neither would they let the door hit either in the ass. Out the back door, away from jackals of the press.

Now Bonnie wished she could hail a police car rather than a cab. Now was the time for sirens, ticker tape, a police escort. A parade to the Intercontinental where a proper shower awaited. Some righteous sex. Burn a few carbs and replace them with beer.

Thirty-six | *Jackie and Steve*

JACKIE WEPT FOR A full five minutes while Steve hugged her, sweat-sticking clothing and all. She forgot all about the Band-Aids she'd brought. She forgot all about Christian compunction for public displays of affection—and Steve did, too.

But she didn't forget about germs. She'd vigorously massaged hand sanitizer into her palms, glad the small bottle in her purse hadn't been confiscated at the airport. Everyone looked like ruffians in that building, staff and prisoners alike. She was glad to be squired out, on her man's bruised, but still ardently lovable arm.

After hugs, a meal, and good old-fashioned sex, Jackie unfurled the tissue embedded in her palm. There were three lawsuits hanging over their heads—well, not hers and Steve's, but over Bonnie's and Carl's, and they should team. She fervently hoped their friends were together and not merely out from behind bars to enter into the other kind. The kind of bars that started this fine mess.

She had to inform Steve of the full extent of their dilemma. But not just yet. Jackie dabbed the corners of her eyes. She needed to fortify herself for an unimagined motherhood task: to phone her son to share the strange turn their vacation had taken. That his upstanding father had been jailed. As difficult as it was for her to accept the reality of her partner-for-life as prisoner, this could fell Brandon.

It was difficult to imagine the conversation, to frame the message adequately, without setting up asymmetrical warfare. Yet Jackie welcomed the connection. She'd had enough of deciphering the slang-heavy Aussie accent. It'd be good to hear another American male voice, especially that of her one-and-only son.

Especially with Steve in the same room as she was. A family united by phone.

For now the call was deferred while she figured out the time zones, to not interrupt dairy chores. Jackie glanced over at the bed. Steve was zonked. Should she wait or phone Brandon alone? Would the kid scoff? Would he empathize? Would he offer support? Even the Magic 8-Ball Jackie visualized on his bedside table in his old room wouldn't be decisive about this prospect.

At least Steve was alive, not dead.

After several yoga poses, including the Happy Baby, Jackie's height resumed its full length of five-foot-two again. She grabbed her purse, retrieved and poked her cell, not even caring what time it was in the US. Brandon was a dairy farmer now, and readiness was required at all hours.

Brandon answered on the third ring. "Mom. Good to hear from you. I've been down lately."

"Sorry, dear. Is there anything your mama can do?"

"I doubt it. Julie dumped me and the cows are pregnant."

Jackie almost quipped, "At least Julie's not pregnant and the cows didn't dump you." She sighed instead.

Though she thoroughly loved her son, Jackie had warned Julie that Brandon looked at her the way he looked at her baked items. Further, Fran warned Jackie the relationship wouldn't last because of Julie's intellect and ambition. Jackie had thought the threat was the other way. The distance to Purdue was a hundred-fifty miles, but with a diamond as big as a searchlight, one would have thought Julie's engagement was everlastingly clear to every red-blooded male on campus. Even among a predominately engineering major population, not noted for their access to social cues.

Fiddlesticks. Jackie had good reason to reunite them. She no longer wanted to raise her son. It was the same old, same old, yada yada, all about him nonsense. She wanted her retirement to be complete.

For cripe's sake, she'd stuffed the closet in Brandon's old room with baby and toddler clothes, leaning heavily on pink. Including a tutu. It was long past time to turn Brandon out to someone else's pasture. *Lord, help me endure my blessings.*

"I'm sorry about all that, honey. I truly am. What did Julie say? Did she return the ring?"

"She said, 'I have four-and-a-half more years of intense studying ahead, and I can't handle your interruptions.' She handed the ring back in its black velvet box." Brandon bleated in a way a grown man never should. A manner never allowed by her or Steve or Coach or his teammates. "I'm not an interruption, am I, Mom?"

Jackie couldn't say, *yes, you were, many times. Especially when your dad and I wanted to make love,* so she switched the topic to food. "You eating all right? I loaded both freezers with meals before I left. How's the dog?"

"The dog's fine, though I can tell he misses Dad. He enjoys the frozen meals as much as I do, by the way. We share. Especially those Lemon Bars in the back of the barn fridge. I found them when I stashed the ring in its black box. Hope they weren't designated for some church bazaar, because they're gone."

Bizarre. What a perfect word to ignore, yet to use as a mental segue. "I've just released your dad from an Aussie police station, Bran. Seems your old man is a chip off of your block. Got into a bar fight and spent the night in the poky."

"Shut the front door! Is he all right? Let me talk to him."

"I'm afraid that's not possible. He's resting, and I don't want to awaken him. Jet lag and jail time are not a good combination." Jackie peered around the bathroom door to smile at her sleeping husband, to assure herself he was wholly safe and sound. She squelched a desire to fondle his hair. She didn't want to awaken her sleeping giant.

"Brandon, listen. Take notes if you have, too. Use one of your dad's many yellow pads—"

"I'm good, Mom. Remember, I have a college degree."

Jackie inhaled. "Some serious charges have been levied, and we need to raise funds."

"Remember when I offered up my piggy bank?"

"Yes. You were ten. Your dad was proud of you then, and he's gratified now. He said to tell you—"

Jackie cut off the thought. She couldn't tell Brandon that his dad already knew what he'd just confessed in this phone call. While Brandon may have been vaguely aware of Fran and Paul's supervision, he could never know about the Bran Cam.

What to do? What to say? Rather than becoming more

centered by this touchstone to home, Jackie felt confused.

On one hand, Jackie desired deeply to return home. While Fran sought peace in yoga sessions, she experienced *the zone* in cooking. She couldn't cook here, not in a hotel room. Foods, especially plucked from one's own garden and augmented by one's own dairy milk fulfilled visual, tactile, sensual smells, sumptuous tastes. Jackie almost began licking her own fingers.

"What's that noise, Mom? If I didn't know better, I'd say the dog was licking your face."

Hearing her slacker, self-involved son reminded Jackie of her longing to escape the bonds of middle age in the Midwest, constantly enmeshed in other people's issues. That was the same old, same old. Adventures here were supposed to be the new, the incredulous, the desirable, but same old imperative prevailed. To be the fixer of men.

"Your dad might enjoy his dog's company, licking his injuries literally and figuratively right now. He's pretty banged up, Brandon, though he doesn't have a concussion. He's embarrassed and, well, he hoped you'd still look up to him in spite of his lapse, just as he'd been of you over the years."

"Pain isn't hard, Mom. Simple pain I could take. Years of football bred pain tolerance into me. Neither you nor Dad nor Coach allowed tears, and teammates would spear chuck you for sure if you whimpered."

Jackie startled as visuals of her poor eight-year-old's early football experiences floated to the fore, but she also startled because he constantly referenced himself. Was he not hearing her? Too much information at the wrong—long distance—time. She was about to say something when she heard Brandon inhale deeply to continue his thread.

"Nothing said love like the klop of Coach's clipboard on your butt. It was the absence of that, the fucking up that was unbearable to contemplate, but you and Dad always returned me to the fold. I can return the favor. Tell Dad I love him. By the way, Mom, thanks for the alarm. It's 4:30 a.m., and I have to go milk pregnant cows."

Brandon hung up before Jackie could chastise him for cursing. Perhaps absence made the mind more tolerant. More open to truth. It was clear. In Brandon's version of the world, mothers were supposed to be blank, receptacles for a kid's personal needs, his issues, his trash. *The warm milk of human kindness,* nurtured by farm food and servitude.

But here I am, squawking and trembling like a wet chicken. Bristling at Brandon's indifference. Bristling at fate. *Maybe it is time to throw the baby out with the bathwater.*

Jackie resolved worldwide escapades would resume, now that Steve had learned a lesson to not willy-nilly follow Carl. No worries. She knew Brandon could watch a YouTube on calf delivery, as he did for everything else. No worries, she could count on Fran to record the blessed event, nine months hence, give or take. Fran might even watch a YouTube on how to email the Bran Cam video to her and Steve. Long distance parenting could be bliss.

Aussie slang wasn't so bad, after all. It was darn useful to ease a troubled mind. But there was something better. Jackie slid her phone into her purse and snuggled next to Steve, who seemed to be coming to.

Like a buzzard riding a thermal, dread had looped in Steve's dreams and lingered when he was awake. A bad movie for a non-movie-going man to fixate on. He felt more morose than since Vietnam. He overheard Jackie's call to Brandon and felt heartened that all went well. He would be alarmed by the lawsuits, but only peripherally. He trusted the Lord to work things out for good.

Steve hoped to agree with the outcome. He shrugged, and then jostled the anguish and self-disrespect from his soul to accept Jackie's spoon. The touch of human kindness personified. Tenderness could heal both body and spirit.

Worry wasted time. He had good times and Jackie was at the heart of everything. Mate for life. No worries.

Thirty-seven | Fran

FRAN CHECKED HER WATCH, automatically converting to Australia time to think of what her friends were doing tomorrow, which was now in Michigan. Secondarily, she noted that Charlene's car moved across town in under fifteen minutes. As rapidly as her Mini, but much more comfortably.

Ms. Prim-and-Mimsy Charlene parallel-parked on the town square, not scraping her Cadillac's white sidewalls once. Fran suppressed applause, the automatic response with her friends, Bonnie and Jackie. Sometimes the trio included self-pats on the back. None of them were too self-important for childish rituals, but such actions might be an unwelcome compliment in a rather new pact.

Charlene and Fran shared a Judge-focused alliance, albeit for different reasons. Only time would tell if the two were well-suited, but for now, Fran smiled, *we are. Charlene's suit may be more costly, with shoulder pads that could carry epaulettes, but mine is empowered by years of administrative experience and blood relation to Judge.*

Fran had an urgent set of lawsuits that Judge needed to address, pronto, for her friends. It had been tough to suppress a gasp as she'd listened to Bonnie's urgent voicemails and then read Jackie's better-detailed email. She'd only dug her phone from her purse to avoid conversation with Charlene. Instead of a sham listening, she'd gotten an ear- and eyeful. *Be careful what you wish for,* the devil on Fran's shoulder said.

The duo bustled inside the hushed interior of the lawyerly sanctum, not bothering to check in with Jillian, the weekend receptionist. They each mimed that the casserole was hot, so the young woman nodded, not even removing her headset to speak.

According to Charlene, Jillian was a dolt who'd blown off Charlene's calls and, if Fran knew anything about the Widow beyond her wealth, it was that she held a grudge. Charlene jangled her slew of gold bracelets and lifted her plastic-surgeried chin, which set off the haughty bobble of enormous pearl drop earrings.

Again, Fran almost applauded. Charlene put on quite a show. Judge had shared that the gum-chewing Jillian was useless, but it was hard to get good weekend help. The young woman mouth-breathed, and gaped overlong at the earrings' swing. Fran feared Jillian might lose her teeth. *Thou shalt not covet,* Fran thought.

Fran allowed Charlene to lead the charge into Judge's inner office. She took over as soon as she saw Judge grip the overlarge desk pad by its rustic leather side rails. Was he afraid of assault? Her brother wore his usual three-piece suit, but with his tie loosened and askew. Above it, his tan jowls sagged to emphasize his eye bags. His hair looked a wreck, a sight Fran couldn't recall witnessing since her teens.

"To what do I owe the pleasure, ladies?" he managed, a crack in the word "pleasure" giving away his true state of mind.

Fran pre-empted *Ms. Mimsy's* interests, which were decidedly different than hers. Who cared about the Widow's personal fortunes when lawsuits and lives were at stake?

Charlene was merely her entry excuse to Judge's chambers, a shield Fran knew to be unnecessary. She and Judge were profound-thinking sibs.

"We're on a mission from God," Fran said, employing *The Blues Brothers'* famous call-to-arms. "Some things have gone awry with our friendly foursome's trip." She winked at her brother to remind him of their promise to reveal neither the source of the funding nor the extent of the trip itinerary. "As you recall, Bonnie and Carl married in Vegas, taking Jackie and Steve along to witness, visited Carl's adult kids in California, and then honeymooned a week in Hawaii."

Fran's vow was to multi-edit the truth, to eliminate the Aussie jailing/release, the attendant media blitz, the lawsuits and more, but she'd been unable to derail Carl and Steve's imprisonment on Paul's Prayer Chain. As usual Marge, his secretary, barged ahead and had likely called key church ladies to sound the alarm, er, the need for Holy intervention. Was the Widow in the know?

If Charlene already knew, Fran could minimize the jailing, its timing and place, by benignly leaving it out, laser-focusing to read the Widow's eyes to assess her level of knowledge—and interest. She counted on Charlene's narcissism to keep interest at bay... And, she saw success.

Fran knew her talents. She could most certainly dole out the triple lawsuits, the tabloid eccentricities, and protect her breath with a mint. That was how she dispatched problems at the high school. One trouble at a time, topped off with a handful of mints.

The first dilemma, how to extricate Charlene from the room to consult fully with Judge. Fran began to sneeze, violently, clutching her sides, then her chest, doubling over her feet, feigning the wheeze she'd once witnessed when Jackie experienced a full-blown asthma attack.

Her brother caught on fast. "Place the casserole on my desk pad, Mrs. Braghorn. It won't harm the wood. Then you can rifle Fran's purse. If she doesn't have an emergency inhaler, hurry to the pharmacy to buy one. The best one Doc Watson recommends. Put it on my account." His body language commanded haste. Charlene seemed exasperated, stalled, so Fran accelerated the pace of her coughing bouts.

Judge softened, using the voice he used to cajole a frightened witness. "You know I can't ask my incompetent staff for help. They only know how to drink coffee, file papers, and write the occasional brief."

Rather than merely dump the casserole and hurry on her assigned chore, Charlene looked Judge square in the eye. "Chief among their talents is generating pages of billable hours, sent in business envelopes that stack my desk." The Widow inhaled to inflate her chest in full proportion to her self-worth. "My cook prepared mac-and-four-cheese with chicken breasts because I was worried about your health, but I can most certainly handle the health of my new best friend myself, Fran."

Despite her feigned asthma writhing, Fran could see her brother's lightly tussled tie twitch, his jowls tense. The Widow's tone had shifted from her usual sugar maple sweet to stern molasses again. Judge wasn't used to whiplash shifts of temperament.

Charlene gingerly tossed the contents of Fran's purse onto Judge's broad desk, careful to disallow anything atop the casserole. She turned the purse over and gave it a few shakes, unconsciously timing her movements with Fran's wheezed breaths.

Charlene didn't bother replacing the contents of Fran's purse. She scooped up her own, dug her keys from a side pocket, and trotted to the door. She looked over her shoulder to wink at Judge. "If I get a speeding ticket, I'll count on you to fix it."

Fran had never seen a woman run in pink heels and, despite her desire to laugh, she couldn't abandon her asthma act. She increased the frequency and volume of her coughing spell and fell to the floor.

As soon as the door closed, Fran raised herself from the dead to collapse in one of Judge's over-stuffed chairs. She felt winded, truly asthmatic for several moments, and used the time to collect her thoughts. Judge folded and unfolded his hands, straightened his tie, and pulled out a fresh legal pad.

Fran leaned in and propped herself on her elbows. There was no escape from the news. "I stopped by your office the other day and found you in a dead drunk and near-naked state. I took matters into my own hands to search your world-wide barrister sites." Judge's eyebrows shot up. Fran shushed him before he could sputter about her access to his passwords. "You'll always be transparent to me, Brother, just as likely I am to you. We've always been good at secrets, you and I, and now we have more."

"Shall I pour us a stiff drink or a slight nip?"

"Neither," said Fran. "I need you at full power. It's for our friends half-a-world away. Steve and Carl were jailed on their first day in Australia." Judge didn't look up nor did his pen pause. His face remained impassive while his scrawled handwriting flew across the page. Even the creases seemed to vanish from his suit, starch reinforced in his shirt.

"They've already been released, on bail, and are with Jackie and Bonnie." Judge's jowls relaxed. "But the media took an interest." Fran's droll tone carried her media disdain with it.

Now Judge looked up. "I'm glad that Australian news doesn't make the States."

"Well, this news might reach our shores. Somehow a Sydney bar manager discovered Bonnie's Boffo Lotto win and is suing for a large sum, as well as pressing full charges for damages sustained in the same bar brawl that landed them in jail."

Fran paused, as if to reflect upon proper wording, but there was none more apt than a football metaphor. "I'm afraid Carl landed a punch that broke the jaw of the local rugby team's star player. The man is out for the season. Since the team was favored to win the World Cup again, I'm afraid the team owner piled on."

Judge started to speak, but instead scribbled in another column, this one headed by "Quash". Fran didn't know what he intended, but she knew it wasn't a game. Judge was fierce, all business. They were going to war.

"The news may not have hit Michigan, but Carl's ex-wife in California got a whiff and slapped a suit for half of Bonnie's lottery win, served by a room service waiter at our friends' hotel. Bonnie wants us to countersue for invasion of privacy and for the hotel's failure to deliver on its promise of food."

"I always admired Bonnie's steadiness, but now, I must say I admire her spunk," said Judge. "This should be easy to take care of, though..." He raised his eyebrows. "...there will be enormous expediting fees attached."

"We know that's no problem, because we know the truth! Money is not an issue. Bonnie's lottery win pre-dates her marriage to Carl. Secure the signed lottery ticket and their Vegas wedding certificate. Make certified, notarized, color copies if need be. Write a forthright letter, enclosing a copy of the lottery ticket and Bonnie and Carl's marriage certificate—"

Before Fran could finish, Judge grabbed the phone. "Who are you calling?" she mouthed.

"In-house hacker," Judge printed, upside down, on the tablet for Fran to read. He winked and then twirled his chair to the wall of bookcases to instruct the person on the other end of the phone, punctuating each with a finger jab in the air.

Fran listened, aghast. Judge knew more legal mumbo jumbo and geek speak than Fran would have guessed. She prided herself in English and Portugese, but these two languages were above her pay grade. Her brother must have sensed her watching him—hell, she knew he reveled in it—because he looked over his shoulder to ostentatiously mouth, "Getting the ducks in a row."

Fran glanced at her watch and drummed her fingers on her brother's desk. The call seemed to be taking over long. Didn't he know time was of the essence? Charlene could bustle in at any moment, with an armload of meds, and she needed to resume her feigned asthma attack.

A realization arrived: that much coughing had loosened her bladder and her diaphragm hurt. She eased from the chair and limped to the restroom during the lull. When she returned to Judge's office, Fran helped herself to his booze, swallowed two Tylenol, and then meticulously reloaded her purse.

"Done." Judge twirled his chair around. "One problem

squashed. All documentation to derail the ex-wife's lawsuit will be emailed within the hour."

"And the other lawsuits," Fran said.

"All of the 'forthwiths', 'persuants', 'whereases' and 'henceforths' have begun." Judge's eyebrows arched. "Anything else?"

"Bonnie has maxed the float on her Capitol One card, misplaced her wallet with her other credit cards, and forgotten the PIN for her ATM. Apparently she's been flashing cash—like she did here immediately after she won—living more frivolously than even she expected. She hocked her mink for Carl's bail bond. We need to unleash one of the LLCs."

Judge didn't speak for a while. Fran watched the wheels turn. Which of the limited liability corporations, set up to shield Bonnie's lottery win from excessive lump sum taxation, would untangle the quickest? And which would trigger the least tax liability?

Within minutes he spoke, finger point punctuation towards heaven this time. "Ah, the Good Dog LLC could be funneled fluidly into Harold Prince's bank, ready to replenish Bonnie's several lines of credit with minimal fuss."

Then he tapped a few computer keys, grabbed the phone again, and barked orders.

Fran, not to be left out of the shenanigans on her friends' behalf, circled 'round the desk and crouched by Judge's side. She watched the computer monitor, which revealed little of the machinations, though the input codes worked like sorcery. She felt certain the other lawsuits would vanish properly with Judge's magic, too.

Her eyes lit up as her brain realized, *the Good Dog LLC*

unleashed. She laughed and laughed and laughed.

When Charlene returned, primed to stab Fran in the haunches with an EpiPen, in addition to stuffing an inhaler in her mouth, Fran was breathing easily. Into the paper bag that had formerly held one of Judge's bottles of hooch.

Charlene plopped the entire bag of allergy pharmaceuticals to the desk, huffing and red-faced, looking primed to swoon. As if she required an inhaler or Epipen. *Or some hooch.*

Judge jumped to his feet and rounded his massive desk with the aplomb of a male ballet lead. Fran lowered the crinkled paper bag and glanced over her shoulder—to watch her brother grasp the Widow's right elbow and steer her to the other client chair. As Judge handed Charlene off to the chair, Fran thought she saw her brother's lips brush the Widow's fingertips.

Fran plunged her face back into the bag and sucked air for all she was worth. Camo for a full-fledged blush.

"Charlene, my dear. As you can see, Fran has recovered, though we cherish your deed of mercy. Your divine casserole was moved to the staff room fridge. With a large black-markered note, "Do not touch or you will be prosecuted."

Goodness gracious, did he wink at Charlene?

Then Judge gestured toward Fran like Vanna White bending elbows to "O". *Oh.*

"Now that our dear Fran is all right, would you kindly take her home? Paul's been apprised of her attack, but can't be called away from a church council meeting." He beamed for all his capped teeth were worth. "Don't worry, Fran won't talk your ear off on the ride, because she needs to conserve her lungs.

I've placed her on voice rest."

Now my brother winked at me! What. The. Hell?

Then, Judge folded his hands, leaned forward—as Fran had seen him do from the bench—to proclaim, "Case closed." Not a furrow of the brow, not a blink, no more winks. Just a million dollar verdict smile.

He swiveled in his high-backed chair, so like a lion in his lair, to charm Charlene. "After you deposit my sister to her door, my dear, I'd like you to freshen up and prepare to dine with me tonight at the country club. I know you may have an issue to discuss because Jillian handed me all 20 of your messages. Pick you up at 6:00?"

Fran peered over the top of the bag to observe—*Ms. Mimsy's* face as pink as her suit. Perhaps the woman wasn't prim-and-annoying after all.

The ride to the church parsonage was quiet, though Charlene's over-powered antiperspirant—mingled with her expensive perfume—spoke volumes. Fran almost gagged, but remembered not to utter a word. She paused before she opened the car door and mouthed, "Thank you."

Charlene beamed, chin tucked demurely, a queen in her Cadillac.

Fran didn't look back. She exploded into her home, knelt on the carpet and laughed, holding her sides, but not in feigned pain. In relief and disbelief. What a life!

While she hadn't been invited to the escapades in Australia, she'd experienced several peripherally. She'd been sole witness to improbable local sights: Brandon, hit square in the kisser with a shitload, and her brother, a judge, smarm a widow. Who needed Hollywood news when one's own town folk were a hoot?

She collapsed into her home office chair and turned on her computer. The email chime sounded immediately. Judge had blind-copied her on everything.

All would be copacetic and *too cool for school.* What a kick-off to retirement!

Thirty-eight | *Bonnie and Carl*

CARL EMERGED FROM THE shower and began to towel dry. When Bonnie tugged his arm, he winced. She motioned toward the Jacuzzi, frothing with bubbles as much as she frothed for sex. Carl demurred. "I'd prefer several ice packs." Then he turned his back, maneuvering the towel tentatively over his bruised body parts.

Bonnie pouted and stomped her feet on the smooth marble floors. Not a smart move, because she was barefoot. The bones of her feet stung and sent a shiver through her knees to her hips. "I'll give you thirty seconds. Your body may ache, but mine hurts in different places." She shimmy-shimmy-shook out of the hotel robe and stepped into the tub.

"Please allow me to brush my teeth. My mouth feels like I swallowed a dirty sponge." Bonnie didn't reply, she just tossed her head and splish-splashed. "The radio is playing our song." She licked her lips, squeegeed bubbles from her chest and blew them toward Carl. He looked at her like she was crazy; there was no music. Only her purr.

A buzzer razzled the still air. What the hell?

It rang again, insistent as the devil. Since Carl was gargling, Bonnie was forced to pull on the hotel's white terry cloth robe and pad to the door. She was so frazzled, she'd pulled the sash too tight and had to release it to breathe. She scooped her hand to release her hair from under the robe and peered into the peephole.

A biker's helmet blocked her view of anything other than the long lushly-carpeted hall. The buzzer rang again. Imperative. Shrill in Bonnie's ear. She turned at Carl's shout, "Answer the damn door."

Bonnie flung open the door so quickly, it slammed the doorstop on the wall. "I didn't order room service, and it's not Halloween."

The black bike helmet bobbled, bony elbows twitched, and knees below black biker shorts quivered as the biker's black Nikes pranced. He looked like he was walking a treadmill to hell, holding an envelope that contained all the secrets of life near his chest.

Bonnie made fists of her hands, which was difficult because of her over-long nails. She kept them low, ready to punch the guy's nose. "This is very bad timing, Mister. Whatever could you want?"

This thinnest of thin men, with bristles of red beard and mustache that wisped like baby carrots above his unsmiling lips, thrust a DHL envelope into Bonnie's hand. His hand was gloved, holey, close-fitting contraptions that looked haute couture. The man's black latex uniform reminded Bonnie of the 1920 era bathing suits pictured in black-and-white photos downstairs in the hotel spa.

Wordlessly, a spindly arm whipped out a device like looked like an '80s cell phone. "Sign here," he squeaked.

Bonnie frowned, clutching the bundle to her chest to cover any cleavage that might appear. "Where and how? What is this? A stick-up?"

"No, ma'am. I'm a Bikey."

"Well, take a hikey. I'm busy here."

"Miss, I'll bugger off as soon as you sign. I assure you the contents are legit. I work as a courier for Barrister Lachian, the solicitor you hired. You could call him if you like."

Bonnie put her head down and signed the small screen. She pushed the envelope inside the robe and slammed the door. Anything to halt that chalkboard scratch voice.

Bikey had the last word, muffled though it was. "No tip? You're really up yourself, Ma'am."

Bonnie shrugged and stepped back into the well-appointed room. It may not be the poshest suite, but it felt like home. Carl was here. Peeking out of the bathroom, apparently catching all the commotion and curious, he asked, "What?"

Bonnie shook her head and shrugged out of her robe. She wanted Carl to see what he was missing. She wanted appreciation and applause. "Don't forget I have White Rapture lotion. It may be Victoria's Secret, but I'm telling you."

Carl emerged from the bathroom, robed in white terry. He was laughing so hard at Bonnie's teasing that the towel fell.

Bonnie ripped into the envelope. She pulled out a copy of a document with the Judge's embossed crest. She lowered the papers, glanced at Carl, winked at his bewildered look. "You've got time to dry yourself, honey. I got something more important than your body to read."

Carl's face fell. He picked up the towel and returned to the bathroom, throwing Bonnie a perturbed look.

"I'll get right with you..." but her voice trailed off as she recognized the doc.

Yes, it was a copy of an encrypted email, with the promise of a certified letter and appendages in Judge's safe, available for delivery by Lachian's courier as needed. The contents were from Judge Blackstone, *their* judge, with a go-ahead blessing. Amen.

Bonnie dropped her head back to the papers, double eye-scanned, and then let go. Truly let go. The papers plopped into her robe on the floor, splaying like lava from a white volcano. Ah, one fire was out.

Bonnie unearthed the robe and donned it. "Woot woot!" she shrieked and shimmy-danced left, then right.

Carl, clad fresh clothes, emerged bug-eyed from the bathroom. "Are you okay, dear?"

"I'm more than okay, I think." Bonnie bent down, careful to mind her back. She needed it to be fully intact for the celebratory romp. She picked up the papers, smoothed them, and assured the proper order in the bundle of six.

Bonnie read slowly, mouthing the words. She pranced and danced and moved to Carl. "You don't mind a bribe, do you, dear?"

"I won't commit until I've heard the details."

"There was an extra wrinkle to our Aussie problem-set, Carl. Your ex-wife behaved badly and slapped me with a lawsuit."

"She's a weird chick. I've got no use for her, just as she had no use for me. Spill it, Bonnie. I have a feeling I'll want to join your dance. The look on your face is triumphant."

"You know, I don't even know her name," Bonnie said, suddenly coy.

"I forgot as soon as I crossed the Michigan border." Bonnie raised her eyebrows. "Okay, certainly when I met you and your sweater sets and pearls." Bonnie hugged Carl, but he pulled back, held her in place at arms' length, and looked her in the eye. "Just get on with it," he enjoined. "I'm impatient, especially when I sense good news."

Bonnie winked. "Ms. Rip Off got wind of the lottery." Carl mouthed 'how,' but Bonnie shushed him with a wave. "She tried to invoke the same puny law you attempted to use, to spurn my hand in marriage. She tried to sue for half of the half of a half billion bucks."

Carl's jaw fell. "The ungodly gall!"

Bonnie nodded vigorously. Who was she to disagree? She held up a finger with its glistening polish.

"We recall the order, and so does the law. Judge's staff secured my signed lottery ticket and our wedding certificate. Notarized copies were sent to your gnarly ex-wife's lawyer. Case closed."

Bonnie began to clap her hand against the papers, as if they were a tambourine, but changed her mind. The papers were a treasure. She went to the safe.

Locked. Bonnie cocked her head to one side, then recalled she'd placed her wallet inside, using their room number as the code. Clever, yet not so clever. She quickly punched in the code to open the safe, stuffed her wallet in her terry robe pocket, placed the papers inside the safe, twirled the dial, and launched into the Macarena.

A little sleight of hand covered by dance moves. She bumped Carl's hips, one side and then the other, not minding what swiveled and swayed. "Open the mini bar champagne! She lost, we won!"

Carl caught on and disrobed. "Killer," he said.

Bonnie'd never seen a naked man run. She'd never watched

a naked man open champagne. She didn't watch anymore. She raced to the tub.

The sex was epic. Rub-a-dub-dub.

When the door buzzer sounded again, Bonnie deemed it Carl's turn to respond.

"The bikey, who delivered the previous papers, had another set, and he seemed very pleased to be greeted by a different person. And he liked his tip."

Bonnie glowered, so Carl lightened his tone. "Whether it's good news or bad news, it'll go better with Scotch," Carl said. "I'm going to pour myself a strong one, while you read. Hop to, Mrs. Edwards. The real Mrs. Edwards."

Bonnie beamed. How could she deny Carl? Besides, it felt very queenly to be sought out by two messengers. She truly felt like an empress, rather than a tourist who'd been in a foreign country less than a week.

This time Bonnie went at the envelope with her teeth. Her fingers were so wrinkled from their prolonged water romp, they didn't work. Besides, Carl handed her a Scotch.

She paused for a sip, letting her eyes fly across the documents. Then she took another sip, to slow her pace. The text contained some awfully big words, but the photos held the truth. She solidified her thoughts and looked at Carl. "The numerous cell phones and bar security camera footage of the bar patrons consistently show that neither you nor Steve struck the first blow. That voids the bar managers and the team owner's lawsuits."

Carl almost gagged. "Lawsuits?"

"Yeah, you launched a trifecta," Bonnie held out her arm as if to stay a dog. Carl devolved before her eyes. "No worries, because with Judge and Solicitor Lachian's help, we've whipped all three." Carl limped over to the over-stuffed chair and dumped his damaged body and soul into it.

Bonnie looked at him. "Plus, this country has a diversion program to allow you to avoid getting a criminal record, since you two are first-time offenders. Drum roll, please, and thanks for the work on your badass behalf."

"Thank you, honey, but I'm still unclear."

"First. Time. Offender." Bonnie near-shouted. "The Aussie cops checked Interpol and U.S. data bases. How ego-flattering is that, for them to consider you as international criminals?

"And the bottom line is?"

"You are verifiably first-time offenders because the offense occurred within hours of our landing on Aussie soil. Within our first hours, you bum with a capital B."

"Bonnie, I'm more than overwhelmed, but I'm not over-impressed. You are one hella missus. Gimme a kiss."

"I already gave you several." Bonnie shuffled more papers and scanned. "Wait, there's more. Solicitor Lachian has already submitted the paperwork so that we can fund a charity in lieu of more jail time and a record. All you and Steve have to do is admit that you fought and apologize."

"I apologize. You write the check. What charity?"

"That detail isn't settled, but likely something for retired Rugby players, or better yet, injured ones, like the star player you decked."

Carl had the grace to wince, then suggested his own half-sarcastic solution. "Or retired and/or dead cops or their families. Scholarships for kids or Alcoholics Anonymous. You know, friends of Bill and Carl and Steve."

Carl snickered in spite of himself. Many grim situations solved by cash. What a way to problem-solve, something he'd never considered with his own windfall. Seemed more fun to visibly bust somebody's chops.

This encouraged Bonnie to continue. "And, naturally, we cover the damages to the bar to reward the owner for dropping the lawsuit and to generate positive publicity and good will. Sort of like a tip for a great waitress. What a lollapollooza vacation start!"

"I apologize for that, too, Bonnie. Sorry for putting my desire for exploring our family's Aussie roots ahead of you. I confess to an unmerited plan." Carl inhaled so deeply, Bonnie almost felt sucked to his chest, which wasn't a bad idea, so she moved into his arms. "My appreciation of family is new, and I'm not used to thinking of consequences for me or anyone else. Thank you for marrying me and winning the lottery."

"Don't forget the order of those two events," Bonnie said. "And thank your lucky stars. Also, repack your barely unpacked bags. I'm afraid we are all too infamous here and that reality could impede our good clean fun. I've heard that Australians are a raucous sort and too many blokes might want to take you on. We're going to Phuket."

"Just what I need. Thai massage on a body covered in bruises."

"Don't forget the unshaven face."

Carl's free hand flew to his face.

"It's okay. I can deal with a scruffy face. Your face can be as free as you are during our extended trip. I'll accept that you look like a bum. But you may not be a drunken bum."

Carl winked. "You stole one of my phrases. Gimme a hug. I'll make you a hella Californian yet."

"No, you won't. Not as long as your ex-wife lives there. I'd have to learn her habits to assure I'd never run into her, and I don't want to adopt stalking as a life skill. I want to rule the world." Bonnie rolled her arm to hurry Carl along. "Read the docs. I'm dying for you to know what's what and what's right," she said.

Carl complied. While he liked the photos, to relive the bar fight he could still feel, his eyes bugged as he read the last clause of the ex-wife agreement. "What's the catch?" Bonnie skewed her mouth with a finger to mime a gaffed fish. "Oh-h, you bribed her, too?" he asked, bug-eyed at her chutzpah.

"Doesn't matter," Bonnie breezed Appendix A under Carl's nose. "Look what she signed."

"An injunction to not come within a hundred miles, to never call or contact in any way for any thing."

Carl stopped smiling. "Not even for my kids or grandkids?"

"We'll wrangle the details later. For now we are unencumbered, disentangled, and free to fly around the world. In my, er, our Learjet."

Carl still didn't grasp, so Bonnie sassed with attitude befitting a millionaire queen, "Nothing says closure like a quarter-of-a-million bucks a year. For ten years, in case there are grandchildren and we want access."

Bonnie paused to hug Carl. "Though she may not live long

if I go serious outlaw on her. There's no cut for your kids ensured via the settlement—let her spoil them, if she wants to pamper and entitle them, but I don't want to watch you *Brandon-ize* anyone like I watched Steve and Jackie for thirty-one years. Isn't going to happen. *I* deserve to be the spoiled brat. I was an in-the-wings person for years. It's my turn to hog center stage."

Carl rolled his eyes. He laughed his trademark thirty-two-teeth guffaw.

And then he kissed her. "Let's gather up Jackie and Steve and watch a proper rugby match somewhere. Maybe the ANZ Stadium. The world champion All Blacks from New Zealand are in town and the roar of 80,000 rabid fans is just the cheer-up I need."

Bonnie gaped, incredulous at his choice.

"I want you to see the Aussie jocks Steve and I were up against."

"Jocks!" shouted Bonnie. "That's it! You just solved the PIN problem, you genius. I used that last four numbers of the winning lottery ticket. Remember? Your high school locker combination? Let's find an ATM."

Thirty-nine | *Jackie*

WHILE BONNIE'S LOTTERY WIN had given her loads of cash, it hadn't come attached with much sense. Her voice intruded constantly during the game, yammering about how cold it was without her mink. Had she forgotten how much the men—and Jackie—enjoyed sports?

For relief, Jackie went to the fan wear booth at half time. She bought team jackets for everyone, dividing equally between the two teams playing. She didn't care if they fit. Jackie had a sixth sense that this wild rumpus would pass—as the recent kerfuffles had—and the men would behave. Well, she knew Steve would, and she vowed to hold his hand throughout the rest of the trip. If they remained on the trek.

Jackie knew she now suffered from a form of mental whiplash. Not that long ago, her longtime relationship with Bonnie had unraveled, like the hem of a store bought dress when one pulled the incorrect/correct thread. Point of view mattered. At the moment Jackie felt unsure of just about everything. Except for her and Steve's abiding covenant and love.

Forty | *Bonnie*

BONNIE GUSHED ABOUT ORDERING a personal plane, now that her homies had replenished her Michigan bank accounts and credit card floats with funds from offshore hidey-holes. Her wallet found without her having to admit it was momentarily lost—or having to cancel the multitude of credit cards, some of which she didn't even recall. It was neat to know that she could resolve a problem on her own.

Judge, aided by Paul, who'd apparently recognized almost all of the nonprofits in the worldwide data base, had selected the proper charities to ensure Carl and Steve's release without a criminal record. If it was graft, it was blessed by Him. God's graft had been the Pastor's game for so long, Bonnie knew she could rely on his choices.

She didn't need to compensate the bar owner who'd succumbed to greed. But it certainly helped her win the publicity game.

Everything wrapped up, faster than a birthday gift. As Carl always said, "We're golden."

Gosh, this rugby crowd was loud. She would most certainly enjoy the quiet of her private plane. Travel would resume after a good night's sleep in the Intercontinental's private suite, no matter what fool Carl had proclaimed. He could only be right part of the time.

After all, he was a Californian.

Forty-one | *Jackie*

THE SUITE WAS AS still as a vault. No sounds, no smells, its inhabitants poised for *what's next.*

During her glance at Steve's watch, Jackie noticed his toe tapping. Because his hand rested against the side of his leg, the time was difficult to detect.

If Steve had longer hair, he'd likely be twisting his curls like her. Again, Jackie blessed the fact that he didn't twiddle his mustache, like every stage villain since vaudeville. Now was not the time, place, or audience upon which to project evil. They were about to Facetime with their hometown crowd.

Bonnie seemed to have adopted the hair curl habit, though her style employed each finger in turn. The undulating action proved strangely hypnotic. Jackie tried it, but to no avail. *Holy crap, I'm wired!*

Carl's general impatience forced him down to the hotel bar, eschewing the ease of room service to deliver a six-pack of cold beer. He must have broken a sworn pact with Bonnie already—to lay off the stuff—because Jackie witnessed an extreme elbow to his rib. She also noticed he left the suite, anyway. Recalcitrant to the bone. Their marriage would be interesting to watch. If she and Steve continued the vagabond.

Fran had emailed and Jackie had replied. The appointed hour was nigh. The community was easy to convene because, while midnight in Sydney, it was 10:00 a.m. in Michigan. This

Facetime call would replace Pastor Paul's sermon. What better message of hope and reassurance could the Lord deliver to his flock than to know that all was well with Bonnie and Carl and Jackie and Deacon Steve?

Jackie felt anxious. When all the ringlets she could reach were tangled, she crossed her fingers and toes. She refused to cross her eyes and prayed that Fran wouldn't bring it up. It was their secret talent, learned during long hours of recess indoors when the weather was overly cold. In the winter of 1958, nearly a hundred inches of snow had fallen by Christmas. Epic.

Most of Jackie's anxiety stemmed from concern that worldwide publicity had undercut the secret of Bonnie's lottery win. If not, she didn't want to be the one to spill the beans of Bonnie's Boffo Lotto win. As far as their troupe knew, only nine people in the world knew, and all but one of them would soon share the screen.

Let there be peace on earth, and let it begin with me. It was a Freudian feature of any brain, but assuredly one as honest and open as hers. Even Fran had agreed that it was best that Jackie accompany Bonnie on her lottery-fueled world tour, if for no other reason than this one. Bonnie's early flash of cash had caused community whispers that she was dealing drugs. What would happen now? Would their community implode?

The sound of "Amazing Grace" tingled from the phone atop the table between the room's club chairs. Jackie liked the song so much, she let the notes fill the air for several seconds. How fitting for a congregational call to begin with that song.

"Hello!" Bonnie shouted over Jackie's head. It had been mutually agreed that Jackie and Steve would be seated in the chairs, with Bonnie and Carl kneeling behind because they had better knees. Who knew how long a chat among several hundred of their closest friends would take?

"Hello," intoned the pastor. "Want to see my new steeple?" His arms swept toward an easel beside the pulpit.

Suddenly, the screen jiggled and Fran's face filled the screen. "Forgive my husband, Lord, of his pride. Shall we open this call in prayer?"

It felt silly to waste minutes of a Facetime call with no faces to behold, but Bonnie and Jackie and Steve acquiesced. Everyone in the church assumed the position. It was the Lord's house—further, Fran acted as the congregational hostess.

The prayer wasn't overlong, but it was filled with sanctimonious, polysyllabic words because Fran exercised her vocab. Carl returned from the bar, popped the top of one of the convenience store cans, and shouted, "Amen." Jackie smiled at Steve. All was copacetic. So be it. Amen.

"Welcome to our service, world travelers. What do you have to say for yourselves?"

Caught off guard by Pastor Rankin's exuberance, the hotel honeys looked at each other, swallowing their tonsils as they struggled for the right words. This was dicey. Who would speak first? Sharing was caring, but giving up unknowns would be a bust.

Carl ended the silence by shouting, "Thanks for your prayers. We're all eager to see the city. Do any of you have suggestions?"

This request puzzled even Pastor Paul, who took the reins of his tablet. "Google likely has better answers than God in that department, and we do have hundreds of people who'd like to give their regards. Most haven't even been to Sydney, Michigan, let alone Sydney, Australia. I considered having a lottery system—" Here the screen warbled again. Clearly, Fran disapproved of his choice of words. She took over the big picture, which was actually a small image on Jackie's cell phone. She was glad she'd taken time to fully recharge the battery.

"We abandoned that notion because Waylon Huffington, the newspaper editor, demanded a quote. He'll be taking notes throughout, if you don't mind. Nod at the screen if you agree," Fran chimed.

Jackie almost doubled over with this one. Of course, he'd want the story, but he wouldn't hear the biggest scoop in Michigan, which was just behind the screen. She shook the phone, remembering Brandon's Magic 8-Ball. *No, I will not slip-up.* To seal that assertion, she handed the cell phone to Steve.

Steve wiggled his eyebrows, their agreement code, and settled the phone in his palms. If Pastor Rankin had, in fact, called the multitudes into the sanctuary, this would be a long call. Jackie knew the Deacon in him hoped that Marge or Paul had had the presence of mind to fill all of the back-of-the-pew slots with new member applications. That would be a bonanza of souls for the pastor, er, the Lord.

Paul appeared on the screen again, having wrested control of his tablet from Fran. Jackie wanted to chuckle, but she didn't. Fran had met her match in Paul. Jackie leaned over to pat Steve's hand, gently to not jostle the screen. "We've already passed the collection plate, for practice, mind you, so if you need any cash, let us know." He winked at the camera to assure that the Boffo Lotto secret was safe with him, the misdirect intended for his flock.

Bonnie snickered. Carl laughed aloud, but Steve didn't move a muscle. He had a responsibility to keep the phone stable and not disconnect the call. Jackie remained mute, following Steve's lead.

Steve reached over, smiling, as he tapped Jackie's thumb, the one she hadn't realized she'd placed in her mouth. Its nail was half-bitten. Old habits died hard. She returned his smile, crossed her fingers, and then crossed her heart. *I swear to keep the lottery and lawsuit secrets. So help me, God.*

"At any rate, I've elected for us to pass my tablet through the congregation, so everyone can smile and say a few words." With that, the background of the call swiveled as he turned to the congregation to repeat, "A few words. Right, everyone?"

The picture shifted on its axis again as Paul's face returned to view. "I think this beats the record crowds of Christmas and Easter. Thanks for bringing them in."

Suddenly the picture flickered, and the tablet clunked to the pulpit. Earthquake?

Pastor Paul had apparently set it down to enjoin applause. Whether for themselves, the Lord, or for the love of the foursome from the flock, none knew for sure. But they all clapped, too. Except Steve, who remained on duty to secure the screen.

Rustling noises ensued as Paul drew the computer back up. Jackie wondered if it tickled through the vestments. Then the pastor ceremoniously intoned, sounding for all the world like a cattle auctioneer at the fair, "Ready, friends? We're going to start with the choir."

Though all she could truly see were the vestments that curtained his bulk, Jackie could see the pastor in her mind's eye as he began to carry out the task. To him all congregational tasks were sacred, so there'd be great pomp in his stance. He wore his best vestments, and she noted that his hair was newly clipped.

One sideburn seemed a little shorter than the other, but who was she to point that out? Not the place. Not the time. Not the pastor to pull that on. He was as vain as the Widow about his looks. Jackie wondered if he covered his gray or if he had Fran do it for him? Most certainly, Maybelline, the town loudspeaker, did not.

She jolted back to attention as Polly's sweet face appeared on the screen. "Hi, ladies and husbands. How are you? I'm chair of the annual Thanksgiving Bazaar this year. Are you going to return in time to help me set up the high school community room and make donations?"

For the first time, guilt overwhelmed nostalgia. Jackie didn't know what to say. She looked at Bonnie and Bonnie looked at her, shaking her tresses in vigorous "No." Jackie pointed at Bonnie and mouthed, "You tell her then. Please."

Bonnie spoke a little more forcefully than necessary. "We're not returning in time, Polly. Sorry to let you down, but we haven't made specific plans."

Jackie began to hum the ancient Carpenters' song, "We've Only Just Begun" to keep herself from crying. Polly teared up, too, but she managed a graceful, "Miss you much." She blew a kiss before she passed the tablet along.

Within moments of the community call, vertigo set in and Jackie was glad she was seated. She closed her eyes to maintain her equilibrium, just as she had on the county fair Tilt-a-Whirl ride during her childhood. She and Steve had ridden it together on one of their first dates. She clearly recalled the extra *feel* he confessed to later, when the carnival ride slammed his body into hers and vice versa.

So long ago and yet so recent. Amen.

The friends procession continued. Handy seemed to have closed his hardware store for the first time ever. He aw-shucked when Steve remarked on the fact. "Before I closed up, I put a sign on the door, directing folks here." Just then the church doors opened and several folks scurried to wedge into back pews.

No Brandon among the crowd, however. Jackie hoped Steve didn't notice. She'd have to have a private chat with Fran later on that topic.

Jackie mentally recorded all the faces, weeping when she sighted some, feeling disconcerted as she saw others. There didn't seem to be a jealous bone among the throng, though she suspected some lurked beneath the Sunday best clothes. She felt truly heartened by this large outpouring of affection and support, but she knew there'd be snipes among the coffee klatches and cliques.

For that, Jackie was glad to be away from the small town. The lawsuits and jailing were lollapaloozas. As much as the lottery win. If that hell broke out, the gossip would be so toxic they might never be able to return. Branded, they'd be.

Not having to confront the tall tales, curtailing false or countermanding the vicious, was no longer her daily role. It was almost as great a relief as no longer having to make beds and make meals. She wondered how Fran would survive.

Then she saw Fran locked, arm-in-arm, with the Widow Braghorn. Shock flashed within and likely colored her face.

Jackie was glad she wasn't directly on screen. Bonnie pinched her shoulder. She felt it, too. Oh well, absence had several nuances.

Slowly it dawned on Jackie that she wasn't necessary to hold up the universe that was their small town. Equilibrium found its way.

Further, she now realized, in living for her family and friends, she'd failed to create a multi-layered life of her own. She didn't even have hobbies, unless potato peeling tallied. Maybe that could become a goal of her travels: to find her will and her way.

While she missed him, there was no gaping hole in her heart with the absence of Brandon to fuss over. The love of her life was beside her. Both of her men survived, despite her guidance and direction. Her menus of home-cooked grace. Had they grown up? Would she?

There was more to contemplate as the good wishes from eager faces congealed into one. Jackie's vision blurred, and she retreated within.

All her life, bad things had taken place, feelings tumbling along with them: a miscarriage, her father dying of cancer, Brandon's career-ending accident. That little marijuana incident and brush with the law, a little larceny for the good cause of returning home. Amy, as ex-daughter-in-law, now incarcerated in the Michigan State Pen.

Calamities. Holy crap! Jackie understood there was no immunity from sorrow, but the last forty-eight hours had topsy-turvied like a Patterson novel, seeming to top all.

She felt seasick. Or was it jet lag, vertigo, or chaos-induced indigestion? Steve admitted he felt like he'd endured a car chase like the *Bullitt* classic, though he hadn't ridden in a car in this country, only a paddy wagon as an extreme form of chauffeured limousine.

Together they had survived life's pounding, uplifting and down drafting, and every emotion in-between. Faith, family, friends mattered. Love of the Lord mattered, too. But self-nurturing held it together.

The Facetime call lasted 64 minutes, a veritable Easter Parade of friends swathed in smiles and Sunday best. There was likely jealousy among the throng. The Widow, for instance, hadn't said a thing, but Fran and Paul Rankin had effectively shushed them in the preamble prayer. Fran hadn't spoken, but she had abundant email and phone contact.

Jackie felt blessed. And then it hit her. She hadn't blurted. She maintained sumptuous self-control. She was officially a grown-up. She threw her arms high, symbolically shredding mistakes, failures, and regrets of the past like confetti. Let it go!

Forty-two | Fran

I'M HERE FOR THE last word. My husband wants to deliver it, but he already preached once today. It's my turn. I'm entitled. You, dear Reader, may have noticed that I missed my rotation in the recent chapters. What a friend I am.

I'm proud of my husband, his church and flock, his steeple-chasing dreams. I'm proud of my place at his side, shepherding a gaggle of everyday people who live the best they can, grinding away at goodness while the world turns. We are but wisps, but large in the Lord's heart. We are blessed.

I'm proud of my friends, Bonnie and Jackie, as they flew the coop to make their way in the wider world. They'll see things up close and personal that I'll only see between the covers of my National Geographics. I'm now pleased that I wasn't able to donate the lot, and that Carl never opened one when I loaned them to him. If anyone is going to dog-ear the issues, it'll be me.

While I purchased a large pack of Bic pens and borrowed a few of the pastor's lined tablets, I've abandoned my planned memoir. I realized that I've lived a white bread life, not scarred or exotic enough to gain even my interest. I willingly yield to the fact that my need for control may have expunged deplorable memories. *The baby with the bath water.*

My brother's in rehab, and I didn't want to trouble him for details. He needs all the concentration he possesses to kick alcoholism. Charlene visits him daily and may do more than hold his hand, but I don't stress. Or inquire. His wizened eyes crinkle more softly these days. His beaky nose is less beleaguered looking red. He's lost weight.

Let's not discuss Marge the Barge. Let's just say that my husband prefers me in the yoga studio, at the Koffee Kup, or on field trips that I've organized for other Seniors. So far we've visited the Henry Ford Museum and Greenfield Village. Next we'll foray to the Chicago Art Museum. I have two tickets left, $65, including entrance fee, round trip bus ticket, and a sack lunch.

I've learned to play poker. Shh-h. Soon I'll learn French horn, maybe even march incognito in the high school halftime shows. Wouldn't that be a hoot?

Speaking of hoot, the worldwide flap about Bonnie's lottery win and all the escapades in Australia didn't enter the local atmosphere. Waylon Huffington squashed his headlines at the behest of Judge, his fellow Rotarian.

My husband appointed me steward of church philanthropy, utilizing Bonnie's Boffo Lotto largesse. I dispense the interest only, generous and regular donations for local and nationwide causes, no tax receipt required for Uncle Sam. No siphon for self-interest. I have a title, but no nameplate. My heroics are more hidden, and that's just fine. My research is vital, and I spend hours online.

The massive expansion plans were downsized when the committee fell apart. That is, when Charlene Braghorn devoted her free time to Judge. And to me. She wears a new chapeau each time we meet for lunch. She even swapped me once, my orange fedora with the duck feather for her black straw halo with the free-floating veil. Our picture, in the showcase window of the Koffee Kup, is often featured in what passes for the newspaper's society page.

The idea of writing the adventures of my crazed-kick-up-your-heels friends tickled my innards. After all, they experienced a truly staggering series of events. In the first two weeks. What a saga the rest of the trip portends.

But then I realized that the compelling buddy movies were too zany to wish on an audience I'd admire, and that the successful ones starred males. Plus, invention of tales might make the implausible come true. My mom's superstitious nature had lodged itself in my views more than I imagined to be true.

Besides, people say to write what you know, and I didn't feel comfortable appropriating my friends' escapades. I shall conserve my mental energy. My friends might be frazzled again and require my counsel. Bonnie mentioned something about owning a Lear, so she could ferry me at will.

I also abandoned my home renovation plans. Contractors didn't return my calls, perhaps because many were the ones I'd most often disciplined in school. I think I didn't paddle them enough. Manners are manners, but I guess that's a parent's duty.

I felt badly for momentarily contemplating soaking my friends for a fee to monitor Brandon. As penance for that faulty thought, I contemplated selling this place, but we've agreed to utilize it as an office for Bonnie's gift-giving foundation. 1600 sq. ft. seemed cozy as a home, but it's quite grand as an office. I finally eclipsed my brother on some measure.

Brandon, bless his jaunty, paddle-bitten butt. He didn't

need as much monitoring as my proprietary self desired. His antics paled after what his uncle and dad were able to accomplish in twenty-four hours. Especially when one considered that the majority of those hours transpired when the men were seat-belted, in transit on a plane.

Brandon is *adulting*, as far as I care. If Jackie and Steve let go of the leash, I could, too. He sought my husband's counsel—twice—to learn tips to mend his relationship with Julie. He also sought Lord's recompense for his arrogance and slacker ways. I'll let community gossip tell me if it sticks.

By the way, the Bran Cam remains in place. I've promised to restart it remotely around calf-birthing time. Steve is going to be so proud of his son. All will be copacetic for Bran.

I'm here in contemplative mode. To see the future is easy—all you need is hope. That's the boon of Christianity, that all will be forgiven. To understand the past is harder. That task requires honesty. Thus, no memoir.

Rub-a-dub-dub. Three friends in a small town. Let's tie their transformations up with a bow:

Bonnie Voss Edwards: She worked through an axiom that, while money can purchase copious happiness in the form of stuff, it isn't the stuff of life. For now, Bonnie thinks adventure is—with a man in tow. The juxtaposition to her prior life is remarkable. It pushes her forward to explore, but she's still wonderful in her core. No more queenly or over-the-top bitchiness. No more tantrums, just joy.

Eventually she'll dial it back to a simple fact: people love her whether penniless or cash-plump. Meanwhile, she adores

Carl and Bonnie abides his beard, which is growth for him and for her. And Carl realizes that he doesn't have to search for his roots: he has them in her.

Jackie Clay Breeden: The archetype good wife/smother mother resolved to let her one-and-only son manage his own life. Her husband, Steve is thoroughly proud of his rascal son, the reflecting pool of himself. He remains her better half, but he doesn't define their life any more than Brandon does.

Or me, for that matter. We're friends, but I'm not imperious. I think.

Jackie knows, *truly knows,* that she need not go-along-to-get-along. Adventure is good, but love is all good, even when the circumstances are not. Endure. Prevail. Life is a wild ride everywhere, no matter what.

Fran Blackstone Rankin: (c'est moi. Yes, I'm learning French) I'm calmer, trimmed down to size. I realize that the only title I need is Self, child of God. I cherish entanglements with town folk, even the outliers of the farm community. I have more friends, including people I formerly despised, like Charlene, though not yet Marge. These friends embrace me for who I am, not who I was. Better yet, *if* you lapse, people might adore you all the *more.* Relax. Abandon *stance.*

You don't need to control others any more than you need to control yourself.

Besides, Paul reminds me, God is in control.

Oops, gotta go. The U-Haul is here, driven by a crew of my ex-students. Soon, everything that's mine will be with everything that is Paul's. *Home sweet one home.*

I'll run Bonnie's foundation from my former residence. I'll like driving to work again.

ACKNOWLEDGEMENTS

Ed and Narelle Cree, who first taught me 'Strine

Diane Rogers and her 'Kevinisms', OZ knowledge, and critique wisdom

Laura Taylor who leaned across the table, placed her hands on my shoulders, looked me in the eye, and intoned, "You are a writer, my dear." At the top of her edit manuscript, she wrote, "Good work, Author!" Years of endeavor's graduation day!! Swoon –

Mike who smilingly, gleefully shared a true incident from his days on a farm and willed me to share... and those who granted permission to purloin their silly and/or pithy lines. You know who you are.

Maddie, who pushed, pulled, and suggested ways to guide me to Story, also sharing a hilarious dog episode that didn't happen to her...

Larry, my first reader and truthful editor, my partner in adventure for life.

The Silly Hats & Caps grammas who continue to model commitment, perseverance—and the value of true friendship.

Kassie Rittman who asked to read my manuscript—and then re-read after I made changes. We each value the tribe of Boomer Chick Lit.

Jeff Lyon, who patiently shepherded me into emotional resonance for characters

Pamela who applauded—and then encouraged me to find Structure!

Early readers: Casey Dorman, Susan Appel, Sister Writers critique group.

Tom McCranie who perked at my first oral read and urged me to up my game in a neighborhood authors' group. I wasn't ready, yet I blossomed. Didn't I, Teacher Tom?

BOOK CLUB QUESTIONS

1 Have you ever been in a group of close friends? Did you consider it clannish or inclusive? Did you name your group—and why?

2 Use one word to describe Fran. What did you like about her? What did you not like or admire?

3 Describe Jackie in one word. What traits of hers did you like? Were there any you despise—or identified with?

4 Describe Bonnie in a word. What did you like about her? What did you not like about her? Did she have a suitable arc?

5 Did you ever live in a small town? In the Midwest? What do you know, think, and feel about the fly-over states after you've read this book?

6 Do you think that Jackie and Steve will continue to world travel with Bonnie and Carl?

7 Is Brandon book-worthy? Describe him in a word, if you can.

8 Could you picture each character with description given? Could you see them in each other's eyes?

9 Why do you think that Fran had to have *the last word* (final chapter)? Did you notice the point of view change? Did it bother you?

10 The working title of this novel was Cash to Dash, contiguous with the rhyming nature of the first two books in the FAITH FAMILY FRENZY! Series, Stashes and Hashes & Bashes. Would you like to read the first two books now?

11 This book was ignited by musing between my husband and me about what we'd do if we won a $500 million dollar lottery that was in play at the time... We determined that $8 million would be enough. Whaddayathink? What would you do with a boffo lotto win?

ABOUT THE AUTHOR

PJ Colando was born and raised in the Midwest, yet unabashedly aspired for adventure elsewhere, following her parents' model. She lives in southern California with her family, hobbies, and pets.

PJ writes comedy and satire with a literary bent. She is the author of three previous novels, with short stories, personal essays, and articles published in journals, magazines, and anthologies.

FEEDBACK

Please take a few moments to pen a positive review on book purchase sites, including those online, your local bookstore and library. Whatever, wherever. Tell all your friends, including other books clubs. It's the highest compliment a writer can receive: that others read and relished their work.

CONTACT

Go to **pjcolando.com** to:
· Follow her boomer humor blog
· Learn more about her and her other books
· Contact her.

Or contact her directly via email: **talklady@sbcglobal.net**.

45511021R00189

Made in the USA
Middletown, DE
18 May 2019